Unscanned

"You deserve your story to be read by as many children and adults as possible."

"If you haven't already, send it off to publishers.
I would buy copies for the library."   (Children's Librarian)

"It is the sort of book I'd like to buy. This is because it is a really good story and I felt like I was one of the children...I felt like I could imagine being in the places in the book."
(child aged 10)

From the Author:

I live in Grimsby, Lincolnshire and write mostly in my front room. I've written stories for as long as I can remember, and still have some from when I was at school! I have an eleven year old son, who always hears the first draft and gives an 'honest' kids' opinion - sometimes meaning sections have to be completely 'scribbled out' and re-written! On top of that, we are a large family, with tons of nieces and nephews. Christmas is a party!

The first book I ever read was when I was four about a sheep dog rescuing a lamb. I still have that very tattered book, and even get it out every so often to flick through it!

I love climbing in Derbyshire and high on my most favourite place in the world is Edale. There is a picture of me on my website, (www.tracytodd.co.uk) showing our last visit this summer. I am standing on an old, wooden bridge, under which is a crystal clear stream, cascading down from waterfalls in the peaks.

Something known only to a chosen few is that I once sneaked up to the top of the highest pyramid in Giza, Egypt, and watched the sun set over the desert.

Acknowledgements

I would like to thank all those who supported me in the writing of Unscanned, including all the kids, (both young and young at heart), who read it in advance and told me what they *really* thought about it!

More particularly, I would like to thank my family for reading and reading and reading, past the point of boredom!

Dedication

I would like to dedicate this book to Adam
for inspiring the tale.

Prologue

The bushes were always a favourite hide-out place when I was a kid, a bit scratchy, but great for spying on the house. I'd watch my Mam come and go without her even knowing it. Sometimes, I'd even take the ancient iPad out there and play games for a while. I could pick up the neighbour's Wi-Fi, as she was quite old and didn't think to put a security code on it. Perhaps she didn't know, but I didn't care. I was a spy and no one ever found me out. They thought I was upstairs under my blanket, keeping warm, playing Minecraft. It was still one of my favourites, even if it was years old.

But it's different now. We don't live here anymore….had to leave in a hurry. The Ejectors were coming. And with nowhere to live and a minor in her charge, Mam said they would've taken us away. Her to the Ejector's Camp and me to an Ejector's Kids' Home. So we ran into the dark night. We escaped. Left everything behind like refugees with nowhere to go. I was afraid then, but not anymore.
That was a couple or so years ago.

The family I'm watching are packing. They're in hurry. The father's throwing stuff in the boot. The mother jostling two young children along; a pretty normal family going on holiday. I am to observe them and wait till they leave. After that, my mission really begins.

I am Adam.
It is the year 2043.
In three weeks, I am 12 years old.
And I am a Downer.

Chapter 1: The Mission

They eventually left. I'd almost been caught. The little girl, with ruddy cheeks and curly blond hair saw me and pointed, gabbling something to her flustered mother, but no-one really listens to a two year old. They should have I s'ppose but then I'd be in trouble, so I'm glad they didn't.

I have to follow protocol. Yes, we do have rules. The leaders are very strict about them…. to protect us, but even so I'm anxious to move forward. My legs are beginning to cramp and I'm getting cold. This is my first mission alone. It's nerve-racking to be sitting here like this, so I want to get it over with, but protocol states I must wait for half an hour after the occupants leave.

Once, we are told, one of the Downers went in too early. The owners came back and trapped him. He was led away by the police and we haven't seen him since. So, we stick to the rules now.

Two minutes to go. I run through the schedule in my head. Open the door. Dismantle the alarm. Find the stuff. Alarm the house. Leave. Ten minute job. In and out. No lights permitted. I'm clutching onto the small LED torch light as if it were my life saver. I want to prove myself, but I'm shaking. I curse under my breath. I can do this. I know this house. I lived here for eight years of my life. It'll be a doddle.

One minute to go. I stare at the luminous face of my watch, willing the seconds to tick by. Thirty seconds…I peak out of the bushes, no one around. It's a dark autumn night, dank and cold. No stars, no moon. Perfect for someone like me.

Ten seconds, I make a move and crawl out of the bushes on my hands and knees. I know I have camera deflector strips on the sleeves and front of my jacket, which I'm confident will scatter any image the security cameras catch of me. (They are truly the best invention we've come up with. Wearing deflectors distorts security photos or videos by turning the replay into a myriad of grey, square, pixels.) Having said that, the same neighbour lives next door and she was always nosey. You could always see her peeping out of the window, watching what everyone was up to, as if their lives were her personal TV soaps. I need to keep low so she can't see me, and to make sure the security lights don't flick on.

Like a snake I slither across the grass as fast as I can until I reach the path in front of the door alcove. Then I am on all fours like a cat, reaching up to the lock with the key.

We have an informer. Informers are always useful, but this informer is the best. She, Sara, used to be our cleaner, cook and nanny until I was eight. She lived in with us and made me laugh. Now she works for this family, but I know she still loves us. A twinge of jealousy strikes me, but I push it back down. No time to think of her now. Distractions could kill me. Rule number three on our list of ten. Don't get distracted! Only the schedule in my head!

The door clicks open even though my shaking hand missed the lock a couple of times. My heart is beating so loudly I think everyone must be able to hear it. The alarm immediately goes off – a piercing noise in the silence of the dark night. It spears me to action and I jump up, pushing open the door and entering the hallway. Gotta reset it as fast as possible before anyone notices. If I get it to stop within five seconds, neighbours forget. At ten seconds, the noise registers. And at fifteen, they start to wonder. If it's not off within twenty seconds, we leave. Another rule though not part of the Downer's ten – more one of the Collectors' individual guidelines for keeping safe! At twenty seconds, people look out of their windows to see what the noise is about. We have to be gone by then. The strips on my jacket don't protect me from the human eye and, as a Downer and Collector, I have to avoid being seen at all costs.

Luckily, our informer gave us the key and the code. Quickly, I close the door, hold up the tiny torch in my left hand, flip it on, and type someone's birthdate with the forefinger of the right. My finger feels numb, as if it doesn't belong to me. I'm sure the digit will trip over the pad and hit the wrong keys, but it doesn't. And the alarm stops, throwing me into a dark, eerie silence that seems to leave echoes in my ears.

At that point we're supposed to move through the house quickly, but I'm trembling. My legs feel like jelly and I slide down the wall, my back to it. My head slumps. It's pounding as if in tune with every pulse in my body. I want to run away, but I can't. I have a mission and people are relying on me. This is to be my final test before I go it alone. And I need to go it alone or my role with the Downers will change. I don't want it to change. I love my role, even if I am terrified.

I know I can't sit there long, but just a minute will be okay. I know this house, know the layout, know where to look. It won't take me long.

I take a deep breath and look around. The hall doesn't seem so dark now. My eyes have adjusted. The torch is still in my hand, a circular light reflected on the wall opposite. I play a little with the light, watching it jump up and down the wall, as if a cat is chasing it. My cat, Sally, the one we left behind.

I shake myself and abruptly stand up. Such thoughts could destroy me. I live in another world now and this is my test to really be one of them. I can't fail, I won't fail!

Suddenly, over my left shoulder something or someone moves. I can see it out of the corner of my eye. My heart goes into overdrive and I stand as still as a deer in headlights, or a person in the middle of their stride, magically turned into a statue; one foot slightly in front of the other. As if that would help me disappear or not be seen by anyone left in the house. Cameras I can handle, people not. If there really was someone here, they'd see me.

Had I made a mistake? Was there someone here?
Slowly, I turn my head to the left and almost laugh in relief.

God, I'm an idiot!

Looking back at me, almost in silhouette are large green eyes. Wisps of thick, dark blond hair escape from under the cap and scarf. It's only my reflection in a large mirror, which wasn't here before. We used to have a picture of red poppy fields hanging on that wall. I remember it 'cos my mother always loved it. I even remember the day she brought it home delighted with the find. She'd been scouting old antique shops for just the right thing. She always said that, 'just the right thing', as if it gave her an excuse for rummaging around in old, dusty shops, but it was her hobby. She took me along once and I hated it. Moaned so much, she had to take me home.

Torch down so neighbours don't see the light, I move on, easily passing through the hallway into the kitchen. The layout's all the same – cupboards in the same place, cooker against the middle wall. Quickly, I open a few draws until I find the cutlery. We need a couple of sharp knives, we are more people now and don't have enough to go round. I find some at the back of the drawer. They look old and used, which is all the better. They won't be missed.

In one of the drawers I notice some AA batteries and a card of electric wire. I know we need them. Our leader mentioned it, but they aren't on my list. I collect them anyway. Showing initiative is a good thing and opportunity can't be ignored. I stuff my treasure into my backpack and turn to go upstairs, feeling quite happy with myself. Only one more thing to shop for and I'm done for the night. I'll have accomplished my first mission.

Suddenly, I hear a car outside and lights shine in an arc, passing across the windows and creating shadows. I hear the father complaining...something about the alarm and why can't she remember one thing.

Oh my God, they're back. They've forgotten something.

I stand absolutely still, terrified, wondering where to run to. I'm going to be found out. Visions of being sent away engulf me. I won't see my friends again, and my Mam will go crazy.

Adrenalin charges around my body as if I've eaten a ton of sweet fudge and have a sudden sugar rush liquefying my cells. My brain screams at me to hide, to move out of the kitchen. They will see me standing here like an idiot of

a statue. Time seems to drag by like a slow motion film.
My legs are heavy, but I manage to reach the utility room
and hide under an old table as someone walks towards the
front of the house. Clip, clop of a woman's heels on a
cement path, screaming child wanting to get out of the car
and follow, irritated father. The heels stop for a moment
and I hear a short, fiery discussion, although I can't make
out the words.

I look up from under the table, wondering what I'm to
do.

Should I wait it out or try to exit?

I need a distraction to help me get out. I look around
desperately and see the two rectangular panes of glass in
the back door. Strangely it has a letter box opening. We
never had that when we lived here. The glass is full of
bubbles and looks black in the dark of the night, but then
something else catches my eye and my heart leaps.
They've left the key in the keyhole and it's the old
fashioned metal type, not a scanner. Don't they know
anything about security?

I have an idea!

Slowly and silently, like a snail, I crawl out. The voices
have silenced and the clip-clopping has started again.
Standing close to the backdoor, I ready myself, clutching
onto the key. I glance back for no particular reason and
notice a notepad on the old table. I can't believe my luck.
My last item just sitting there for the taking. Quickly I grab
it and stuff it in my bag. I can hear the key turning in the
front door. Beads of sweat are sitting on my forehead.
Surely she will notice when the alarm doesn't go off. My
stomach is churning cheese painfully and my legs have
started jelly-wobbling again. I have to get the right timing
on this or else I'm done for. She'll hear me.

She pushes the door open noisily. Without hesitation, I unlock the back door, slip out and close it. Then, I lock the door again and push the key through the letter box. Just as I turn to leave through the back gate, I hear it hit the floor. No-one will ever know I was there.

Leave no trace. The last and most important rule.

Chapter 2

We're trained to become invisible. We have a whole
science on invisibility, like how to block wireless trackers,
computer signals, phones and even where we live. We've
had some success; the strips on the jackets are amazing.
But invisibility is not just about technology – it only goes so
far, and obviously we're not magicians. From being young,
we master certain talents, one of them is to avoid being
noticed. It's a whole class in itself and no one can go out
until they've proved they can do it.

So, I don't charge down the street in an effort to
escape. I walk casually. I'm disguised as a boy coming
home from a school club, wrapped up warmly in the cold
November weather. Wearing a scarf, that covers my face,
and a dark blue hat with a peak. I keep my head down and
walk close to the walls and privets to shelter me from the
whirling wind.

No one would recognise me. Not even my Dad, if he
was around. He left way back when we lived in the house,
just before all the troubles began. I can barely remember
him, and as we don't have any photos – everything was
left behind the day we ran away – I'm slowly forgetting his
face, his voice, what we liked to do together – if we ever
did. Apparently, I have his curly hair and height, but that's
all I think.

I'm tall for my age and could pass for 13 or 14, so no
one stops me anyway, even when I pass a local policeman

– none think much of the boy with the school backpack. He's on his way home, of course he is.

And it's true. I am, but not the kind of home they would ever understand, nor even dream of. I walk quickly though. I'm shivering, both from the cold and the release of tension. Just as I'm about to turn the corner, I notice a girl sitting on the corner step of an empty house. She looks vaguely familiar and I stare for a moment. Her short, wavy brown hair sticks up at varying angles as if it's been gelled, but in this case, I think it's just matted with dirt and mud. She wipes her face and leans into her knees, head down in her hands as if she's weeping. Then she quickly wipes her face again as if ashamed of being seen weeping. She's sitting in a corner so forlorn, I almost approach her. Why hasn't anyone else seen her? She looks like she needs help. She glances at me for a moment. Our eyes meet, I turn away quickly, not wanting to be noticed, but she looks so familiar. I wonder if I've seen her in the street before.

Perhaps I should chase after the policeman I saw earlier and tell him she needs help, but no, police don't help our kind. He might start asking questions. I look at the girl again. Everyone walks passed as if she doesn't exist. As I walk passed, she pulls a dirty collar high and pushes herself further into the corner, hugging her arms into her waist, trying to escape the cold winds. I wonder where her family are. I know I should do something, but I don't know what and daren't get involved.

"Adam?"

A voice shouts my name and instinctively I turn. A mistake, I should have just walked on. No one must see me.

"Adam, is that you?"

It's the girl. She's standing now, looking straight at me. Our eyes meet again and then I know who she is - my old friend from another world, another time, the time that will never be again. She's taller now, but I recognise her as she does me. We were at the same school, played together for endless hours.

The almond shaped, brown eyes, the pretty face, but where have the long, auburn curls gone?

I'm unsure what to do. Should I turn and run away? I don't know what to say.

"I can't believe it's you. You're bigger."

Her voice is croaky, her nose red. She sniffs and wipes it across the back of her hand and then shrugs.

"Sorry, I've got a cold."

Tissues?

I don't say anything about the gruesome mucous or the dirt, her eyes are still bright with tears and she's obviously upset.

"Don't you remember me?"

I give in. I can't help myself. She looks so messed up, so dirty, so bedraggled.

"Of course I remember you Alicia. What are you doing here?"

I indicate the doorway, but really mean how did you come to be in such a mess.

She understands and stares at me for a moment before the full blown tears streak down a filthy, miserable face.

"They've gone Adam….my parents. I don't know what happened to them. I tried to find them. I even went to the police, but they wouldn't tell me which camp."

The words are stuttered and garbled. They seem to come out faster and faster as if she has to tell it all before she breaks down completely.

I look around. Has anyone noticed us yet?

"They put me in one of those non-contributor homes. It was horrible, they beat me every day and I just had to run away. I came back to find my mam and dad, but our house has been sold. Someone else lives there now. I have nowhere to go. I don't know what to do. I can't go back to the home. You can't imagine what happens there."

Wet with tears and snot, she tries to wipe it all away with both sleeves. As if that would make her appearance any better! I know she wants me to hug her, to make her distress go away, but I'm only eleven. Eleven year old boys just don't do that, even if they are Downers. I feel awkward standing there, staring, not knowing what to say. I chew on the inside of my lip and wonder what the odds of meeting her here are, and on a day like this are. I hesitate before I speak and then it is more like a conspiratorial whisper.

"Come with me!"

She nods and follows like a lamb being rescued from a storm. She doesn't ask where or why. I'm her only hope.

I'm even more nervous now. This is breaking one of the rules. She attracts attention. Not only is she younger than me by ten months, but she's a head and shoulders smaller. And she's grubby as if she has been living rough...which in fact she has. There is a button off her coat and her trousers are splattered with mud. Her face is dirty and her hair matted up.

I, on the other hand, am suited up to look like a typical young teenager. I'm clean, well-dressed in blue jeans and a padded jacket, and look full of bouncy energy as I walk down the street.

Together, we are noticeable as extremes. I suppose I could be the older, bullying brother, but I look more like a person dragging a young girl away to some devious way of life. People are staring at us. I'm not sure what to do. She's jabbering on, trying to lighten the mood, trying to be normal – whatever that is!

"Remember the time we went to the park on your tri-scooter?"

"Mmm…"

She doesn't need much encouragement.

"And I tried to outdo you on the curves…well I did outdo you actually."

My pride can't resist.

"No, you didn't. I twisted into the curves much faster than you."

"In your dreams…"

"What are you on about? You didn't even have a scooter at that time. You were borrowing mine."

"So, I was a natural."

"Come off it."

She was grinning. She'd done it. Somehow we'd managed to slip into our old, competitive ways without even realising it. Flashbacks of a 'yesterday' that would never be again. The world had changed. Children suffered and no one even blinked. The voice in my head sounded bitter, but I quickly shook it off. I'm not the same person now. Not a scared child in a cruel world. Glancing at her for a moment, I quickly look away. She reminds me too much of then – a time when we'd been best friends and things had been different.

"Where are we going?"

The dreaded question! What would she say if I told her the truth? Would she tell me I was crazy? What if we got there and they wouldn't let her in. No one had ever said we couldn't bring someone in. I wasn't sure what to do or say. I couldn't just tell her about it. What if she changed her mind about coming with me? She would know then and she might tell others.

"We live in a different place now."

"Who, you, your Mam and Dad?"

"No, my Dad left, remember?"

"Oh yeah, and you disappeared after that. Where did you go?"

"None of your business!"

"Why is it none of my business? It's not as if I'm being nasty or anything, just asking."

Seemed like the three years hadn't changed her much. Same girl, same attitude. I didn't respond to the jibe. Silence lay between us.

"Well if you're going to be like that."

"Like what? It's you that needs help, not me. Don't come if you don't want to."

I'd have been relieved if she'd said she wasn't coming. This night was not turning out how I'd planned it, but her mouth stayed shut for a while as I traipsed on, taking longer and longer strides.

It had slowly dawned on me that this was probably a reaaaallly bad idea. I shouldn't have turned round...should've left her on the corner. Remembering how stubborn she used to be, and how many arguments we'd had because of it, I was beginning to feel uncomfortable, and glanced behind me. She was still there. Had I expected her to disappear? Not sure, but it hadn't happened; her head was down, her shorter legs scurrying to keep up with my giraffe-like bones. Sighing, I slowed down. She did need help and I s'ppose I was the older and wiser one now, in much more ways than just my age.

"We're going to the outskirts of town, but that's all I can tell you for now. I'm sworn to secrecy."

Before she could form the next 'why' I interrupted.

"More lives than just mine depend on me not saying anything, so don't ask questions. At least not until we get there. Okay?"

I heard her mumbling,

"You've changed."

I pretend to ignore it, but know she's right. Everyone says it. Even my mother keeps telling me not to be so serious, that I don't need to grow up so fast. On my eleventh birthday, she made me a card with 'seventeen today' on it, as a joke. I smiled, but didn't really get it. I don't feel like I've changed or behave older, I'm just me.

Chapter 3

"Adam, are we nearly there yet?"

She drawled like a kid out of a silly Disney series. It had always been a joke between us. We'd sit at the back of her mother's car asking the same question every five minutes, giggling at how it drove her mother insane.

I smiled. I couldn't help it. The smile turned into a grin and she grinned back. Like a secret piece of our past had bonded us, a memory that would be ever part of who we were.

She had the same look about her, even though she was older and her hair looked like someone had hedge-trimmed it with a blunt saw. Her brown, almond eyes crinkled, her nostrils flared for a second, daring me not to share her moment of joy. I had the impression she'd have thumped my arm if I'd refused to join in. She needed a connection with someone, anyone after being so alone, and I had turned up in the right place at the right time.

Nope, that would be the wrong place/wrong time!

"Ah...the best of times..."

Her voice faded, she sighed and slumped a little.

I couldn't help myself. Even though we'd had no contact for years, I wanted her to feel better. I knew what it was like to be so desperate. My Mam said it was my one weakness.

"You can't save everyone Adam..."

I could hear her voice in my head. But she wasn't here, I was and I had to make a decision.

"They were good times, but maybe better are to come…"

"Not in this world."

"Perhaps not, but there are always other worlds."

She snorted.

"Other worlds as in stepping off this planet. Has the scientist in you actually found a way to do that?"

I'd always loved 'anything science' and had planned to be a scientist.

"No, but there are other places, other ways of living."

And with that, almost unknowingly, I'd made my decision. I'd gone past the point of keeping silent, not saying anything… being invisible. I needed to make it okay for her, even if I had to do more work to let her be one of us. For now though, I couldn't tell her anything more. I needed to gain permission first.

We'd been walking through an old industrial estate for a while. It was the fastest route back, but pretty dangerous, and so I was keen to get through it. Fortunately, I knew the short-cuts, but I'd never travelled through it alone at night. Alicia being with me didn't count as far as I was concerned. She wasn't street wise, more of a child still.

Most of the businesses had closed down years ago. The buildings were drab and weather beaten. Dilapidated signs advertising such things as 'packing warehouses' or 'dog treat factories' hung off their hinges. Doors swung open, rubbish littered the ground and whirled around in mini wind cyclones. It was deserted except for the drug dealers who had made it their home. People died here for little more than a few pounds, or so the stories went.

"Eh you two...what are you up to?"

Number 2 rule: Stay invisible!
Number 3 rule: Don't get distracted!

Two rules broken, and now look what had happened, someone had seen us. Alicia and I glanced at each other before turning round. I mouthed,

"Let me do the talking."

She nodded imperceptibly, her eyes as scared as I felt. Neither of us wanted to be sent to camps. I'd only heard about them, but what I'd heard was horrific. It was too late to run or hide. We'd been spotted in a derelict place where no-one came. So, I pushed my shoulders back, (to make me look taller), put on the best 'teenager' face I could muster and used the voice I'd been taught at the private school, pronouncing all the words correctly.

"Good evening sir. How may we help you?"

I was quaking in my shoes, no, not quaking, more like a full volcanic eruption, I felt so sick with fear.

The Special Forces Policeman standing in front of us had climbed out of his armoured car, leaving his headlights on, to glare angrily out at us so he could take a proper look.

Why hadn't I heard an engine?

I protected my eyes with my left hand so I could see better, but it didn't help much. I could barely see his face as his helmet covered everything but his eyes. He was obviously tall and wide even without the bulk of his black protective clothing. He held a stun gun in one hand, ready to fire. His hand hovered over his waist were a pistol was already unstrapped and probably cocked.

On hearing me speak, he hesitated a moment before continuing, as if weighing me up and down, not quite sure what he was in for. He hadn't expected a well-spoken teenager and although the girl next to me looked like a ruffian, I did not. He was used to routing out drug dealers and dragging them off to gaol, but this situation was mildly confusing. He went ahead with his usual drill anyway.

"Name, address and ID card."

I tried to stall him.

"Have we done anything wrong sir?"

"I don't know, have you? This is not the kind of place I'd expect to find two kids of your age, especially at this time of night."

He was being obstinate and following procedure. After all we could be drug transporters or even buyers. Kids were apprenticed into gangs as young as five nowadays.

"I'm Jake Sartan. This is my sister, Alison. She was stupid and had a bit of trouble. I'm taking her home now."

"What a good kid you are."

The sarcasm ripped off his tongue. I couldn't hold his stare and looked down.

"Name, address and ID card."

For a moment, I wondered why he was alone. Surely in such a dangerous place, there would be a partner.

By law, everyone, of all ages, had to carry an ID card, as well as being scanned by the age of ten. But Downers didn't. We burnt ours out of a matter of choice, and no child was ever scanned. We opted out of a society which had gone too far into the 'devil's arena' to ever have our support. (Of course, I don't mean devil literally, he doesn't exist, and besides which, it's a 'stuck-in-the-head' quote from my mother. She uses it to mean 'evil doings'.

Whatever they may be!) The government no longer offered what we needed, so Downers defied their rules.

But Collectors, along with trackers, always carried fake ID cards when out on a mission, just in case. 'Just in case' was exactly what was happening now. This was a real mess.

The name on my fake card was someone around my age who had died about five years ago. The address was a street in town. I knew 'cos I was curious and checked it out one day.

The card was fine, as long as they didn't examine it in too much detail. If they used a computer to reference it with the morgue's records or a personal scanner, I'd be done for. They could easily do it of course, if they thought we were trouble and they wanted to do the extra bit of work. I was hoping this lone cop would just let us walk.

I tried to control the shaking as I passed over the ID card. He scrutinised me with dark, suspicious eyes, as if he knew I was lying and wanted me to know he knew. As he took the card, Alicia did the worst thing. She started crying. I don't mean little sobs, rather huge, racking, bawling noises that seemed to reverberate off the silent walls. In shock, I almost said her real name.

"Al....."

Quickly I corrected my error.

"Alison...what's wrong?"

She needed to keep quiet. Why wasn't she doing as I said? She was going to get us both into so much trouble.

Wheezing, she tried to speak.

"I...I'm scared, cold and tired...an'a' jus' wanna go home. Mam'll be wonderin' where we are Jake."

She'd taken on a strange dialect as if she were from the north.

The cop looked at her, then at me. Alicia cried even louder and began wiping her nose across her dirty sleeve. For the umpteenth time that night I didn't know what to do or say. I wanted to be quick witted, say something clever, but my mind had gone blank, and so I just stood like an idiot staring at the bawling girl in front of me. What would an older brother do anyway? Immediately, I wanted to cuff her, tell her to shut up, not to ruin everything. We were in so much trouble, but she really did look like the upset little sister, and bigger brothers just wouldn't do that, would they?

Instead I surprised myself by casually slinging my arm around her shoulders and giving her a one-armed hug.

"It'll be all right sis...honestly it will."

I couldn't do dialects even when I tried. They sounded awkward, so I didn't try to hide my dialect, which was 'posh' according to most of the Downers I spoke with.

She was hiccoughing still, but the sobbing had slowed down and she'd become embarrassed, I could tell. I figured the tears had been real. She did want to go home, her non-existent home.

Suddenly, from out of nowhere there was a loud noise – a metallic clang that echoed in the street parallel with ours. Both Alicia and I flinched in surprise. The policeman looked distracted, searching into the night, wondering what to do.

"Right you two", he looked back at us in a much more matter-of-fact manner, "I don't know what you are doing here, and to be honest, I don't really care. I have more problems tonight than two kids in the wrong place at the wrong time. And believe me, you really are in the wrong place, so get out of here now before I change my mind and take you in."

He handed me my ID and headed back towards his car. I couldn't believe our luck. I just stood there watching him pull his vehicle away from the curb and speed down the street. I was so shocked I didn't realise I still had my arm around Alicia.

Abruptly, I pulled away, embarrassed at the closeness and muttered,

"Let's go!"

"Aren't you going to thank me?"

I stood for a moment not at all comprehending what she was talking about. Was she on a different planet?

"For what exactly?"

"Well, don't you think my acting was good? He'd never have let you go if you'd been on your own."

I could have screamed, shook her and even pushed her away, leaving her to another street corner, but instead I just scowled and spoke to her coldly, before turning on my heels, not caring if she followed.

"If I'd been on my own, none of this would have happened."

Chapter 4

I knew she was following. I could hear her feet shuffling along the pavement. Every now and then she sniffed, probably using the back of her hand or sleeve as a tissue, but I didn't look back. We had to hurry, she was noisy, and if I could hear her, others could. At the back of my mind the policeman's comment had bothered me. I rolled the thought over in my brain, repeating it like an irritating, repetitious song that gets on your nerves.

Wrong place, wrong time!

I looked around, but couldn't see much. Most of the lamp lights had been broken in this district and it was really dark, so dark we couldn't see the buildings up ahead. My other senses kicked in. Not just hearing, which seemed to zoom up a level, but fear and the knowledge that someone was around, if that could be called a sense. I was sure someone was watching us and turned round to grab Alicia. Suddenly very scared, I knew we had to get out of there. I seized her shoulder in panic.

"Run Alicia."

"I can't run. My feet hurt."

"More than that will hurt if you don't pick up and keep up."

Suddenly, I sounded like my father. I wondered when he'd said that to me, but the thought left my mind immediately. I didn't have time for stupid 'think-backs'.

Think-back was a word my Granddad had used as a joke when I was young, and it had stuck.

"We have to. There's someone around, watching us."

"How do you know?"

"I know, so don't argue or I'll leave you behind."

I pushed her forward a little more aggressively than I'd meant to and she slipped. Her hands flaying, she hit the ground and screamed out.

"Oh sh...."

I stopped myself swearing. It wasn't really my thing, although lots of Downers swore tons. It was frowned upon around kids, but I wasn't perceived as a little kid anymore. My mother hated it, but many Downers didn't even think of it as swearing anymore, and it didn't really bother me. It was just part of who we were.

"...sugar."

I corrected myself using my mother's word. I felt bad. In my own fear and hurry, I'd actually pushed her over. I crouched down next to her.

"I'm sorry. I didn't mean to."

She scowled at me, trying to hold back the tears in her eyes. Why do girls always seem to be crying? She saw my look and quickly wiped the falling trickles away, leaving dirty smudges down her cheeks. At least she was trying to be brave.

"I can't go faster Adam. I have blisters. These shoes aren't mine. I was in a hurry and stole them from the kids' home 'shoe box' when I ran away. They don't fit me properly."

"Right!"

She could tell I didn't really understand.

"When we entered the home, they took everything away. We weren't allowed to own anything....Do you remember 'Tiger' – that old rag toy I'd had since I was a baby?"

I did, although I hadn't thought about it for years.

"They even took that. When I cried, they slapped me and told me I wasn't good enough to own anything. That I was a burden to the state."

Silent tears fell. The pain in her eyes was acute and I had to turn away. I couldn't say anything to make her feel better. I had no words. Grabbing her hand, I pulled her up.

"We have to leave this place Lissy. It's dangerous."

Lissy was the nickname I'd used years ago.

She smiled through the tears.

"Okay Ad…"

My long ago nickname.

I took us down an alley to the left. It was so dark, so pitch-black, it was as if we'd gone blind. We trod carefully so as not to slip, and I knew at the end we could cut out onto a field and leave this horrid place behind us. I reached for the torch in the pocket of my backpack. I was so tense, it was as if there was static in the air. My heart began to thud in my ears and beads of sweat formed on my forehead. A sure sign danger was close. I wanted to flee. I knew I could get down the end of the street in less than ten seconds, but I couldn't leave her behind now. She limped along lamely, every so often making a little squeak of pain. I shone the torch on the ground ahead of us, trying to focus on the rules, our code. It helped me to breath slower.

Number 1 rule:	Never tell anyone about the Downers even if you are in trouble.
Number 2 rule:	Stay invisible!
Number 3 rule:	Don't get distracted!
Number 4 rule:	Downers are all equal
Number 5 rule:	Downers all have roles for the benefit of everyone
Number 6 rule:	Downers do no harm
Number 7 rule:	Downers do not barter for money in any form
Number 8 rule:	Downers always help their kin as long as number 1 rule applies
Number 9 rule:	All are free to leave and return, but always number 1 rule applies
Number 10 rule:	Leave no trace!

I wondered distractedly if Lissy would accept the rules, immediately breaking number 3 and putting both our lives in danger.

From a side alley, out of the darkness, came four boys. It was as if they weren't there and suddenly they were. They carried old fashioned gas lamps I'd seen in one of those Victorian films my mother used to watch.

But there was nothing Victorian about them. Each wore dark blue jeans and a black leather jacket with a diagonal red stripe from shoulder to waist, as if they had taken a paint brush and smeared their coats. It matched the blood red streak across their faces, cutting across their left eye and ending on the right hand side of their chin. It marked them out as the red-striped gang; one of the drug-mobs selling illegal drugs that 'owned' the district. Jumping in front of us as if they were ghouls had the desired effect; we were immediately terrified.

Lissy moved closer to me and grabbed me with her sticky hand, her arm leant in towards me. I didn't push her away, she was trembling. God, I was trembling!

What was far worse than their gruesome makeup, was the long scythes they carried, flashing them around menacingly as they danced forwards and backwards, as if they were going to attack, but then change their minds. Their intent was clear. I wondered if I should introduce them to rule number six, but the joke was on me. What was I going to do now? Absentmindedly, I switched off the torch and slipped it into the side pocket of my bag. And then the one in the middle came forward and spoke.

"Out for a liddle romantic walk wiv' yer girly-friend then?"

He was about my height, although at least three years older, with spikey, black hair and strikingly blue eyes. His voice was deep and teasing.

"She's not my girlfriend."

They all burst out laughing. What a stupid thing to say! I'd blown my age cover. I could have used bravado and said I was older…I looked it…but now they would know. Only a younger kid would give that response. When Lissy and I were kids, we'd been teased the same way but my mind wasn't working properly. I must think more clearly. We were in deep trouble.

I felt Lissy squeeze my hand to comfort me. I didn't let go.

"Well, not-girlfriend, we 'ave a liddle prop' fe' yer not-boyfriend."

He waved the scythe so close to my face, I could feel the air around it.

"And then we'll letcha' be, bin good 'n' all."

I didn't believe him for a minute and had to think of a way to get out of this.

Lissy was quiet until the scythe stopped in front of her face.

"Priddy liddle t'ing...wun't wanna' scar 'er, would yer now?"

'Red-stripe' still goaded us with that strange mispronunciation and lilting dialect. He wasn't from around here, but then lots of people had been displaced. I had to concentrate to understand him.

Lissy flinched and stepped back, a mouse-like shriek erupting from inside her somewhere. Our palms were sweaty, but we clung to each other.

"What do you want?"

Somehow I was able to find my voice though it sounded so unlike me, so distant.

"Dat's bedda'."

He toyed with us, playing his own warped game.

"A liddle faver'. Jus' a tiny t'ing!"

Looking at us for a moment, he stepped back, ordering his gang, by way of a hand signal, to lower the scythes, stop their entertainment. I glanced behind me. Somehow they had surrounded us without me noticing. It was impossible to escape.

Red-stripe was now all business, his voice no longer goading.

"S' easy. You..."

He pointed to me.

"Deliver a small package t' a location we tell yer wivin' t'our and she..."

He pointed to Alicia.

"...is delivered back t' yer all safe and sound."

"Noooo!"

Lissy screeched. The thought of spending any time with them terrified her. I could see her point.

"I'll go. He stays."

I looked at her horrified for a moment, even though I knew she was right. She was a girl, all alone. She shouldn't be left with them on her own.

"Nope, too dirty. Yud be spotted 'n' picked up. We need a bruvver who looks like a propa' liddle school boy 'n' speaks posh. Yer jus' the part. We 'eard ya talkin' to that cret'n coppa'."

Damn, I knew someone was watching us.

He was pointing at me with his scythe. I swallowed, but there didn't seem to be any spit to go down my dry throat. I just didn't know what to say. It was exactly the cover I used myself. He was right. I did make a good schoolboy look-alike. I tried to stall whilst I thought of something else.

"What's in the package?"

"Let's jus' say, we provide a service."

I couldn't help myself. Sometimes, my mouth spouted words before my brain gave a thought to the consequences.

"Drugs. You make money on the poor, the addicted and those who just can't help themselves."

My tone was one of disgust. My brain was horrified. We were not exactly in a position to mock. To my surprise, he frowned and, for a moment, I thought I saw a look of pain pass through his eyes, but then they hardened again.

"Bag and tie 'em!"

Suddenly, all went dark. Lissy yelped and began to whimper. Someone from behind had put a bag of rough sack cloth over my head. It smelt of rotting mud and did its job really well. I couldn't see in front of me at all and sounds became muffled. The next thing I knew, our hands were being tied with a coarse rope and we were being dragged along. I could hear Lissy shuffling next to me, trying to keep up the pace with her poor, blistered feet. Only now did I have sympathy for her feet!

"Where are you taking us?"

I tried to sound brave, though I was terrified enough to blubber, but tears wouldn't help and I swallowed them back. I just couldn't get it. Why was this happening? Why now? I should have been celebrating with my mother and receiving my full status as a Collector. That's what happened when a newbie successfully managed a trip out on their own. Everyone celebrated with you. It was supposed to be a passage of rites – of sorts. I would now be a provider. I knew mine had been particularly easy, as I knew the house and had an insider to help with keys and the alarm system, but I'd still done it.

The ground beneath us changed from road to gravel. I could feel little stones under my boots, and the normal street sounds disappeared completely. We seemed to be on a sloping path and I had to make an effort not to fall forwards.

It was about then that I heard Lissy slip and tried to pull away from my captors to help her. I don't know why I suddenly had a hero complex, 'cos it was useless. They just yanked me back. The rope tore into my wrists, burning and causing shooting pains up my arms. Lissy had started crying again. I wanted to put my arm around her, which was unusual for me. But I couldn't make it all better for her or for me. I could only move forward into the unknown.

The air around us changed. It became dense and heavy, difficult to draw in to my lungs. I started breathing deeply, craving more oxygen through the tiny holes of whatever very itchy bag they had thrown over our heads. The more I tried, the less I seemed to get. My heart thudded and I started panicking. I was suffocating, going to die in this place without ever seeing light again. I tried to calm down, take deep breaths, but my heart felt like it was going to burst. Not only that, I was going dizzy. There was not enough oxygen getting to my brain. I really was going to die. These would be my last moments on earth. I'd never get back.

And then, I really did do the most girly, embarrassing thing I could ever think of doing. I passed out! The last thing I remember before hitting the ground was a base drum in my head getting louder and louder, beating faster and faster, before my legs turned into unset, quivering jelly.

Chapter 5

I woke up confused. My head was pounding. The world was dark. Someone was putting something cool on my forehead. I could hear strange noises around me. People whispering close by, and movement of some kind not far away. My nostrils flared at the smell of dirt, but more my stomach growled, as I realised I was starving. The necessity of survival kicked in and I opened my eyes.

The first thing I saw was Lissy looking straight at me. She was kneeling at my side administering the wet cloth, playing nurse. She smiled.

"Oh Ad, you're okay. I was worried. You fainted coming in."

In a flash the whole situation came back to me and I sat up too quickly. Pain shot through my eyes as if someone had stabbed me.

"Ow…"

I squinted and held my hand to my head; the gesture didn't help the agony in anyway at all. There was a huge bump on my temple. Rubbing it made it worse. I tried to look around, but there wasn't much light. Lanterns hung here and there giving off gassy fumes. A few people, perhaps six or seven in all, mulled around, most sat in a group a few metres away. There was a small fire in the centre; its smoke curled up to the ceiling and seemed to dissipate.

"Where are we Lissy?"

"Dunno, looks like a cave to me. Don't you remember what happened?"

"We were mugged, dragged away."

The feeling of panic sickness hit my stomach again.

"We have to get out of here."

I tried to move, but a shot of tormenting head pain stilled me. I responded by screech-whispering. I could feel my face contort.

"It's okay. Don't worry. I don't think they're going to harm us."

"Harm us! Don't you think they already have?"

Anger and pain made the words sharper than I meant. It wasn't her fault...well not much. I guess if I hadn't brought her along...but I didn't want to go there. Better to think about how to get us out.

She looked scared; the pupils in her eyes had dilated until I could barely see the brown irises, although that could have also been because it was so dark....or because I'd shrieked at her.

"I don't think they really mean to hurt us."

I knew she wanted to believe it. I didn't have the same faith, but I tried not to take it out on her.

"What do you mean?"

"They just want something."

"What?"

At that moment, Red-stripe came over and crouched in front of us. It looked like he'd rubbed off some of the red streak across his face, but it was still noticeable in the dark. At least he was minus the scythe this time, although he still wore the black jacket. Without the horror-story make up and killing knife, he looked fairly normal with his spiky hair and pale skin. But I knew better! I tried to shuffle backwards, but he held up his hand as if readying it to shake mine. I looked at it in confusion, then stared back up at him. I imagined myself spitting in disgust at his feet. I would have done too, if I could've, but I wasn't that tough or practiced enough and would probably just end up embarrassing myself by hitting my shoe or something.

He grinned. Grinned! What sort of game was this? After a few seconds, he lowered his hand. The smile went with it.

"Who are you?"

I spat the words out at him. I was angry and my head hurt like crazy and he was the cause.

"Hi! Let's say fer now, ma' name's Dillon. Yeh, that suits me well, duncha' fink?"

His name obviously wasn't Dillon. He didn't even look like a Dillon, more of a Peter or Oscar, if you didn't count the attitude. And he had the strangest dialect. He missed off the end of half the words he spoke and slurred everything into one long sentence.

"Yer right to be scared, in fact, yer should be scared, but we' ne'er gonna 'urt yer, not right now anyway."

He spoke in a self-congratulatory manner, as if he had done me some great favour.

"What are you talking about?"

"'ere..."

He handed me a packet and a bottle of water, which Lissy took from him, avoiding eye contact and muttering a thanks. Her upbringing demanded she was polite, even in a situation like this.

"It's drugs. Yer 'it yer 'ead 'ard when yer went down. I bet dat 'urts."

He grinned again, as if it amused him.

"We 'ad such trouble bringin' yer in."

"Bringing me in where exactly?"

He spoke again; the strange words squashed together and lilting in some sort of sing-song tune.

"'Ar 'ome."

He gestured around and, for the first time, I really looked. Although it was dark, it was not completely black. The walls were made of some sort of granite stone, the floors rocky. I looked up. There was no ceiling.

"A cave. We're in some sort of cave."

"Sort ov'."

"Where are you all from? Why are you here?"

"I could ask yer t'same questions. Who are yer? Wha' were yer doin' wonderin' 'round t'estate?"

Silence reared its ugly head between us - neither willing to give way, both staring each other down.

"We dun't ask questions 'ere. We are who we are. We live by our own rules. We're not interested in who yer are, only what yer cun do for us."

I breathed an internal sigh, partially relief at the fact that he didn't care to know who we were, and partially due to nerves. I didn't want to do anything for them. Our priority was to find a way out.

He stood up to go.

"When yer feelin' less of a sissy, come and see me."

Sissy...sissy...what was he talking about?

He must have seen the confusion in my face.

"Even yer girl dint faint."

I could feel my face turn beetroot as I watched him turn round. I knew he was goading me, but I couldn't help it. At that moment, I hated him. He glanced back after a few strides. The aggressive attacker had returned: his voice angry.

"Duncha' steal the food or we'll 'urt yer. Yer not one of us."

I wanted to be indignant, to shout back I didn't want to be one of them, but his words and manner confused me. One minute he was just a boy, teasing and messing around, another a life threatening drug dealer. I stared at his back as I questioned Lissy.

"Time Lissy, what time is it?"

"Not sure. Can't tell in here. You've been out about half an hour I think."

"Oh my God, we have to go. They'll start getting worried soon and be sending search parties out..."

"Who will?"

I ignored the question and made an effort to stand, wincing as I did. I'd never suffered from migraines, but my mother had. I was sure this had to be up there with the worst. I thought I was going to black out again and bent over leaning on my knees. The dizziness passed and I was able to take a first step. Lissy was instantly by my side.

"We have to leave now."

"We can't leave."

"Why not?"

My screeching angry tone appeared again. I didn't mean to take it out on her, but the pain in my head was unbearable.

She looked away.

"I didn't get us into this mess."

I was about to get into an argument with her again, but realised there was no point. Firstly because she was actually right, it was me who had decided to take a short cut through the estate – although I would never admit it – and secondly there was no point. I needed to try and focus to get us out of this place.

"Okay."

I lowered my voice.

"Why can't we leave?"

"Because we don't know the way out. They covered our heads, remember?"

She pronounced the 'remember' with sarcasm. The 'nursey' sympathy had long gone now that I was standing and able to screech at her. She was still holding the water and medicine out towards me.

"What did he give you?"

She looked at it.

"Aspirin I think."

I took it from her and squinted as I tried to read it in the dark. Could I be sure it really was aspirin? What if it were some other sort of drug?

My head screamed at me not to care, the pain was colliding around it like a fevered tornado trapped in a box. I was angry and upset. I felt sorry for myself and I didn't care. If it killed me, it killed me. At least the pain would go away. Ripping the top off the paper, I took out the two white pills, threw them to the back of my throat and swallowed some water. Done!

I waited a moment. Nothing happened and as there was no immediate threat, I decided to move on.

"Where's that kid, what's his name...Dillon? We need to see what he wants from us."

I kept my head down and let Lissy guide me. I didn't want to look at anyone. I had the feeling the more we knew, the less likely it was they'd let us out.

Chapter 6

Red-stripe/Dillon, it turned out, was their leader, although how a fourteen year old boy, (he looked fourteen), could be a leader, I wasn't sure. I was about to find out.

"So, yer on yer feet then?"

It wasn't really a question, so I nodded briefly, wary of the remark and everything it implied.

"At least t'girly dint pass out on us ag'in!"

The comment was aimed at me, not Lissy. The kids that surrounded him laughed and did high-fives as if it was a hilarious joke. His gang all looked between ten and fourteen, though I couldn't be sure in the dark.

I scowled and stood over them, ignoring the jibe.

"Why dun't yer join us?"

"I don't want to join you. Which is the way out?"

I was stubborn. This was a no-name, no-question society. I didn't trust them.

To my horror, Lissy sat down on the hard, black plastic bag covered floor. I stared at her. What was she thinking about? Whose side was she on anyway? The Dillon kid offered her some crackers of some sort, which she took and greedily ate, stuffing them hurriedly in her mouth. She looked like a starving vagabond from a Dickens' novel. Guiltily, she looked up at me, trying to justify her actions.

"I'm tired and hungry."

I harrumphed like a child before giving in. I was as big as any one of them. They wouldn't take me easily again. I looked around. The younger one with pale skin and fair hair I would kick backwards. The one next to him – dark hair and dark eyes – would be knocked sideways in the thrust of his neighbour's kick. That would leave only two. The one on my right had mousey hair and a long nose. He looked as if he hadn't washed for weeks he was so grubby, and I was sure he smelt of rotting rubbish. The shock of my attack before he stood up would leave him unprepared, so I'd easily get to him next. And finally Mr. Oh-so-clever-Leader I'd push his shoulders, buckle his knees and grab his neck, forcing everyone to stand back before I did some real damage.

Even though I'd never done any karate, or kick boxing, the plan made me feel happier, more in control, so I squatted down where I could see all of them and stared out the leader, daring him to speak first. When he did, his question surprised me.

"How old are yer?"

"Fourteen."

I lied. Lissy said nothing. At least if she wasn't completely loyal, she wasn't giving me away.

"'Ad say 'bout 'leven or twelve. Yer jus' look olda' and try to act tough."

I tried not to show surprise or argue. That's what little kids did.

"How old are you and what's this place?"

Change the focus to him.

He stared at me for a moment and diverted his eyes. To my surprise, he actually answered the question.

"'I'm sixteen and I'm the leader of this place."

He looked young for his age. Maybe he was lying, wanting to be older than me.

"This place is our 'ome. We're refugees in t'is won'erful world of ours. All of us!"

"What do you mean?"

Were we actually having a conversation? What happened to the no-question rule?

"Well Posh Boy, look at us. Waddya' see?"

Looking round at the gang, I was surprised. There were only about eight people, all of which had gathered around us to listen to what was going on with the newcomers. None could be older than fourteen or fifteen, a couple were younger, perhaps seven or eight. They were kids. All of them! I snapped my head back.

"Where are the adults?"

"We dun't need adults. They're t'ones that 'arm us now. They're t'enemy."

He spat on the floor as if he had a nasty taste in his mouth.

"We set our own rules. Look after ourselves."

"How…?"

And then it hit me.

"Drugs…illegal drugs. That's the life you lead them in?"

My voice showed the disgust.

Pale Face, Long Nose and Stinky made as if to move, and I readied for an attack, going through my fictitious karate sequence in my head, but their pack leader stopped them.

"No, 'e dun't understand. 'Ee's new 'ere. And besides which, there's t' task."

He looked back at me.

"Yeah, we survive usin' drugs. Yer got owt to say?"

I looked at Lissy. She was strangely quiet for her. She just shrugged her shoulders and looked away as if she had lost all strength to do battle. Red-stripe continued.

"Medical drugs like that cost tons."

He was trying to explain to me, give reasons. It was odd. It was also odd that he seemed to dip in and out of his dialect as if he were trying it out or making it up. Didn't anyone else notice?

"It's 'ard fer normal people to pay a lot. T' state 'as made it impossible for people like us to survive illnesses, so we help. We steal t' drugs from pharmacists 'n' sell 'em to the less well-off for food and stuff."

I said nothing, my face blank in thought, trying to comprehend what he was saying.

"'A like t' think of us as modern day Robin Hoods. Yer know t'story of Robin Hood, duntcha?"

I did, but I didn't want to respond. I didn't want them to be the good guys, so I ignored the question.

"Where are you all from?"

"Remember t' no-question rule?"

I didn't respond. They were probably escapees from Ejector Homes. I couldn't be sure, but they looked the part.

And then the horror of what had really happened to them all hit me. Lissy saw it in my face. She'd realised before me what this was all about. She'd met kids like this before – skinny, dirty and hungry for food and freedom. They weren't really drug dealers –well they were in a sense –but at least not illegal drugs, (not yet anyway). They were just kids trying to survive in a world that didn't care anymore.

I was silent for a moment, mulling it all over in my head.

"Why the whole bags on the head stuff...the secrecy..."

"Protection. We dun't know yer. We cun't take t' risk of yer knowin' who we are or 'ow t' find us."

"Right."

It struck me, they would fit in well with the Downers' ethics, except of course the 'hate all adults' theme.

"And what is it you want from me?"

"Well, t's like a liddle barta', y'see. We 'elp yer and yer 'elp us."

"How are you helping me?"

The thought made me sound angrier than I really felt, but it was true. I just couldn't believe they were actually helping me at all.

"Well, let's see. That policeman was chasin' us when 'e saw yer;. If it 'adn't bin fer us distractin' 'im, eed've dragged yer int'station. And then yer'd 'ave been Ejector Home Meat!"

"How did you help us?"

"Dint' y'ear t' noise?"

He watched my face register the realisation.

"Dat was us."

It had a weird sort of logic.

"And then yer fainted, causing dat bruise on yer head, and yer friend 'ere....."

He actually spoke with a strange sort of kindness and offered her another cracker, which she accepted and wolfed down. Protective jealousy cursed through my veins. We needed to leave now.

"...'ad blisters t'size of stones."

I looked at Lissy as she swallowed, hiccupping at the dryness of the food.

"We gave yer precious medicine free of charge."

He looked at me, his eyes boring into mine, daring me to disagree. His whole body was tense, ready to attack should I cause problems, like a pack leader in a wolf community. Dare I face him down?

No, he was sixteen, older than me by five years and he had a gang with sharp implements ready to peal our skin from our bones! I decided to get this over with.

"What do you want from us?"

"Neer 'us', just yer."

He pointed at me with a dirty finger.

"And?"

"We need yer t' deliver a package t' an address 'n' pick up t'trade."

"The package?"

"Drugs."

I sighed, hoping I wasn't breaking rule number 6.

"The trade?"

"Food."

Chapter 7

"Why me? Why can't one of you go?"

"The district t'is a bit more up-market. We'd be outta place. But not yer."

"And Lissy?"

With horror, I realised I'd accidentally given her name away.

He smiled sarcastically.

"Ah…liddle Lissy….she stays with us till yer return wiv' t'trade."

Lissy's ability to fight back was drowning in fear. She looked at me, her eyes flooded, begging me to rescue her from the situation, but there was little I could do but make a deal.

"How do I know she'll be safe?"

"No…"

She was shocked. Somehow she'd thought I could get her out of this, but I was doing my best. What did she expect?

"I'll take care of her."

A girl behind me had spoken up. She had short mousey hair, a long face and dark eyes. She looked the elder of all the girls – there were three of them, and as if to prove it, two youngsters were leaning on her like they might their own mother. She hugged them into her, comforting the lost children.

For a moment I stared. All my training with the Downers and still I couldn't help it. Under the grubbiness and dirt, the little kids had dark skin. Not only dark skin, but ebony black! They almost dissolved into the gloom around them except that the white of their eye balls stared out from scared faces and raggedy hair. Other than a couple of Downers, who would only risk being out at night, I'd never seen black people above ground. It sounds stupid even to my own ears, but the purging was before my time. I didn't have anything to do with it, but I know the history.

My mother still speaks of its horror. It started with the changing environment, and something called the jet stream causing floods. I don't know the details, but large parts of the country to the south and west were lost to terrible floods. It was an environmental disaster. With no money to fix it, the land couldn't be recovered and England shrunk in size. The survivors moved into London and further north to find work. There were suddenly less jobs to go around. Those applying for permission to work in England from another country had new laws and regulations to follow. They were only permitted to stay for one year and then only if they had a job. Anyone caught without a job or living on the streets was immediately 'ejected' from the country. That's where the term 'ejected' originally came from.

Then came the riots. Money was scarce and jobs hard to find. White people attacked those who didn't look British, those who were not white-skinned, those with different beliefs. Hundreds of people died. Businesses were set on fire. I've seen the old photos and news footage. It's hard to believe normal people could be so violent.

In an attempt to control the situation and keep power, the government responded harshly by sending in government troops and kicking out anyone who hadn't been in the country for more than five years, then more than one year. Eventually, it was anyone who didn't 'look' British. Those who refused were put in camps or just disappeared. England went from a population of seventy million to less than forty million almost overnight.

The look on my mother's face when she talks of this time is painful. She is ashamed she did nothing. I tell her she probably couldn't have done anything anyway. But it was only the beginning.

After the purging, the government couldn't seem to stop. They started on those left – the weak, the poor, those who didn't contribute to society. Contribution became the word by which everyone was judged. 'Ejection' became a word to fear and still is.

I try not to think about these things, they're frightening, even to a kid my age. I can't believe I live in such a world…it's a nightmare that I put away in a box to ignore, pretend it's nothing to do with me. I didn't do it after all, but all the Downer kids are taught recent history…. so we understand how we became what we are, so we understand how not to be that.

The older girl interrupted my thoughts.

"What'yer starin' at? D'ya 'ave a problem?"

Her voice was hard and protective. She looked towards her leader.

"Yer shun't 'ave brought 'im 'ere. What if 'e tells?"

"He wun't tell."

Red-stripe cut her off sharply. She didn't respond, but looked away from me, speaking into the dark cave.

"The little ones are starvin', so as long as yer bring back food, no one shall 'urt yer friend. She'll be under my protection."

I wanted to believe her. I didn't know whether to, or really whether I had a choice.

"Come 'ere Lissy. Yer stay wiv' me now."

Resigned to not having any say in the matter, Lissy obeyed the order, crawling over to the girl and sitting down at a slight distance, as if she had been claimed. She wrapped her arms around up-bent knees and rested her head on them, not wanting to register the world, or me. Guilt engulfed me.

What had I done?

"All settled then."

Red-stripe was talking again.

"We'll go wiv' yer as far as the edge of the estate, but then yer on yer own."

He handed me an old shoe box with faded writing on it, and a piece of paper. I read the scribble - 18 Albert Gardens. I knew the address; it was not far from my old street.

"I know it."

"Good. When you get there, knock on the back door and say you are here to trade. That's all, nothing else."

"But what if it goes wrong."

"It wun't as long as yer follow instructions."

"What if they take the box and don't give me anything back?"

"Make sure they dun't or else."

He dragged a threatening finger across his throat, making a guttural noise as if slitting his own gullet. It was overly dramatic, but his goons found it amusing, snickering from out of the shadows.

"What if it goes wrong and I can't get back? What if I'm taken? What happens to Lissy then?"

My mind was flashing with images of supposed drug carriers being found dead in the street or floating face down in rivers. I heard Lissy squeak behind me.

"Then we'll 'ear 'bout it soon 'nuff 'n' liddle Lissy can stay or go. Weel also know if yer just run off."

I said nothing, just stared at him. I wasn't sure what to do, how to keep Lissy safe, but as there was nothing more to be said, I stood up. I wanted to get this over with. Then I noticed something.

"Where's my things...my bag, hat and scarf?"

"They're mine now."

"No, they're not, they're mine. Give them back or I'm not going."

This time I was obstinate. They were my disguise and I felt safe in them, hidden under the cap and protected by swathes of wool.

We locked eyes once more. It was as if we were challenging each other to a mental duel.
Everyone around us stared, looking from one to the other, silently wondering who would give in first.

His eyes were dilated, causing them to look weirdly black and haunting. I wondered vaguely if my eyes looked the same in this cavern.

"Food or bag? I thought the little kids were starving?"

It wasn't really a fair comment, but I wasn't feeling much like being fair. I didn't see why I had to be. They were forcing me into another dangerous situation. Keeping Lissy as a bargaining tool.

Dillon's eyes flicked towards the older girl, before dragging my bag from behind him. He delved inside and took out the knives, electric cord, notepad and batteries.

"I keep these."

It was a trade-off. He couldn't lose face and I knew it. I wanted to disagree, they were my symbols of victory, but my head was still throbbing and I really didn't care anymore. Getting the task done and getting out of there was more important now. My test didn't seem significant right now.

"Fine...take them."

I snatched my bag out of his hand. Inside was my cap and scarf. I pulled them out and slung the backpack over my shoulder. The weight of the LED torch in the side pocket gave me a sense of victory – they hadn't even noticed. I loved that torch, it was a gift from my Mam one Christmas, when we could afford such things. I kept my personal Gabber in there, slipped down the back of the batteries. It was a tracking device. Hopefully it was working and if I didn't return soon, they'd send someone to find me.

"Let's go."

Lissy was watching me. As I was about to pass, I stopped and bent down close to her, whispering so only she could hear.

"Don't worry. I'll be back soon and then we'll leave. You can come and live with us until we find your Mam and Dad."

Her eyes teared up again.

"You will come back, won't you Ad?"

"Of course I will. I said so, didn't I?"

"Promise?"

"I promise."

Another childish bargain from our past, but it brought a wan smile to her pale, tear-smeared face and that helped me move on. Strangely, I felt like Lissy was a child that needed protecting. I now had to be the adult that makes things right.

I stood, squaring my shoulders as if I were some sort of tough guy-villain, and followed Pale Face, Long Nose and Stinky to the back of the cave. They seemed to be the deputies, but none of them had spoken much, just provided the sneers and grunts. Watching the backs of their heads, I stepped carefully over rocks and gravel, sure I would fall in the darkness. Suddenly, they turned round. Long Nose was holding up a dirty piece of material.

"Blindfoldin' time!"

"What...no one said anything about blindfolding me!"

The recent horror of walking through dark caves with a hood on my head sent a curdling shiver up my spine."

"Be glad t'sn't the hood."

"Be glad...!"

But by then, Pale Face and Stinky had grabbed me by my arms. I struggled and kicked out, shaking my head from side to side.

"No, I won't."

Long Nose put his face close to mine. His breath was disgusting, like rotting fish. I held my breath as he spoke, the thought of inhaling any air that had already been down his throat or through his nostrils, repulsed me.

"S'either this, or we go back. Do yer wanna go back and explain why yer din't finish the task?"

His voice was menacing. He was now the scythe-holding drug dealer, and from his expression of glee, he enjoyed the terror in my eyes.

"Fine..."

I conceded, but only because there was nothing I could do. I hated it that they were controlling me. I wanted to attack them. Anger welled up inside of me as he tied the dirty rag across my eyes, pulling it extra tight and trapping hair in the knot. I said nothing, I didn't want them to have the pleasure of hearing me screech. I wasn't a sissy and at least I could breathe.

It took us about ten minutes to get out, during which time I was arm-dragged and back-pushed in the direction they wanted me to go in. After a while I felt the ground beneath me change. There wasn't so much gravel and then suddenly, I could breathe fresh air again. I knew we were outside. The wind still howled, and had been joined by cold, spitting rain which lashed at my face.

I bowed my head to my right shoulder, trying to wipe freezing water off my cheek. In doing so, I managed to move the blindfold ever so slightly across my right eye, allowing me to see where we were. To my relief, I recognised the area, but as I'd never known there was a cave around – or maybe it was a mine shaft – it would still have been impossible for me to locate it. I wanted to look back to check, but then they would know I could see and so, as they grabbed me, I purposely put my head down, imagining myself the frightened, tired, captive for their benefit. Every so often, I kept looking up, to check our progress through the grassy field so I could find my way back – just in case they weren't around and I had to get Lissy back on my own. I didn't trust them one bit. Only when I could feel pavement beneath me, did they wrench it off.

I stood for a moment, squinting, waiting for my eyes to fully adjust to the dark. I knew approximately where we were. I'd taken this route with a Downer before, we were back in the old industrial estate – a murky alley.

"This way...keep quiet, we'll take yer a way no one'll find us. Dun't make a noise. Others live 'ere too. We'll 'and yer ova' if they see us."

Stinky's voice was a mixture of deep tones and high pitches. His voice was breaking, so he must have been a bit older than his skinny body showed. Reluctantly, I nodded in agreement, doing what he said. I was afraid of getting lost if they suddenly decided to leave me stranded. I didn't actually know the way.

It was hard going and tense. I gritted my teeth - my jaw was rigid. The wind batted against us, throwing us backwards, as if warning us not to go any further. The freezing rain had begun pouring harder and I could barely open my eyes. All my instincts said 'run', but it was pitch black in the 'lampless' streets and impossible to see anything. I could only keep to their pace as the second in a line. We pressed ourselves against buildings like spies creeping against walls and peeping out around corners to see if the enemy was there. It was a slower pace than I wanted to go and sent my nerves jangling. I didn't know what time it was and I shouldn't be caught out on the streets at night, particularly after seven o'clock. The Downer's enforced a curfew for kids. It wasn't safe for them at night. No one under fifteen was allowed to break the curfew.

At one point we heard a car engine, probably that cop that stopped us before. We stood stock still for endless moments, but we were lucky. It went in the opposite direction. After ten long minutes, we eventually arrived at the edge of the estate. They turned to face me. Stinky spoke.

"We'll wait fer one 'our and then we'll leave. If yer run away, we'll know – dun't expect yer liddle girly-friend t'live."

I believed the threat. Long nose was cruel and angry with the world. And I could tell he didn't like me. He was the type that would hate you just for the way you looked or spoke, and I spoke of 'money' and 'class' to him. I represented all those who'd stepped on him, treated him badly, made his life everything he didn't want it to be.

I felt like defending myself, but I said nothing. He wouldn't believe me anyway, but I was not one of those people. Not any more anyway. But he didn't know that and didn't really care. I turned to go. I could feel six eyes watching me from the shadows of an old one-story office building as I quickly made my way across the long grass towards the city lights.

Thank goodness I could find my own way back!

Chapter 8

I felt an enormous sense of relief ditching my 'guardian angels', but the fear still lingered. Tense, I flicked my eyes from left to right warily, not knowing who might be around the corner. My stomach curdled tight and my teeth ached with clenching so much. The next time I looked in the mirror I'd see nothing but ground down stubs. Alone in dark streets, probably after the curfew, all I felt like doing was running home, but Alicia's life depended upon me succeeding. Surely they wouldn't really carry out their threat. I couldn't be sure. But I'd promised to go back for her, and to do that, I needed the trade. For that reason alone, I was now a drug dealer.

Do no harm!

The rule stuck at the back of my throat. What if they had lied to me? What if the package I carried wasn't medicinal at all? It wouldn't surprise me. I hitched my bag higher on my back – the straps had slipped uncomfortably down my aching arms. To compensate, I took to striding faster down the street. The sooner I got this over with, the sooner I could leave it all behind and I really didn't want to be caught out when the lights changed to red.

The government had installed red street lamps on the side of buildings. Not only were they cheaper, but when they glowed, you knew you were an 'illegal' in the street. Any 'illegal' could be caught and hauled off, thrown into the back of an armoured van, never to be seen again – or so the story goes. I can't say I've ever observed someone being 'hauled off' myself, so I s'ppose it could be a fairy tale nightmare to warn kids to stay off the streets at night, but who knows? I wouldn't put it past the government and I didn't really want to test the theory tonight.

I was getting hot with the exercise and the thought of the meeting at Albert Gardens. Beads of sweat had formed on my forehead. I could feel my face burning. I didn't mind the 'exercise heat', it was a cold night, but the fear I had to get under control. Usually, I was very good at controlling my emotions, hiding what people saw, but tonight was making that very difficult. Pretending I was a temporary drug dealer was horrible, but I had to make it work or the deal might go wrong. That would be the worst thing. What would they do with us then?

My mind wandered on thoughts of what I might do once I'd found the cave, how I might find my way in, not really taking in the streets or people who passed me by. Most had their heads down anyway, protecting their faces from the wind. Fortunately, the rain had stopped, although it was still too dark to take in much. Street lights were far and few between until I hit the richer districts, and the clouds had covered any chance of light from the moon and stars.

Instinctively, I kept as close to the buildings as possible, trying to melt into the walls. I didn't want anyone to see me. I needed to be invisible again. Every now and then I passed a sewer grate and my nose wrinkled at the waft of rot which shot upwards. After a while, I just covered my nose to lessen the disgust, hoping I wasn't breathing in any harmful gases.

Maybe when I got to the cave, I could just hide outside, wait to see if one of the kids went in and then follow them. One of them would have to come out or go in at some time. I followed through a plan in my mind. It was a bit of a long shot, but it might work. I imagined myself sitting behind a bush or hiding in the shadows of the cave and seeing Long Nose enter. What then? I'd have to follow him in of course, shadow him so he showed me the way. Yes, that would work. I was almost pleased with myself.

How would you find your way back? No tech to guide you!

A voice in my head asked.

Good question!

I was having a crazy conversation with myself.

The answer was immediate – I'd read it in some kids' adventure book once, an old turn of the century thing whose title I couldn't recall at that moment, but the answer was clear.

Chalk or string. Mark the walls with something to guide you out.

That sounded like an even better plan and I felt a little happier. But the voice snapped back at me.

Now all you have to do is remember how to get to the cave and to collect some chalk or string.

The cave I didn't know existed until today.

Suddenly, I was at Albert Gardens. It seemed between all the planning and brain-yapping, my feet had walked me there without my consent. I had a friend once who told me about his mother's sleepwalking habits. Once she'd manually driven her car to his grandmother's house whilst still in her sleep. She'd arrived on the step in her nightwear and rung the bell. His grandparents awoke to find her standing there, unaware of how she got there without crashing. The car hadn't even been on auto-drive.

That's how I felt, standing in front of 18 Albert Gardens, staring at the tall, detached townhouse, with its large, jutting out windows beaming light into a dark street. I just stood there and stared for a moment, dizzily not recalling how I'd managed to get there. Obviously I had, and now was the time for action. I was the drug dealer come to trade. I had to keep telling myself this. I had to leave with the food. I had to make the trade, or else!

I almost went to the front door, a large black thing with a golden knocker shaped like a lion's head, before remembering I had to go to the back door. I wondered who I'd meet back there. Maybe the owner, or maybe a servant. A house like this probably had several. With so few jobs around, working in a rich house was a privilege, even if poorly paid.

What if they don't know what I'm talking about?

I pushed down my doubts, gulped and took a deep breath. I needed to do this before fear took over completely and I ran in the opposite direction.

Walking around the black iron railings of its small front garden, I found a dark alleyway. I dragged my torch from my bag and switched it on, shining it towards the ground so no one would see it. Not wanting to make any noise, I placed my feet one in front of the other carefully, almost balancing on the tips of my toes.

Unexpectedly, a black cat jumped out in front of me and hissed, its slanting eyes daring me to pass into its territory. My heart jumped out of my chest, flashing red and booming to drums only my ears could hear, like the old cartoons I used to watch. My pulse raced and blood gushed into my temples. My brain was preparing me to either 'fight or take flight' – from a cat. I giggled inwardly to myself and leant against the wall until I calmed down a little. A drug dealer afraid of a cat, who was now rubbing itself against my left leg and purring as if it were my best friend! I bent down and stroked it for a moment. Funnily, it helped calm me down and sent my feet forward to their destination a little faster.

I can do this!

The back door opened a fraction – a thick brass chain preventing anyone from pushing their way in. A small woman of about seventy peered out.

"Yes?"

She had a pale, extremely wrinkled face and grey hair tied back behind her neck; her voice was croaky. I stared for a moment, forgetting my lines. She stared back with squinting eyes as if she found it hard to see me.

"Em....I'm here to trade?"

My voice came out embarrassingly squeaky and I managed to make it sound more like a question, rather than a statement.

She stared again for what seemed like endless seconds.

"You'd better come in then."

Chapter 9

I stepped into a small, dimly lit utility room with machines for washing clothes and stuff. On the floor boots and shoes were scattered and on the wall, coats of all colours and types hung. After my strenuous walk, it seemed extremely hot and stuffy. I had the urge to pull off my hat and scarf, but instead made sure they covered my face as high as my eyes. I didn't want anyone to remember me, or even worse, recognise me. Although I didn't know the people in this house, I had only lived a few streets away once upon a time.

"The package?"

The woman was shorter than me, bent over and older than I'd first thought, her back was bent with a bulge between her shoulder blades. She could have been eighty, although it was really hard to tell. She was holding out her hand, palm upwards, waiting. I stared at her bony fingers, my brain not engaging. All I could think was that she reminded me of a witch. Her finger nails were so long, they could scratch out your eyes. She even wore an old, black, woollen shawl across her shoulders. My pulse was racing. And I was so hot, not only were my hands sticky, but sweat was also running down my spine. I could feel the slow trickling.

"Are you deaf?"

The witch croaked. Perhaps she was planning a spell to turn me into a frog, or to capture me and put me in a pot.

Don't be so daft!

The voice in my head woke me up. Nerves were getting the better of me and quickly I pulled myself together. I had to.

"Where's the trade?"

I didn't care if my voice squeaked; I needed to get out of here. I was in danger. I knew it.

"You don't trust me?"

She said it like an accusation, as if I didn't trust a little old woman….which I didn't. She looked far too much like a witch for anyone to trust her. I rebuked myself. I needed to focus and not drift again. She wasn't a witch!

Yeah! Well what about the black cat?

I ignored the remark in my head.

"I don't trust anyone. Show me first."

She dragged out a medium-sized, blue plastic bag, seemingly too heavy for her to carry, and opened the top. In the dim light, I could see loose potatoes and a small packet of sliced bread. Food!

"Okay."

I was trying to sound tough, but she knew I wasn't. I was just this skinny, little kid from nowhere. I dug out the shoe box from my backpack without taking it off, but left the zip open, ready to pack the goods. I wanted to be out of there as fast as possible. I slowly passed the package over to her. As I did, I noticed her foot shoving the food backwards. Immediately, I knew what she was trying to do. Her hand was on the drugs, ready to grab them and then what? Was she stronger than she looked? Would she try to push me away without the trade? I pulled back the shoe box just in time.

"Wait!"

She looked at me curiously, unsure what I was going to say. She knew I knew she'd planned to trick me. I tried to see it from her perspective. I was a stranger, my face was covered and, after all, it could just be paper inside the box, but all my instincts were screaming at me to be cautious, not to get too close. Without even thinking about it I took a half step back.

"Put the bag over there against the wall and I will put the package on the washing machine over here. Then we both cross over and take what we want."

She hesitated before muttering.

"Open the package first."

Fair enough request. I was curious myself. Perhaps it was scrunched up paper! Then I'd be in trouble. I should have checked before. I cursed myself for not doing so.

I pulled off the dirty newspaper, screwing it up and throwing it on the floor. I really didn't care at that moment if I was making her house untidy.

Perhaps it wasn't even her house!

Inside the shoe box were eight smaller boxes; they looked medicinal to me.

"Open the boxes! All of them!"

She ordered. Was it my imagination, or did she seem suddenly taller...and her voice...less croaky? Hairs on my arms stood up, adrenalin shot around my veins. Something was wrong. I could feel it in my bones and hear alarm bells ringing in my head. I needed to get out of here quickly. I started undoing a box as fast as I could, but my fingers seemed like toes. I couldn't open the boxes fast enough. Her eyes flicked to over my shoulder for a moment longer than was normal, causing me to turn round to see what she was looking at, but my instincts were too late.

The door I'd come through was opening, I could see the handle turning. I was about to move out of the way, when a man with dark, bushy eyebrows and short black hair pushed the door so violently into my back, that I screeched and dropped the medicine. Although I immediately bent to pick it up, the woman knocked me out of the way. The pain shooting through my back caused me to be off-balance and she used it to her advantage. I fell to the floor on my right side, moaning again. The woman disappeared into the house with the medicine, the man stepped over me, kicking me in the stomach for good measure. I doubled up, gasping for breath. In his hand he held something dark and heavy. I couldn't see what it was, my eyes were seeing a myriad of flashing lights and then I began to feel so sick. Salty saliva burnt the glands at the back of my mouth and ran over my tongue furiously trying to find an escape. I knew I was about to either vomit or faint. His crazy, threatening voice was distant in my mind.

"This is a warning. Tell your little friends not to trade on my patch."

And then the heavy thing was brought down on my head. My skull had been split open, I was sure of it. The razor-sharp pain was agony. I could hear myself screaming on and on, but it all seemed so distant.

"Shut up! Shut up! Do you hear me?"

Was he telling me to do something? His lips seemed to be moving, but I couldn't understand what he was saying. Almost in slow motion I saw him as a blurred object moving towards me. Saw him lifting his arm with the heavy thing in it. I knew what he was going to do, knew that this was my end, but just couldn't do anything to prevent it. He brought his hand down towards my head. He really was going to kill me, and I wasn't going to stop him. My brain wasn't working my body, had stopped giving it orders. I tried, I willed myself to move, but I just lay there watching, screaming.

After only one moment of pure agony, one knife-hit to my skull, I knew no more - the sweet oblivion of unconsciousness and a blackened world overcame me.

Chapter 10

I registered the hurt first. Hurt wasn't the word for it really. It was as if someone was hitting my head with a mallet every two seconds. Throb...throb...throb! I tried to move, but it sent sharp, shooting pains up the side of my neck and face. I could barely think. I didn't know what had happened or where I was. I tried to open my eyes, but they were impossibly heavy and it was so much easier just to lie there with my eyes closed.

I tried to think, but every thought was a painful ache in a damaged skull. Every cell willed me to go back to sleep, but something else pushed me to survive, to think. Slowly, I remembered the old woman, the bag of food, but nothing after that. My mind was blank. What had happened to me? But it was too much, the pain took over and I faded again.

Eventually, I woke to a noise, muffled voices somewhere. I was coiled on my right side, knees to my stomach and my hands holding onto the sides of my head as if to keep it from falling off, or perhaps just protecting it from the jolts it was receiving. The pain was still there, but I seemed to be able to move a little. I was lying on a hard, cold ground, shivering; my right arm was numb with pins and needles and my stomach clenched. I thought I might puke at any time. Still I tried to concentrate, tried to figure out what had happened.

The voices became clearer....two men talking somewhere in front of me. I knew I had to hide. If they found me, I'd be in trouble, I was sure.

I tried to sit up. I felt sick and dizzy. White hot searing pain shot up the side of my head and I groaned, as I leant on my dead elbow to look around. I lifted a heavy hand towards the searing pain and found a sticky patch on the side of my head and down my face. I couldn't see what it was in the dark, but it smelt like rusty metal, like blood.

"'e's awake."

A gruff voice reached my ears.

"Don' matter. We're nearly there... jus' round the corner."

Shocked realisation that the cold ground was actually a moving vehicle made me jerk upwards. The only light came from a small grid which led into the front cabin, but my eyes soon adjusted enough to realise I was in the back of a small van and the two voices were up front.

Although my brain seemed to be working in slow motion, my whole body shook, my heart pounded. I had no idea what I was doing in the van but I was in a dangerous situation and every instinct told me I had to escape.

We were slowing down, I could feel it; the creak of the gears changing and the hand break being pulled up.

"We're 'ere. This is the place. Give us a good price, they will, well at leas' 'nough for a few suppers."

"Can't throw that 'way."

What are they talking about? A price? Supper?

I was confused. I heard the front doors slamming as they got out.

Doors...of course. Where are the doors? I need to get out.

My heart fully charged with blood, it sent it streaming around my body, readying my legs to run as I tried to crawl to the back of the van.

But before I had a chance to figure out anything, the doors were opened, and in the dark night stood my captors, both tall and heavily built. Their faces were hard to make out as the night was pitch black behind them, but their eyes shone white like evil spirits ready to take me to hell and I immediately knew they were dangerous.

"You...come 'ere."

The one on the left had a hoarse voice as if he had been screaming all day. I wasn't about to do as he said and scooted to the back of the van on my bottom to avoid him, although I wasn't sure where I was going or what I was going to do. The movement caused more pain, more sickness and suddenly I was seeing the non-existent flashing lights and spots before my eyes again.

"You get outta the van now, or suffer!"

I didn't respond. I couldn't. I was trying to cope with the waves of sickness flooding through my body from my stomach to my head. I felt like I was on a nightmare version of a swing boat I'd once rode at a fairground when I was a little kid. My Dad had taken me on one, even though I'd been too young. I'd been terrified, but hadn't wanted to admit it, I was trying to be brave and please him, make him proud of me. When I'd stepped off the ride, my legs were shaking so badly, I happily ran into my mother's arms and then couldn't help the flood of tears. My mother and father had argued about it all the way home. She'd been so angry with him.

Unsure why the split second of a memory had entered my brain at such a time, I tried to focus, tried to take deep breaths to stop the dizziness. This was not the time to faint again, I had to stay awake.

"If I 'ave to climb in there to get yer…'"

The one on the right gave me a warning. His tone said it all. I didn't want more pain and there was no way out. I wondered if I could run away once on the ground. I doubted it. Between the pain, the sickness and the fear, I just wasn't strong enough!

"What do you want with me?"

My voice was scratchy as if I had a sore throat.

"Nuffin', so get out."

His voice was menacing.

"NOW!"

There was nothing for it but to go along with them and find out what they wanted. I crawled towards them, head doing its own version of a rock band. I was sure I would vomit. I pictured a projectile of carrots splashing across their faces, the acid blinding their hateful eyes, allowing me the time to run away. But my stomach wouldn't respond to my call of protection. Trying to focus on moving, I wondered which would burst first, my head or heart. It seemed both were in competition. I was heating up. Even though I'd been cold, a sudden flash of hotness enveloped me, causing me to sweat. The smell was sticky and sweet; sickness.

Although it seemed like forever, I reached the opening and found strong hands pulling me out of the cabin and dragging me to my feet. If they hadn't held me up, I'd have probably just sagged to the floor and lain there like a heap of wet blankets.

"Move."

The order came from the guy on the right who kept a tight grip on my shoulder. He smelt as if he'd never washed, of a dank cave covered in fungi and seaweed, or something.

Cave!

The thought brought it all back.

Alicia, the drugs, the food. It was all a trap. Oh my God, I have to escape. I promised I'd go back. They might hurt her.

I tried to struggle, wriggling my arms, kicking out my legs, but they pinched my shoulders harder and shook. The pain shot through my head.

"Arg...stop...please stop."

"Do as we tell yer or suffer."

"Okay."

They led – dragged me to a dirty, black door around the back of the house and banged loudly. I was beginning to realise were I might be and was terrified. They were Clearers of illegals – those on the street at night. Clearers emptied the streets of the homeless and the beggars. I was being cleared.

I began to struggle again. Instinct took over and I fought with my captors, kicking Righty's shins, and biting Lefty's fingers. Lefty immediately swore and let go. Righty hung on, shaking me like a rag doll. I shrieked, tears forming in my eyes; the agony in my head was unbearable, but he kept shaking. I tried to grapple with his hands. Tried to stop him, kicking out, but he dodged this time and slapped me hard across my cheek. The unexpected sting shocked me into stillness. The shoulder pain as Righty grabbed my arm and twisted it behind my back deterred me from struggling further. He grinned and took delight in the pain he inflicted as if I were a mouse caught in a trap and he knew it.

At that moment, the door opened.

"Yes."

"We 'av' anuver."

"You'd better come in then."

A man with a large, industrial torch stood aside and opened the door wider.

They shoved me over the doorstep, Righty using my twisted arm as leverage. I was sure it would break, surely an arm can't go that far. The pain was excruciating and temporarily outdid my head. Once over the doorstep, they forced me onto my knees and held me there.

"Bow to your betters Non-Contributor."

Chapter 11

I couldn't do anything for the moment and so kept my head down, looking at the worn floorboards. It was dark other than the glare of the torch the man held, but my nose was so close to the ground that I could see the planks. They were about as wide as my two hands and ran parallel to each other. Some were cracked, others had swirling patterns in them; all were bare.

I could see the feet of the person who'd opened the door. He wore a dark red pair of slippers and grey-striped, flannel pyjamas that were a little too long for him.

"How old is he?"

"Dunno...looks about eleven."

Righty was talking.

"He looks older to me."

Pyjama-man was wrong, but I'd go along with that.

"How old are you?"

The question was addressed to me. I didn't want to answer. If the only way I could defy them was not talk, then so be it, but a kick from someone behind me soon changed my mind. I couldn't take any more pain. I was sure I was going to be sick soon. Pain was crippling, and I needed to be strong. Strong enough to get away as soon as possible. Escape plans were already entering my mind, but I had to pay attention. Alicia needed me and so did my Mam. She would be going crazy by now. I vaguely wondered what time it was.

"Fourteen."

"He's too old. Take him to the compound."

"'Ee's lyin'"

"How do you know?"

"Look 'ow skinny 'e is, 'n' 'is voice 'aint broke yet."

"Mmmm...perhaps."

"But 'ees big. 'E'll be strong."

Pyjama-man ignored him. When he did speak, he sounded like he was sneering at the two.

"Where did you find him?"

"Up by the park."

That wasn't true, but it was fine by me if they lied, unless of course they were telling the truth and I'd been dumped there. Still, the less anyone knew about me the better.

"Right, I'll give you half the normal price."

"'Arf...bu' that 'aint the deal."

"He's damaged goods. Look at his head. He'll be useless for a while."

"Bu'..."

"You should have been more careful where you placed your boots."

"We found 'im like it."

"I don't care. Half it is, or nothing."

"But 'ees strong."

"And will be with me less time. He's really too old for here....Now make up your mind, or take him away. It's the middle of the night and I have a bed to go to. I care not whether he stays. We have enough here anyway."

I could hear them whispering to each other behind me. Deciding my fate. Deciding whether to sell me to a Non-Contributor kids' home. This was where Evictors' kids were brought, where Alicia had been placed. I wondered if she'd been sold to this place. I wondered how she'd escaped.

"So…."

Righty seemed to be in charge.

"…make it three quarters the normal price and we'll leave 'im wiv' yer."

He spoke as if he were doing Pyjama-man a favour.

"Take half or leave. That's it. That's the deal."

There was silence for a moment as if he were contemplating a very difficult calculation.

"Fine…take 'im. What would we do wiv' 'im now anyway?"

I heard the clinking of money, wondered briefly what half the payment was.

"Now get out of here. I don't want to see your faces for at least a month."

My head was spinning and the pressure of my stomach on my knees made me feel faint. I couldn't have moved had someone asked me to. I heard the door open and close behind me and the almost silent whirring of a high tech lock. My heart sank, security was tight. How would I escape?

One threat had passed and another loomed, and then, without warning, I threw up all over the wooden floor boards.

Chapter 12

"You will scrub the floorboards in this room every day until I can't smell it anymore. Do you understand?"

I nodded. I actually felt better now that my stomach contents were no longer behaving like a wave. My head was clearer and I was on my feet, although my legs still trembled and my head throbbed.

He screwed up his dark eyes menacingly as a reminder of how I should address him.

"Yes, sir!"

He was a tall, narrow man in every sense, even his head was long and thin. His bones stuck out at every opportunity – high cheek bones, long nose, pointed chin, long fingers, as if they were trying to escape his pale, dry skin drawn taut across his skeletal frame.

"This will be in addition to your normal tasks. Do you understand?"

I wondered whether I looked stupid and was almost inclined to ask him, but I didn't want another clobber. I decided it was probably him that was stupid instead. It made me feel better anyway.

"Yes sir!"

He looked at me as if checking I wasn't being rude with the tone of voice I'd used. There had been a slight edge to it, but that was because I was so angry and could do nothing about it. I wanted to kick out at him. How dare he buy me? I wasn't for sale. It was one of the first things we learnt as Downers. We are all free people. No one is for sale.

I looked up, knowing even then he was the type of man that might hit me just for staring at him. With short, dark hair, dark eyes and a sallow face, all I could see was cavernous nostrils under a large nose. In fact, it stuck out from his face so much it was all I could focus on. I imagined bird poo hitting it every time he went for a walk. They couldn't miss it. I could tell he was about to slap me for spending so long glaring at him, and so looked down.

At the moment he was very irritated and I was the cause. Instead of going back to bed, he'd had to stand around watching me clean up carroty sick - I hadn't even eaten carrots that day – with cold water and a hard scrubbing brush. Every time I hesitated he screamed at me to hurry. Being such a 'tall' man, I'd expect a deep voice, but his got squeakier with anger.

After twenty minutes of scrubbing, I had no doubt what place I was in although I wasn't sure where the location was exactly. I'd already asked and received a slap across my face for being impertinent. Apparently, one didn't ask questions, one was seen, not heard. And if possible, one was invisible! At least I was good at that!

Vomiting had temporarily cleared my head, but now I felt sick again. Having thrown the carroty-filled bucket down some back alley, scrubbed the bucket and replaced it in a cupboard, my head pounded and to add to my complaints list, my fingers now stung with the freezing water, and my knees ached with kneeling down.

Shut up!

The companion voice in my head chirped up.

Stop feeling sorry for yourself or you'll never escape.

It was right of course, but I still felt sorry for myself. I was no longer the brave Collector, but the weary eleven year-old. Every part of me hurt. I was afraid and tired, and I wanted my bed. I didn't want to be in a non-Contributor's Home and I didn't want to listen to the man in front of me. Already I knew he enjoyed cruelty and that if I moved at all, he'd slap me again.

"We have three rules. Obey them or be punished. It's as simple as that."

He waited expectantly, hands piously clasped in front of him.

"Yes sir!"

I hated him already and giving him any title almost made me gag.

"The first rule is respect! You will address all your Carers as 'sir' or 'madam'."

There are more of them to 'sir' and 'madam'?

Of course there would be, it just hadn't occurred to me at that moment In time, with everything that was going on.

He looked back at me with those dark, squinty eyes again.

"Yes, sir."

"The second is cleanliness."

His face contorted as he looked me up and down. He was disgusted with me. I didn't care. I wasn't staying here long anyway.

"The third is work hard and obey the Maker."

I didn't immediately respond. 'Work hard' wasn't a problem, but 'obey the Maker' was. I'd been taught to have freedom of thought, fight against the ruling classes' control devices, and the Maker was one of them.

Around twenty five years ago, street wars had taken place between different religious factions. People literally blew each other up just because they believed in one God or another. It started here, but is now a world-wide phenomenon. It caused major riots, and still does, but our wonderful government continues to fight back. They ended up banning all religion and established their own form of worship, with their own 'bible' and 'God'. Everyone is given a choice, 'believe or leave'. Many people choose to leave England, others just go underground.

The nationally accepted religion involves the 'Maker'. A 'God' who only has three primary rules: Respect, Cleanliness, Work Hard. This national religion wasn't something I heeded, nor did I care to, in fact, it was something I would fight against when I grew up if I had to, but one look at the face in front of me, told me obeying the Maker wasn't a choice. I gritted my teeth. I'd tell him what he wanted to hear until I figured a way out.

"Yes sir!"

"If you pay attention to the rules and do as you are told, your life here will run smoother. Do you understand?"

He was now purposely glaring the torch in my eyes, blinding me, amusing himself.

"Yes, sir."

"Then we are now clear. One more thing, make no mistake, there is no escape from here."

I will escape.

It was as if he could read my mind.

"Some have tried, but have failed and suffered for it. It is better you accept this is your home now. You are new, but there are no exceptions. Behave well and you will survive."

This is not my home.

It was as if he was purposely trying to wind me up, as if he knew the routine and relished watching me squirm, waiting for me to respond so he could hit out at me. He loved the power and control, and used it to his own personal advantage. He was more than a disgusting form of humankind, more like a praying mantis, waiting, watching for the right time so he could hit out at and eat his victims whole.

We had reached the bottom of some large, winding stairs that started in the middle of an extremely large hallway with an open, be it dead, fireplace. The bannisters were huge – the span wider than my arms spread out – and made of some sort of dark wood.

"Take off your outer clothing and shoes. They now belong to us. I have no doubt you stole them anyway."

I didn't react to the jibe as I knew that's what he wanted. After only a short hesitation, I did as I was told. I wasn't embarrassed to take off my clothes in front of a stranger, I was too angry for that. It was only at that point though that I noticed the jacket wasn't mine. It was a dirty, brown colour and old. At least the trainers were still my own. But my bag, scarf and cap had gone. I whimpered, causing the Mantis to smile. I no longer had my tools of invisibility, but with further horror, I realised my torch was missing. I no longer had my tracker. They couldn't find me now. Bile rose to the back of my throat. I'd never been out without my tracker. Never been so alone and unprotected.

Slowly, I peeled off the clothes and handed them to The Mantis. He held them away from him with the tips of his finger and thumb, as if he would catch terrible germs just by being in close contact with the material and quickly shoved them all into a cupboard under the stairs. All I could think was that the Clearers must have stolen my things. It wasn't fair. I hadn't harmed anyone.

Why is this happening to me?

I was having difficulty controlling the anger I felt; my chest pounded with both fear and rage and I wanted to hit out at the man in front of me, but a small part of me knew I couldn't win right now. I was still weak. I needed sleep, rest, until my body had recovered its ordeal. Then I'd fight back. Right now my head still pounded, my legs wobbled and I was standing in my underclothes shivering.

I made a note of where my shoes had been stored. I would get them back at least. What right had he, or anyone, to treat me like this? It was totally opposite to the Downer teachings.

"Non-contributors are not permitted to own anything. Do you understand?"

That question again! That expectant look in his squinting, foul eyes! It took a major effort to control myself, not to blurt out 'you're the stupid one!" My pride had been insulted and my mind raced. I had to get out of this place.

Stay calm. Do as you're told. Let him think you're stupid. He won't notice you as much. Stay invisible.

It was as if I could hear my Downer Trainer in my mind, reminding me of the Collector's code. It helped a little, but not much. I doubted they'd found themselves in this situation. I stood in my underwear shivering, arms dangling in front of my body as if to protect it. Looking down at the floor, I quietly stated the obnoxious, but required response.

"Yes, sir!"

"Good."

He smiled a thin lipped, nasty smirk. He knew he'd won - at least for now. I hated him!

"I'm not interested in what you were before. You're now a Non-contributor. As such you own nothing, not even the rags on your back, and you must earn your keep. It's the law."

We were now climbing up the stairs. My legs felt heavy. My nostrils flared at the sweet smell of some sort of lavender polish. It seemed so out of place.

Casually, I wondered if I could trip him up or push him down the stairs. I pictured him breaking his sinewy neck and me escaping out the front door. I shuddered, a cold tingle down my spine. I'd never actually killed anyone and rule number seven jumped to my mind.

Do no harm!

I wondered if that could be changed to 'do no harm unless someone was doing harm to you'. He still blabbered on.

"When you're old enough, you will be transferred to an adult compound."

I will never stay here that long.

"There, you will be expected to work under the government's new 'food for work' scheme. Trust me, no matter what you think of this place, the adult compound is worse."

He turned to me at the top of the stairs to gage my thoughts. Was he scaring me into submission? I kept my face blank. It didn't satisfy him and he snorted as we reached a huge landing.

"I'm only permitted to keep children until they're fourteen, so I'm doing you a favour, unless of course you really are younger than you say."

I still didn't answer. I didn't want him to know anything about me.

"The silent type I see."

He sneered.

"Well, tonight I don't care. Tomorrow we shall see. If you still refuse to cooperate, you'll be moved in two days. I can sell you on quite easily, and it will be a long way from here. Bear that in mind as you ponder how to run away tonight."

Was he reading my mind? I shivered at the thought.

He pointed to a thin, dirty mattress on the floor, a rough blanket was folded neatly at the end of it.

"Tonight you sleep here on the landing. You're filthy. Filth is disgusting."

He paused before repeating his favourite question.

"Do you understand?"

"Yes sir!"

And I did. As I lie down on the hard mattress, shivering from cold and fear, I understood very well. I understood that I'd been sold to the highest bidder, I understood that this was the worst place in the world to be and that worse was to come. Hot tears erupted unbidden, streaking down my cheeks. I hurt, and was so tired and so lonely. Roughly, I wiped them away and forced myself to focus. A 'long ago child's voice' came to my head,

I'm not crying, only sweating from my eyes.

I saw my mother's smiling face from years gone by, almost felt her comforting arms around me. I cannot stay here. She is waiting for me to return, as is Alicia.

My final thoughts before drifting into a troubled sleep were the absolute certainty that I would escape. I promised myself I would not stay in this place long.

Two more horrible days and I'll be free. Only two more days!

Chapter 13

I hid under the blanket pretending to be asleep. I didn't want to get up and face whatever the world had to offer this morning, nor did I want to see The Mantis before I had to. It wasn't long before I heard footsteps and whispers around me. I lifted the corner of the blanket, peeping out from under it, only to see bare floorboards again, on which were feet – kids' feet of various sizes in worn, black plimsolls, all shuffling to fit into a straight line across the back wall.

Suddenly, someone was gently shaking me.

"Wake up…wake up! If you don't get up, you'll be punished."

The voice instantly caused me to pull the blankets away from my face. It was a boy with short hair that couldn't decide whether it was blond or red, and large, transparent blue eyes. His face was pale and he had a shower of freckles across his cheeks and nose. He looked about my age. In a strange way, he seemed familiar, but I didn't know him, I was sure.

"Quickly, get up. You'll be punished for laziness if you don't move."

He looked around nervously, as if scared to be caught kneeling down and talking to me. I glanced around. Everyone seemed to be staring at us.

"Elliott, what are you doing?"

The boy in front of me flinched and stood up quickly, straightening his narrow shoulders and thin body as if a soldier.

"Trying to get this lazy boy to obey the Maker and understand the rules sir."

I glared at the Elliott boy. What was he talking about?

"Really!"

The Mantis stared for a moment, as if he could delve into Elliott's mind to see if he were telling the truth. I admired how Elliott didn't flinch.

"Then you shall be his teacher for the day."

He was enjoying this too much. I could tell from the gleam in his eyes. This was leading somewhere, even though I wasn't sure what was going on. Elliott went red from his neck to the roots of his hair. So red in fact, he wouldn't have been spotted in a beetroot patch. Whether he was embarrassed or angry, I couldn't tell, but The Mantis smiled, relishing his discomfort.

"It would be my honour to serve the house and the Maker sir."

Talk about 'kissing boots'. What exactly was he up to?

The Mantis wasn't entirely convinced either.

"Mmm… if he doesn't know how to behave by the end of the day, then you will both be punished. Do you understand?"

His favourite question again. I wondered if anyone ever said 'no'.

"Yes sir!"

"And you, Lazy-Boy,"

He had now turned his sarcastic words on me. I looked up from the lumpy mattress I'd suffered a night on.

"Do you understand what will happen if you don't conform?"

'Conform' was my least favourite word, although 'understand' from The Mantis' mouth was definitely competing. It was the second time he'd asked that question in less than thirty seconds.

Whenever I was nervous or upset, I began counting. I'd done it since I was a little kid. Once my mind latched on to something, I'd just keep watching out for it the whole day. Once I'd counted how many brown shoes I'd seen, for no particular reason other than it was my first day at school. I spent the whole day with my head down looking for brown shoes to count. I knew I'd be counting how many times he asked 'Do you understand?' the whole day and maybe into the next. It was totally irrational, but I didn't care.

"Yes sir!"

"Good, then you will both report to me for punishment at the end of the day."

We both looked immediately surprised. I couldn't help myself.

"But we haven't done anything!"

"Make that two punishments."

"But..!"

"Three...I am really going to enjoy this day."

He walked away grinning evilly, his black, cassock-like clothing swishing as he walked down the line of kids inspecting them, like victims caught in his web.

"You, report for punishment."

The little kid in question didn't bother to ask what the infringement was.

The Mantis spoke to Elliott without even turning away from the scrutiny of his charges. How Elliott knew he was speaking with him, I wasn't sure.

"Bring him for scanning at seven-thirty sharp."

"Yes, sir."

"And get him cleaned up now."

"Yes sir."

As I pulled the blanket around me – I was still in my underwear - and stood up, I watched as The Mantis repeated the 'report for punishment' phrase several times. There must have been around thirty kids, some my age, some younger. A few actually looked around fourteen or fifteen. All of them behaved like soldiers, arms down, shoulders pushed back, hair short and tidy – even the girls. And they all wore the same dull brown, baggy, button-less tops and even baggier trousers, as if they'd just thrown on the nearest piece of clothing they'd found, independent of the size. Perhaps they had!

"Do you understand?"

He was at it again, only this time he was screeching. That was number three by my count, although of course, he might have said it several times this morning already. I wondered if I should allow a percentage for all the times I hadn't heard him that day, and start counting at three, which would make it nine times instead of six, but immediately discounted it and turned to the slime-ball standing next to me.

Elliott was shorter than me and skinny. He'd already stepped away and was indicating I should follow him down the landing. As I shuffled forwards, I looked back once more at the kids, watching as they began what was obviously a morning ritual. Each child in the line was made to step forward to chant the three rules:

"Respect, cleanliness and hard work is the will of the Maker and the will of All. I will obey."

It made me cringe! They behaved like robots. I wanted to scream at them, to make them see this was not the way, that there were other ways to be, but I was sure it involved a punishment, so instead I caught Elliot up, hoping to have some questions answered.

Chapter 14

We were down a long corridor with identical white-painted doors on both sides.

"This is bedroom one."

He indicated to the left.

"And this is bedroom two."

He pointed to the right.

"One side is odd numbers and the other even. Boys take the even numbers and girls the odd, so you'll sleep in one of the bedrooms on the right. Got it?"

"Yes, but what is this place?"

"Elliott, what are you doing in the bedrooms at this time of the morning?"

A sharp voice made me look up. In front of us was an ostrich disguised as some sort of woman. With a long, sinewy neck, a flushed skin and grey-pink hair piled on top of her head, she strutted towards us, her long grey dress swirling around her ankles.

"The Warden 'as 'onoured me with the position of being teacher for our lucky newcomer Madam."

There he goes again. Crawling up to them all. He's a real creep!

"That is an honour indeed."

She held her hands grasped in front of her like The Mantis – as if contemplating the thing before her with disgust.

"He's filthy."

"'e was on the landing this morning Madam."

"Night arrival then. I suggest he doesn't touch anything until he showers."

"Yes madam."

"And make sure he knows how to behave properly. You know the consequences for bad behaviour."

"Yes madam."

Her voice was screeching although seemingly a little more caring than The Mantis, but I wasn't to be tricked into trusting anyone, least of all one of the carer-gaolers, and definitely not an Ostrich.

She stared at me with large, dark eyes. On the back of her head was a white cap, under which sat uncontrollable fuzzy hair, escaping at all angles around her head. She stood straight backed and pointed a short-nailed finger at me.

"And you, what's your name?"

I didn't answer. My face blank. Refusing to give information was the only way I could defy them.

"Your name boy?"

She looked first at me and then at Elliott, as if she couldn't quite comprehend what was happening.

I still said nothing, so she looked at Elliott.

"What's wrong with him? Is he deaf, or just plain stupid?"

"I don't know madam. It seems 'e 'ad a knock to the 'ead madam."

"Well, The Warden will knock whatever it is out of him, be sure of that. The Maker does not like those who are stubborn or proud. It's a mortal sin."

She paused for emphasis before Elliott chirped up.

"It certainly is madam. I'll do my best to teach 'im the Maker's ways."

He was mad, he actually believed the rubbish they fed him.

She looked at him again, not sure if he was being sarcastic. Deciding however that his face was sincere enough, she continued.

"What did the Warden call him?"

"Lazy-boy."

Creep!

"Well, let's hope he isn't. You'd better teach him well Elliott, or you too will be punished."

"I'll try my best madam. And with the Maker in me, I shall surely succeed."

She ignored his last comment. He was too slimy for words, even for an ostrich carer-gaoler.

"Let me pass then."

Elliott immediately bowed his head low and stood aside. She looked at me to do the same.

"Do you have no respect for your Elders? Move Lazy-boy before you receive a punishment."

She frowned, confusion in her eyes, but I was stubborn. I hated them all. I would not be controlled. I didn't care what punishments they had.

My decision to defy the world around me was not long lived. Elliott took me by surprise and pulled me aside to allow the Ostrich to pass by. She went two strides before looking over her shoulder.

"Oh Elliott, do get him some clothes. He can't walk around in a blanket all day."

"Yes madam."

I was annoyed and as soon as she had turned the corner, I rounded on him.

"What did you do that for?"

I was referring to him pulling me aside for the Ostrich to go passed and he knew it.

"What do you mean what did I do that for? Do you want a punishment?"

His voice had risen in disbelief, his blue eyes alarmed, his arms flinging out.

"I don't care. I already have three and I'm not the slime-ball you are. I don't crawl to them or believe in anything they say. I'm leaving this place."

By now my voice had risen, but he returned to his usual subdued way, standing quietly, hands clasped in front of him. The only indication that he was nervous was the flickering of his eyes from left to right, like a bird on a branch watching for possible danger.

"That's what everyone thinks when they arrive, but it isn't true. You're not leaving."

His eyes lowered. He sounded sad, but I couldn't feel sorry for him.

"How long have you been here?"

"I dunno. Maybe a year and a half."

"Why don't you know?"

"We don't 'ave clocks, calendars or date-keepers. It's 'ard to know. Days just run into each other."

He paused for a moment before continuing.

"You 'ave to learn the rules quickly."

"I won't…"

He paused before taking a different tack.

"Remember, anything you get a punishment for, I get punished too."

"Then you'll be scrubbing floors with me this afternoon."

"What?"

Chapter 15

"Dirty clothing and blankets go in the baskets at the end of the corridor."

He lifted the lid of a large wicker basket outside bedroom two and stuffed the blanket in, taking care to make sure the lid was properly closed.

"I'm in bedroom two."

He pushed open the door and held it until I walked in.

"What's your name?"

I didn't answer.

"I won't tell them if you don't want me to, but it won't get you anywhere."

"I'm going to escape."

"Sure you are."

I looked around the room. The only window was small, high up and had thick, metal bars across it. There were four bunk-beds, all neatly made, squashed into a tiny room. Other than the beds, there was nothing, but a wicker basket similar to the one outside.

"Clean clothes in this basket. Dirty ones outside. Got it?"

"I'm not stupid, y'know."

"Can't tell from the way you're be'aving."

I was about to respond, but he interrupted me, whilst at the same time handing me a set of brown clothing. I hastily dropped the blanked and dressed. The material was rough and barely took away the shivers, but at least it covered the embarrassment of standing in underwear.

"Play the game, don't fight, blend in, that's what I do. If you fight their rules, you can't win."

"I don't need to win, I'm leaving."

He looked at me and sat on the lower bunk-bed to the left, sighing and looking at his fingers fidgeting with each other.

"I thought that too...but it's impossible."

"Nothing's impossible. They come and go, don't they?"

"Some come in from outside, others live-in, but some kids 'ave tried to escape y'know. They were caught and the punishment was 'orrible. The warden beat them in front of us until they 'ad to be 'ospitalised."

I gulped nervously, my eyes drifted to the barred window.

"I'll take my chances."

He sat there quietly.

"I was one of them."

Without saying any more, he stood up and lifted up his shirt. He was so skinny, his rib cage stuck out like he'd been starving for weeks. For a moment I wondered what he was doing, and then, as he turned around, I saw. Scarred tissue on his back stood out like lines of blood in the snow. It was horrific. I couldn't imagine the lashes or how painful it must have been. I couldn't understand why this happened to him and didn't know what to say.

"They did this to you?"

His face hardened, his eyes were full of hatred, his body rigid.

"'E did this to me as punishment for trying to escape."

"The Mantis?"

"Mantis?"

I realised he didn't know who I was talking about and quickly explained.

"That's brilliant!"

"Yeah, but be careful who you use it around."

"'E's cruel Lazy-boy. We're just his excuse for inflicting pain. 'E loves it, lives for it. 'E uses the Maker as 'is reason, but really it's just 'im."

I was silent for a while, contemplating Elliott's words, watching how his frightened eyes kept flicking to the door, as if he was terrified someone would come in and find us. Again I thought he seemed familiar and was about to ask him, but he spoke first and distracted me.

"Since then I am 'seen to obey'. It's the only way, until I find a chance."

"So, all that 'yes sir, no sir, the Maker is great' is just talk."

"You don't think I really believe all that rubbish, do you?"

"Well, I thought...."

I really didn't know what I thought. My mind was in a whirlwind of confusion and uncertainty. I didn't know whether I could trust him. Maybe he was a spy, maybe he was working for The Mantis. How was I supposed to know? Why was he telling me anyway?

"I need them to look away....to look in another direction, and then..."

He didn't finish the sentence, leaving the rest to my imagination.

"You could be my distraction if you continue to behave this way."

His face took on a grimace, though his eyes were full of sadness and at last I remembered the question I'd been meaning to ask since we'd met.

"Do I know you?"

"No, not really, but I know you Adam."

He smiled at the shock registering on my face. How did he know me? Why hadn't he given me away? As if responding to my thoughts, he answered.

"My mother worked at your 'ouse on odd occasions, when your servant needed help."

The word 'servant' irked me, we never thought of Sara as a servant and never treated her as such. She was a second mother to me. I said nothing. I wasn't sure what to believe. I didn't know if he was telling the truth.

"Once, she took me with her. I was playing under the table in the kitchen when you walked in. I was probably about six at the time."

The story jogged a memory, but so faint, it flashed like the beat of a second, and was gone.

"Of course, I was just a nobody to you and you ignored me."

He said it with some resentment, and I was ashamed that it sounded probable. I was a different person then, but still I wasn't sure if he was telling the truth.

He'd replaced his top and was staring at me as if he were considering some point. He was shorter than me, but had learnt the hard way and was tough and, in some ways, wise. I was actually beginning to think 'fitting in' might be a good idea, might be part of my plan. I certainly didn't want to be his distraction. If I wasn't noticed, if I were invisible, no one would be looking when I walked out the door. And I knew very well how to be invisible. This was just a different 'invisibility' game.

"Where would you go anyway? They will catch you and drag you back if you stay on the streets with nowhere to go."

"I have a safe place...a mother."

"You're lucky. They took my mother away to one of those 'ard labour camps. I 'ave no idea where she is, or even if she's alive."

His hands were fidgeting nervously and he looked towards the wall, trying to hide the sadness.

"Right."

I didn't know what to say. The shabby, metal sprung bunk-beds behind him suddenly seemed the right place to stare. Some of the springs were broken, leaving the thin mattress on the top bunk to sink down. I didn't know much about the hard labour camps although I'd heard they were another form of 'food for work' for criminals.

"I know what you're thinking, but she wasn't a criminal. We were starving, living on the streets...she stole some stale bread, that was all."

I didn't know why he was telling me, we didn't really know each other, weren't friends or anything, so I didn't respond. Suddenly, his eyes lit up.

"If you find a way, take me with you."

"What?"

"I can't stay in this place. I'll go mad or die first."

He was excited at the thought as if I were some kind of last hope.

"I thought you'd given up after the last punishment, that you were one of them now."

"Never! I'll never give up. I will get out and I'll rescue my mother too."

He was still terrified at the possibility of being caught, but his voice was hopeful, his face flushed with the ideas charging through his mind, his eyes suddenly lit up.

"If you 'ave a place, we could come and work for you like before. Then we'd be contributors. We'd be safe."

It only then occurred to him then to wonder why I was there.

"What's someone of your class doing 'ere anyway?"

I hesitated. How did I know he was telling me the truth? He might be working on their side. Getting information out of me. I decided to be cautious.

"I was attacked in the streets and sold to this place. My mother will be going crazy."

It was the truth and it seemed that was enough for him. Either that or he wasn't truly interested.

"I'll 'elp you. I know this place."

His mind was racing forward, wanting to cut a deal with me.

"I'll show you around, show you how to survive unnoticed."

He tried to smile, to seem trustworthy, but his face was desperate and he leaned forward as if to grab onto me, to plead with me.

"I even know this area, I can get us away fast."

"Where are we?"

"We're in Dempshire, on the coast, about five miles from town, but we're in the middle of nowhere, on a cliff. No one else lives around here. It's even a drive to the nearest village."

I'd heard of the place, but wasn't sure where it was and I'd never heard of a cliff house.

"If we can get to the village, I know how to get back to town without being noticed. I did it before, I can do it again. I'll show you, but promise me you'll take me with you... to your house. I can't stand it here any longer."

He was now begging.

"How do I know you're not on their side...tricking me, getting me to say things so you can report back?"

"Give me a chance. I'll prove it to you."

We stared at each other, trying to tell if we could trust one another. His eyes were imploring me to agree. He was genuinely desperate, but was it to escape, or to run to his masters with tales of disobedience. To have one up on me, score a point with The Mantis when he handed me over.

"Okay, I'll give you one chance to prove yourself, but that's all."

He smiled for a moment as if I'd given him the world, before his face took on a grimness.

"Come on, I 'ave to take you to be scanned."

Chapter 16

"Scanned? Is that what I think it is?"

Having washed my hands and face in an attempt to obey the cleanliness rule, (although it was impossible to get rid of all the dried blood still caked in my hair), we were trotting down the main hall stairway, the one I'd come in the previous night. The house was strangely quiet and spooky even in daylight. Where were all the kids?

"Probably, but it's nothing."

"It is if you've never been scanned."

He stopped for a moment to look at me.

"You 'aven't been scanned...ever?

"No, never!"

He pulled a strange face, as if he couldn't believe what he was hearing.

"But isn't that against the law?"

"So!"

Scanning was one of those things my mother and the Downers didn't believe in. It was hard to stay invisible, if you had your ID and details imprinted on your hand and registered in a government file somewhere. The police can pick you up and easily find out who you are and where you live, whether you are a Non-Contributor, whether you'd escaped from a camp or home. It's worse if you're found without a scanned ID. The law states all UK citizens have to be scanned by the age of ten. But the Downers are outside the law; anyone who isn't scanned by the time they enter our world, don't bother getting it done. I was one of those people. I was eight when we entered and hadn't even thought about it for three years. It was as if it didn't exist for me. I was about to find out it did.

"What happens to those who don't have an ID?"

"Not sure. I've never met anyone our age without an ID. The warden changed mine when I came in. Instead of belonging to my family, I now belong to this 'ome. That's 'ow they knew to bring me back 'ere."

A look crossed over his face as if he had been jabbed in his stomach for a split second. I knew he was referring to the time he'd escaped and that the memory was painful. I wondered who had caught him and brought him back. Probably the police.

"How can I get out of it?"

"You can't."

"But I have to. They can't find out. There has to be a way."

I sounded desperate, but I didn't care.

He stood watching me, considering whether I was worth the potential risk.

"There might be a way, I was once told of it, but I don't know if it will work, and it will 'urt."

"I don't care."

"You can't scream out."

"I'm not a baby."

"Come...quickly, it's almost seven thirty, we can't risk being late."

We headed back to the bedroom. No one was there, no one was supposed to be there. If we got caught we'd be in trouble again.

"Turn round."

I wasn't sure why, but I did as I was told. I stared at the white, plastered wall. A hairline crack from the top right corner cascaded down the wall into a web of thinner cracks. Following the splintery path, I listened to the noises coming from behind me. It sounded as though Elliott was pulling at something wooden, yanking at it. It grated at the floor level somewhere near his bed. I had an urge to turn round.

"Don't look!"

Was he reading my mind?

"I'm not, just hurry up."

I heard him move and suddenly he was standing before me, a sharp kitchen knife in his hand.

"Where did you get that? What are you doing?"

"Give me your 'and."

He grabbed my left palm, turning it to face upwards.

"Why?"

"Don't scream!"

He was so quick and the knife so sharp, I didn't feel anything for at least ten seconds, but then I saw the blood welling up across my palm and the pain hit me, a sudden shock to my body, as if I'd pushed my whole arm into a meat grinder.....and I yelped.

Elliott covered my mouth.

"Shhh..."

"Why?"

Tears filled my eyes. I didn't want to be a baby, but it hurt. He was wrapping a piece of old rag across it to stop it dripping. I bent forward, squeezing my wrist, trying to numb the pain. The rag immediately filled with dark red blood as it oozed out of my hand.

"'old your arm up!"

I did as I was told, more out of shock than reason.

"It will stop the blood."

But the blood just ran down my arm and up my sleeve.

"Don't get blood on your sleeve. You'll be punished."

"We'll be punished."

He didn't comment. He was pressing on my blood-stained hand, trying to stop the blood.

"You'd better have a good reason for doing this."

"It's supposed to be impossible to scan your palm when the skin is damaged."

"Supposed to be?"

"I've never 'ad to try it."

"Do you know anyone who has?"

"Nope!"

"You could've told me, before you attacked."

"Better to get it over quickly...less resistance!"

I grunted half angry, half in pain...and yet another part of me admired him. He was defying those he was terrified of, just to help me...a stranger, a person who'd ignored him when he was younger.

"Why are you helping me?"

"To escape of course."

And that was it! He needed me to get him to a safe place. He'd already said so.

Chapter 17

It was my sixth day. Every day passed my second was depressing. I'd promised myself I would escape within two, but I always had eyes on me. Newbies were kept under a stricter watch because they were more likely to try escaping. And it was true. One chance and I'd have walked out the door by now...no, not walked, ran like crazy.

I hated the place, hated the people, hated the regimented routine. From seven in the morning until seven at night we were bossed around, told what to do, what to think, what to eat, when to wake up and when to sleep. We had a schedule for every activity, even going to the toilet. It was stupid.

And my hand hurt constantly. I made sure it never healed. Elliott had been right, the scanner didn't work if the skin was damaged. It couldn't measure the palm print accurately and find the data associated with it. At least I had that to thank him for.

The Mantis had impatiently tried twice already. The last time he told me to go away and not come back until it was healed. I made sure it didn't, but it throbbed constantly like a drum beating, as if I had a pulse in my palm.

At seven we were woken by a clanging bell in the corridor, no-one dared ignore it. Everyone jumped up, made their beds and grabbed clean clothing from the wicker box as fast as possible. (Now I understood why clothing didn't always fit – who had time to check the size?)

We were all expected to be standing outside our bedrooms within five minutes. I was in bedroom two with my teacher, Elliott! If anyone delayed, they received an instant punishment, which was usually a slap across the face. Next we were pushed through freezing communal showers. Heating water cost money, so they didn't heat the pipes unless necessary for cooking or washing clothes. Washing bodies could be done in cold water as well as it could be done in hot, so cold it was.

The shower routine was my worst nightmare and I dreaded it every day. They were the old-fashioned type. They didn't even look like they were from this century. But the embarrassment was worse. There were four shower heads set high on a white, square-tiled wall, all turned on by one rusty, tap that squeaked. The boys had to stand in a queue, (girls had a different shower room), covered only by thin, hand towels. There weren't any curtains for privacy so the four in the showers were a spectacle for all to stare at. I tried to cover myself with my hands, or turn my back on the eyes that watched, but the monitors insisted we use soap and wash properly as cleanliness was a major rule. Every person had to spend one minute scrubbing and rinsing. The soap smelled mildly of disinfectant. At the beginning of the week, I cringed at the thought of using a bar of soap some dirty person had used before me. By day six, all I could think about was getting through it as fast as possible – just like everyone else!

One new boy was made to stand under the shower for a full five minutes whilst everyone watched because he didn't clean himself properly. By the time he came out, he was bent over double shuddering. I could hear his teeth chattering, the cold was so bad. I felt sorry for him, but Elliott had at least warned me. Not that it had made it any easier.

Over the last six days, I'd received various punishments for infractions to the rules, but they were planned punishments and so more bearable. I was clever, but Elliott was devious. I watched him perform for the Carer-gaolers. He knew if I obeyed all rules without making mistakes, they would think something was wrong and watch me more closely, making it impossible for us to escape. They had to believe they were 'taming' me. So the 'planned' punishments were ones Elliott said were the easiest to take. He also had to suffer with me as he was my teacher, so he had an interest in making the punishments as easy as possible.

If it wasn't for him, I'd have broken many more rules just out of sheer anger and obstinacy.

On day one, Elliott and I already had three punishments for opening my mouth to The Mantis, plus the floor scrubbing, so we avoided anything else. Punishments from The Mantis consisted of anything from three stinging ruler slaps on the palm of the hand, to full beatings with a leather belt across the back and butt.

Standing outside his office door, waiting for 'my turn', I could hear the poor girl inside already screaming, begging for forgiveness as the belt lashed out at her. What she'd done, I didn't know, but it made me want to storm in there to beat The Mantis up myself. If Elliott hadn't been standing there calmly, holding his fidgety hands still in front of him and quietly glaring at me every minute or so, reminding me of the plan, I just might have done it.

By the time I entered the room, I was shaking. It didn't matter that Elliott had prepared me. The Mantis was evil, anything could happen and no one would help. I briefly glanced around and was shocked. I'd expected the room to be as austere as the rest of the place, (grey/white walls, and minimal, tatty wooden furniture), but The Mantis's office was different. One wall was covered from the ceiling to the floor with old fashioned paper books – the type you only saw at antique fairs now. I'd never seen so many in one place. I wondered why he collected them. He just didn't seem the type. On the other side was a painting with an idyllic country scene; trees, a stream, a couple of cows. It was summer and the sun shone happily on children playing in long grass. .

"Stand over there on that line."

To my surprise, there really was a yellow mark on the wooden flooring. I did as I was told without comment, Elliott's instructions in my mind. Facing me now was a large wooden desk on which papers were piled neatly, behind which sat a chair. I wondered why so much paper was being used. Surely, the environmental laws applied here. No one is supposed to use paper when a screen is available. I looked around for the screen, but the walls were bare. Oddly, there didn't seem to be any tech in the room at all. It shouldn't have been a surprise. The whole place was backwards.

He stood in front of me. The light from a window behind caused him to be in black silhouette. Quickly I looked to the floor, remembering 'respect'. I'd even taken to holding my hands in front of me like a devout priest. He noticed immediately.

"Elliott has taught you something I see."

"Yes sir!"

"Today I am lenient. Tomorrow I am not."

He paused.

"Do you understand?"

Number seven, (at least!)

"Yes, sir!"

"Good."

He walked around me tapping the ruler on his hand, sneering.

"So, boy, what's your name?"

He asked me this question as if I would automatically lie until he could scan my ID, and he was just waiting to prove it in order to deal out more punishment, but I was ready for this, so I didn't hesitate.

"Alan, sir."

"Alan what?"

"Alan Brown sir."

It was a name Elliott and I had chosen. I didn't want anyone knowing my real name.

Suddenly, his face was close to mine. I flinched and stopped breathing for a moment. I felt his sour breath on my right cheek.

"And your father's name?"

"Don't know, sir."

"Don't know?"

He mocked me, as if I were stupid. I didn't care, this was part of the plan too.

"My Mam never told me sir."

"I bet he ran away when he saw your face."

His cruelty didn't affect me. I just wanted to get out of the office alive.

"Yes sir."

"Yes sir, no sir. Is that all you can say?"

Now who was being stupid?

"I don't care who you are anyway. I think I shall always call you Lazy-boy. Are you happy with that?"

"Yes sir."

I felt I was swallowing rage as he began his humiliating pace around me again. The hate in me began to grow. I loathed him and he knew it. The perspiration on my forehead smelt of it. My body trembled with it. I was big enough to do some real injury if I took him by surprise, but he would eventually stop me, and then he'd have a reason to give me worse pain, and that wasn't the plan."

This plan is killing me.

I looked down at the floor, twisting my fingers tighter, willing myself to stay calm. I took a deep breath and looked across the floor, noticing a colourful mat with a design of blue swirls. My mind began counting the repeating pattern to calm me down.

One swirl…two…three….

He stood behind me. The room was silent for endless seconds. I was sure he was going to attack me.

…four…five…six…

"Hold out both hands Lazy-boy, palms up."

Suddenly, he was in front of me, pushing up his sleeves, readying his hitting arm for the attack. I was so close to him, I heard a strange clicking noise, and without thinking, glanced up his sleeve. Glinting in the darkness of his cuff was something silver, something metallic which for a moment held my curiosity. I realised it was not a real arm. It was some sort of substitute, possibly an old bionic one linked to his own muscles, obeying his thoughts, that's why it's clicking. I was vaguely wondering why he didn't have stem cell treatment to replace the arm, when the strikes come down, and I couldn't think anymore.

I hear the ruler whistling in the air six times; three on each hand. He gives out punishment slowly, relishing each flinch from his victims – daring them to move their hand before the strike. It stings, but is manageable on my right. My left palm is a different story. It screams out in agony as the mending skin splits all over again. He watches me suffer, making a conscious effort not to pull away before the hit is placed, laughs in my sweaty face.

My temper is hard to control, I want to scream and strike out. My eyes sting with tears I try to hold back, not wanting to give him the pleasure, my stomach feels a wave of sickness. I will not faint! Instead, I grit my teeth and smile to myself. He has just done me a favour, made it impossible to scan my palm for a few days longer – long enough to escape.

The mat, with its twelve repeating patterns, helps. I count the patterns methodically, breathing in and out, trying to be calm, waiting for the initial sting to throb less. I will not cry or scream out in front of him. I will not give him the pleasure.

Elliott told me the next day that I had passed the test and would be allowed to stay. If The Mantis had decided to sell me on, I'd have been gone already. Now we had a plan, I didn't want to be sold on to an adult camp. Security was even tighter over there …. impossible to get out, once locked in.

On the morning of day two, I didn't get the commitment right, ("Respect, cleanliness and hard work is the will of the Maker and the will of All. I will obey.") For this, I received an immediate slap across my as yet un-healed head.

For not finishing the lumpy, milk-free, sugar-free, disgusting porridge on day three, I had to stand in a corner throughout lunch and starve. On day four I had to scrub out the boys' toilets for not being on time. On day five, I was sent to The Mantis again. He was happy to see me as was the mat. Counting its swirls helped me cope with the six ruler slaps. Apparently, the pain he inflicted on you doubled each time you entered his lair. My hands were raw, my left palm split open again and dripped blood, and I decided to avoid the warden as much as possible. I didn't know if I could take twelve hits, even if it meant my palm couldn't be scanned for another week.

Day six I tried to stay out of trouble, but one of the boys tripped me up purposely, which caused a chair to overturn. The Carer-gaoler made me wash all the boys' underwear by hand – disgusting! Even Elliott couldn't hide his annoyance at that. He was still my teacher and still doing my penalties.

Records were kept of all punishments. If at the end of one week you'd received more than three, you received an extra one, just to teach you a further lesson. It involved missing a meal and reading from the Maker's version of the bible. There was always a queue of people missing dinner. I think they did it purposely to save money on food. One night, there were more kids reading than eating. I watched them out of the corner of my eye as I stuffed some sort of fatty stew and stale bread down my gullet. I was always starving and I never refused anything they gave us now. It was why we all looked like prisoners on a hunger strike.

My days were easier than some of the kids just because I could read, write and do maths. The law requires a kids' home-gaol to educate children in English, Maths and Reading to the level of an eleven year old in a normal school, for which the Wardens are paid money for each child. As I am beyond the level required, it was decided I should teach the younger kids instead – of which there are two. It's cheaper than bringing in another teacher. So, for two hours in the morning I teach a couple of sisters reading and maths, after which I'm sent to the laundry. In the afternoon, I spend another two hours assisting the teacher in preparing for the next day. Apparently, we are switched after a week to the kitchens.

It's a joke really. I'm not a teacher and don't know what to do. I didn't even know how to use the chalk and chalk board to start with, but at least I'm not in the laundry all day, which some are.

Josie is seven, but looks older than her sister Lacie, who's eight. Josie is broader and taller, she has blue eyes and cherub features although she is a tomboy at heart. I can imagine she'd be the sort to climb trees and kick a ball, if she ever got the chance. Lacie is quieter and shy, her brown eyes soft, her pale face sickly. They both have northern dialects and I try to teach them correct pronunciation, but mostly they look down and mumble. They have nervous head twitches they can't control and so I pretend it isn't happening. They are frightened. Every few seconds, one of them looks towards the door as if they are going to be punished for sitting there. They were scared of me to start with and barely spoke. I made it my personal mission to get them to laugh. I drew stick figures doing silly things, pulled faces and made funny animal noises.

We aren't supposed to laugh at all as learning is serious work. 'Work' and 'serious' are words I understand completely, they're already ingrained in me, but somehow I want to do the opposite of my nature just because of the Maker. Apparently, the Maker approves of learning and anything from the Maker is always classed as 'grave and solemn', something to be obeyed without question. As we are in a separate room, no one bothers us and so I do everything I can to disobey the rules. I've come to look forward to seeing them. I pull faces, and do silly things to get them to smile, or react normally, making them, and me, forget the horrors of our daily life.

They hide their mouths behind their hands, not wanting to smile or giggle in case it is a bad thing to do. I try to encourage them, try to show them they can trust me. On the seventh day, Josie lets out a little, squeaky giggle and Lacie copies. They stare at me with frightened mouse-like eyes, waiting to see my reaction, to see if the cat is going to pounce, preparing themselves for an attack. I clap my hands, approving, smiling with delight, and cautiously, they smile back. I'm elated that they've found the courage, but more so, because we've defied the Warden in this one small thing.

The kids' home-gaol supports itself by washing clothes, bed linen, towels and anything anyone sends in really. The laundry room is large, noisy, full of steam and slippery floors, and generally is horrible to work in. Only kids of a certain height work there; mostly because they can reach the machines. If The Mantis could make seven year olds work there, I'm sure he would.

The machines are old-fashioned, they use water and soap that destroys the cloth. Most of the Middle and Upper Classes have a dry-cleaning device cupboard, something even the Downers have. Poorer people either wash by hand or use 'wet devices' such as these monster machines that make so much noise, my ears are ringing when I leave to help the teacher.

There are three large washing machines, two dryers, (to be used as little as possible due to the cost), five huge steam rollers in the centre of the room for sheets, and six sky hangers for smaller clothes. I don't know their real names, I'd never seen them until I came here. They are a contraption that you hang washing on. When it is full, there is a pulley system that strings it up as high as the ceiling to dry out the clothes. It continually drips water on our heads. Around the edge of the room are deep enamel sinks to wash by hand.

The Carer-gaoler who manages the place is a large woman with dark hair, small eyes and big mouth. She wears a knee-length, white apron over a ball-like stomach, her short legs sticking out like sturdy pins under a table. She hates her job and consequently is mostly miserable, taking it out on the kids. She dashes around the place like a rat skittering through a tunnel, lashing out at our legs with a stick if the clothes are not washed to her standard, (although what that standard actually is, I'm not quite sure). You can tell which kids are in the laundry by how fresh the wounds on their legs are.

Most of the time she forces us to wash as much by hand as we can, again to save money on energy, but due to my ever bleeding hand, I have to wear a protective glove. Not to protect me, but the clothing of course.

She constantly reminds us we are non-Contributors, our parents are non-Contributors and we should be glad we are not on the streets or in camps. It is our duty to work and bring money into the home to pay for the food, our beds and the clothes we wear. Bent over scrubbing , no one says anything.

Some seethe, I can tell. Some don't care anymore. You can see it in their faces, in the way their shoulders hang or the way they are always tense – frowning and gritting their teeth. I sag and look down, obeying the rules, obeying the Maker. I play the game until I too become invisible.

Deep down every comment screamed at me, every punishment I receive, every piece of work I perform makes me sick with anger. In turn that sickness makes me determined to escape. Soon they will be satisfied they have trodden me down. Soon I will not be noticed.

Chapter 18

We sit at long, wooden benches, like picnic tables, but even longer; boys on one side, girls on the other. There are candles lighting the room, but mostly it's dark. The government has decided to switch off all energy from seven at night until seven in the morning to save money. Our Wonderful Warden has extended that to begin at four in the afternoon, with the exception of those working in the laundry and kitchen.

We aren't allowed to talk, so I am now very good at reading Elliott's body language. We've created a code and he's telling me he needs to talk tonight. His left forefinger is crossed over his thumb. This is the urgent signal, something must be wrong. I cross my own finger over my thumb to show I understand.

We continue eating the foul smelling food, which could even be gone-off, street-rat for all I know, it tastes peculiar, and listen for a while to the five unfortunates reading tonight.

They stand side by side, contemplating the floor, wishing themselves anywhere but were they are, awaiting their turn. A pale-faced, blonde-haired girl of about twelve begins. She reads a verse nervously...

"Our Maker leads us out of darkness.
Our Maker leads us to light.
Follow the Maker, find the truth...."

...and then, without a sound, passes the book to the tall boy standing to the left of her. He has difficulty pronouncing the words and stutters, suffering for his trouble, but no one comes to his aid. Face red and sweaty, he passes the book to the next person. Once the book comes to the end of the line, it is passed back up, each person reading again.

"Our Maker loveth little children
Who are good and kind
And follow the Maker's three rules.
The Kingdom is theirs..."

They are like statues, not hearing the irony of their own words. It's so boring, I zone out. For a while, I just stare at my empty bowl and listen to the gulping of food. The boy to the left of me almost chokes, but manages to swallow whatever disgusting chunk is threatening to kill him with a slosh of water. He looks around, has anyone noticed? Is he in trouble?

I think about my escape idea. Elliot still doesn't know it, I'm not sure about him. I've decided to keep the whole thing a secret until the very last minute. That way, he can't tell on me...just in case.

But we need some stuff. I told him about it last night, that if he wanted to be part of this deal, he had to get what we needed. I know we'll need clothes and food. Lots of food and I'll need a torch. He thought it strange, but didn't question it too much. Maybe that's what the meeting tonight is about. Maybe he has the answer on how to get the stuff we need, or maybe he's backing out of the deal. I don't care if he is.

The food is for Alicia. I figure trading for her is the only way. It means we have to take as much as possible with us. I picture myself meeting with Dillon again and instantly I punch him in the face. Inwardly I smile. He's caused all this. I wouldn't be here if it weren't for him. He must have known the trade was risky. That's why he didn't send his guys. I hope Lissy's okay. I wonder if the Downer search party has found my tracker and given up on me. My Mam will be going mad with worry, but there's nothing I can do right now.

I force myself to focus again. Stealing keys in this place is impossible. Only two people have them, The Mantis and the Head of Kitchen, and even they are card-keys, linked to their palm IDs. The only way to get out is when the doors are already open. And the only time they are open for any period is when the laundry is brought in or sent out. My choices are limited. It has to be then. I still have to figure out exactly how. To do that, I need to be in the kitchen at the back door to see what happens, or in the garden when the van arrives and leaves.

Elliott told me the government also require kids under sixteen to spend a minimum of half an hour in the day light. They don't specify what we should be doing, so The Mantis makes us work in the vegetable garden, planting and weeding. I haven't been allowed out yet. No one is in their first week, but tomorrow is day eight and my schedule changes.

We have to wait until the Carer-gaoler on night duty has checked that everyone is asleep. Few are, but everyone pretends as he flashes the lantern around the room. It's hard not to hold your breath, but I breathe in and out normally enough that he passes me by. I hear him closing the door and then I wait. The other two kids in the room need to be asleep before Elliott and I can talk. It's hard to stay awake, I'm so tired, so I quietly sit up, pulling my knees towards me, and wrapping the rough blanket around me. I feel my eyelids closing, my head falling forwards on my knees. For a split second I'm unconscious, before I jerk awake and shake my head. I hear Elliott move above me and slip off the top bunk, using my bed to climb down as quietly as possible. We pick up our blankets and tiptoe in the dark across a cold hard floor, relieved we reached the door without waking our room-mates.

The door is so old and creaky we're sure it will bring the 'night watchman' running. We stand outside our bedroom, waiting, my heart beats so loudly it's as if it is trying to bang its way out of my chest. I pull my blanket higher over my shoulders and shiver, but still behave like a statue. The house is silent and so dark, I feel like I'm about to fall into an abyss. It makes me dizzy. I hate not being able to see in front of me. How we'll find the bathroom, our agreed meeting place, I'm not sure. I reach out to the wall that I know is on my left hand side somewhere, to steady myself. Just as the tips of my fingers touch it, I hear a click and a light goes on. My heart skips a beat, but Elliott turns round and smiles. He is shining a torch under his chin, into his face like we used to when we were kids to scare each other. He's a grinning ghoul with red eyes. I gasp for a moment and then try to act as if he hasn't startled me. I push him forward in what I think is a manly, 'I'm way cooler than you' way.

I can't believe it though. Where did he get a torch from? Was it that easy? I follow him as he slips into the bathroom. It's strange to be here at night, it smells damp and the floor is freezing my toes off. There is a little light from one small window to the left, which my eyes adjust to quickly. We sit in the furthest most, darkest corner. If someone came in, they wouldn't be able to see us.

"Where did you get the torch?"

I'm impressed and he smiles, looking pleased with himself.

"Trade."

"Huh?"

"Everything's a trade in here. You just 'ave to know what someone needs."

He hands me the torch and I switch it off, throwing us into darkness again. We don't need to see to talk.

"Batteries might go."

I say by way of explanation before he asks,

"What are we here for?"

"I think I know 'ow to get the food, but we need to bring someone else in."

He's whispering. We are both sitting with our knees pulled in tight to our chests, our backs to the wall. We cocoon our blankets around us, tucking in our toes, trying to keep warm.

"What...who?"

The more people who know, the more likely we are to be caught. The thought terrified me.

He turns to face me. I can smell his stale breath, feel it on my cheek as he speaks.

"'E's the Kitchen Manager's assistant. She trusts him."

I look at him in the dark night. All I can see is the silhouette of his encased body with a head on the top, and white eyes and teeth. It's a little eerie.

"So...?"

"So, 'e 'as access to the food cupboard."

I'm silent for a while, thinking. Elliott continues.

"E's the only one who works in the kitchen full time. We'll be switched soon, but they can switch us back at any time, and..."

He stops talking and we listen, peering towards the door. There is a noise...a floorboard creaking. This is an old house. It may be nothing. He continues whispering.

"We can only take food after the evening stock check, or they'll notice."

"Stock-check?"

"They count the food in the pantry and cupboards to check for stealing."

"Right."

I suppose I shouldn't have been surprised, but it did put a spanner in the works of my plan.

"The Kitchen Manager's lazy. 'Er assistant does the stock check."

"Who's this assistant?"

"Alex."

Of course, I knew him. Everyone knew who everyone was in the home-gaol.

"The big kid with blond hair that serves food?"

"Yep!"

"But he'll never come on board. He's horrible to everyone."

"'E's playing his own game. Everyone 'as a game 'ere. That's 'ow we survive."

"No...definitely not. I don't trust him."

A scratchy voice came out of the darkness.

"What? Yer mean I stayed awake for nuffin' Posh-Boy." The tone was nasty.

"Still...now that I know, I'm sure I could 'ave a little chat wiv' the warden."

"Alex...you've been listening. I told you I'd come and get you."

"So yer did!"

"And don't call me Posh-Boy!"

"What yer gonna' do 'bout it then?"

"Stop Alex! That's just the way 'e is. 'E's a thinker and 'e's thinking about 'ow to get us out."

I looked at Elliott. A little kid protecting me made me feel stupid. Of course he was really around my age, but was smaller and skinnier than me.

"I can fight my own battles, thanks."

Even through the darkness, I can see Elliott glaring back.

Alex is taller and broader than me; he is possibly older, but it's difficult to tell. His hair is still short from the barber's last visit, his wide cheeks shine pale in the dark night. He kneels down in front of us and I switch on my torch to see better. I don't trust him. He might have brought the warden with him for all I know.

"So, why don't yer bofe' welcome your fird member...unless yer wanna' visit the 'ole."

I vaguely wonder what the hole is, but my annoyance with Elliott takes over and I ignore Alex's threat. This is Elliot's fault. I snap at him.

"The more that know, the more likely it is we'll get caught. I knew I couldn't trust you."

"We need someone in the kitchen though, and Alex is the best person."

Alex said nothing for a moment.

"And I 'ave a condition."

"Condition....you aren't even one of us yet."

"Oh but I fink I am."

He was right. We had to take him or he'd tell on us. I was so angry. He continued without any response from Elliott or me.

"Me' sisters come too, or else…."

"Sisters…"

This night was turning into a nightmare.

"Girls? That's impossible! How many do you think can escape at once without being noticed?"

"Well yer the brains, aren't yer? Yer comin' up wiv' the plan. Yer figure it out."

Even though the whole conversation was a whisper, his voice was a little quieter, less demanding. He had a strong northern dialect. I'd heard similar, but couldn't quite place it. He couldn't seem to pronounce 'th' or 'h' properly. But if he was just using it to make him sound tough, it was working.

"I can't leave 'em behind. The warden makes 'em suffer if I do somefing wrong. Once 'e put 'em in the 'ole. They'll be 'urt if I escape. I can't let that 'appen. They're little and I promised me' Mam."

His voice was almost pleading. I paused for a moment.

"Easy then…none of you come, no one gets hurt."

"Not an option…."

My mind suddenly picked up on one of his words, 'little'. There were only two 'little' kids in the home-gaol that I knew of.

"Who are your sisters?"

"Lacie and Josie. You teach 'em."

I sighed. I knew he was telling the truth, if only from the dialect. The Mantis would be cruel enough to hurt them and I couldn't let that happen. They were good kids. I pictured their little faces trying to smile… but they were little. Would they be able to run fast enough?

"No matter what happens, you would be responsible for them."

"'Kay"

"They can't slow us up."

"They won't."

"Right...okay...that makes us five in total. That's it! No more. If anything needs doing, we do it. And we talk to no-one about it. Do you understand?"

I felt like The Mantis suddenly, but they both smirked, Alex raising his left eyebrow, but I could hear the hope in his voice.

"So, what's the plan?"

"No-one but me knows the plan. That way we can't betray each other. I'll tell you what to do and where to be on the night. You just have to turn up with the stuff you've collected."

"I'll need to know which night to collect the food."

"I'll tell you that in two days."

"Fine."

I suddenly had the urge to go to the toilet. Bad timing I know, but the floor was cold. I couldn't help it. I crept over to one of the urinals and was just finishing when I heard a deep voice. A lantern shone and blinded me.

"What yer doin' outta' bed?"

Shock hit me. We'd been caught. They'd find out. I stuttered the words nervously.

"I had to go to the toilet sir."

It was the night watchman staring down at me with his frog-like eyes, bulbous nose, thick hair and non-existent neck. He looked like a Neanderthal man who couldn't carry his weight properly, rocking from side to side as he walked, swinging out gangly arms.

"Yer not allowed outta' bed for any reason. Yer 'ave disobeyed a prime rule."

I wanted to point out to him that being out of bed wasn't a prime rule, but I didn't think it would help much.

"But sir, I was only going…"

"Yer dare speak back to me…"

He was another northerner, though I didn't recognise from where. I stared into the glaring light for a moment, knowing the others sat there watching, praying he didn't turn the lantern on them. Some stupid instinct in me decided to protect them.

"Sir…"

"'gain…"

He slapped me across the head and caught hold of my shoulder. Pain shot through my skull, but I was getting used to that.

"Move."

As he pushed me out of the door, I glanced back at the corner of the room. I knew they could see me, but I couldn't see them. I didn't need to. They'd both look relieved that they hadn't been caught.

"It's the 'ole for yer tonight laddie. Teach yer a lesson in 'ow t'obey the rules."

Chapter 19

He pushed me along the landing and down the stairs. I didn't know what was happening and the little amount of bravery I'd shown earlier had diminished into fear of the unknown. No, not fear, I was terrified. My mind went through everything I knew about this place. What was the hole? Elliott had mentioned it to me. I wondered why. I imagined a hole was something deep and dark, like a rabbit's burrow. I began to panic, not sure what I'd let myself in for, I didn't like confined spaces.

He was an angry bull and in a hurry to get wherever we were going. A sharp pain in my right toe felt like a splinter or perhaps a small cut, caught on the many nails in the wooden floor.

We were on the ground floor. His lantern swung from side to side, creaking in the silent night, throwing shadows across hallway. I could see the big front door ahead and imagined hitting him over the head with his lantern and charging for the door, but there wasn't a key or a handle. A gruesome picture entered my head. I was running to the front door with The Mantis' hand, dripping blood and gore where I'd chopped it off at the wrist, so I could escape using his palm ID. The thought made me smile. The 'Do no harm!' rule didn't even enter my mind. Still I'd never do it. Instead, I consoled myself.

Only a little longer!

The Neanderthal turned me to the right with a push to my left shoulder. We faced a small, wooden door, on which was strung a sign over the knob of the door.

"See what that sign says Lazy-boy?"

I couldn't help but read it.

'To those who follow the path of sin,

Let this be a lesson well-learnt.

For Eternal Darkness is the only reward for your evil ways.

A taste can be a cure. Let this be yours!

Learn from it.'

I had no idea what he meant, but was sure I was about to find out soon.

"Turn over the sign."

I did as I was told. On the back was a notice:

'Hole Occupied!'

"Yer'll be its occupant 'til I come and get ya!"

He seemed to take pleasure in the idea. Could he leave me in the hole for as long as he liked? What exactly was the hole? My legs began to shake. I was sure this wasn't going to be nice.

He opened the door and gave me another shove, almost pushing me down a short flight of steps. At the bottom, he pointed to a trap door and told me to open it. I unbolted the heavy bolt, lifted the large, metal ring and pulled. The door was thick. It took me all my effort to slam it back against the floor. The noise echoed with a loud clang. Half the house must have heard it. I looked down into the small hole below. It was the colour of complete blindness. My whole body trembled with fear.

He snorted with pleasure.

"Get in!"

I looked at him and then at the hole. I couldn't do it. Couldn't condemn myself to such a terror! Suddenly, he was behind me, using a booted foot to kick my butt. I slipped forward and fell face first. Putting out my hands prevented a head crash, but caused sharp, shooting pains in my wrists and on my palms. I screeched without realising it. He laughed, taking pleasure in the suffering.

"See yer when I see yer."

I looked up from the dark. I had to get out. He saw it in my eyes, saw I was about to leap up.

"Mind yer 'ead Lazy-boy."

The trap door slammed down above me, just missing my head, forcing me to sit. The bolts slid across. Instantly, the world disappears.

I am a blind rat in a collapsed tunnel with no exits.

"Let me out..."

I screech, panic taking over.

"Let me out.....you don't understand."

I bang on the trap door, slamming my fists into it.

"...small spaces...I can't breathe..."

I hear his boots treading the floor boards above me. Hear him go up the stairs, closing the top door, sealing me in where no one will hear my cries, burying me alive.

I scream and kick until all I'm doing is hurting myself, but I don't feel the pain. All I feel is the panic, my breath getting shorter and shorter, my heart pounding, trying to take in enough air to feed my brain, but there isn't enough. There isn't any air in here. The room is small, it is a box without oxygen. He won't come back. I'll die here in this box. The darkness will take me over. I'll never see my mother again. I grapple at my throat, trying to get air, trying to stretch my neck, to reach the gaps in the floorboards above me. I'm whimpering now....tears cursing down my cheeks. Fear taking over. I have no strength to cry out.

I know I've gone into quiet hysterics, but I don't care...the cold is turning me numb, the minutes pass without me having any idea of the time. It could be hours for all I know. I'm so afraid, I curl into a ball, cling onto my knees and close my eyes tight. I have lost all reasoning and logic. There's no escape, no way out. I sob to the terrifying darkness...a child again.

Suddenly, I hear the bolt above me slide back. A slither of hope. He's come back. He's not leaving me here. Relief floods me. The trap door lifts up and I see Alex's face.

"Shhh..."

His finger is pressed to his lips. I don't understand. He smiles in the dark and whispers.

"Cun't let our escape planner go crazy, could we?"

He watches me. When he receives no response, he continues.

"Elliott's at the door, keepin' watch. Are yer comin' out or do yer wanna' stay down there?"

There's a light shining down, he has the torch, but I'm confused for a moment until it slowly dawns on me. How much they're risking. I try to stand, but am shaking so much I slip back down to the floor. Alex doesn't comment, but speaks quietly.

"This is 'ow they punished Lacie 'n' Josie the last time I disobeyed 'em."

I can barely focus on what he is saying, but I understand the horrors now, understand why he can't leave them behind.

"They were put in durin' the day so I 'ad to wait 'til night to reach 'em. They were so scared, they din't even recognise me, and then din't speak for a week. Slowly, they've got betta', but they're not the same anymore. "

His talking seems to help. Gradually, I stand up and he helps me climb out. My heart is still not playing its normal tune, but at least I feel sanity coming back. I sit cross-legged, shoulders hunched, fresh tears dribbling down the dried ones on my cheeks. I feel like a baby and rub them away, and wince. My knuckles are bleeding. I manage to speak, though my throat is soar.

"How long was I down there?"

"'bout an 'our. We 'ad to wait 'til everythin' was quiet."

I nod.

"Thanks."

Suddenly, I realise I am glad Alex is coming with us. He is someone who will stick up for you, fight your battles.

"We'll 'ave to put yer back in 'fore everyone wakes up. Crap-Face will let yer out at 'round six o'clock, 'fore 'e goes off duty."

"Crap-Face?"

"The Night Warden that put yer in 'ere. 'e's worse than the warden 'n' 'e's not even s'pposed to put anyone in. Only the warden can do that and it's only for the worst punishment."

"What did yer do?"

"I tried to escape one too many times! After the third time, they decided punishin' me wasn't workin', so now they punish me' sisters for me' wrong-doin's."

I stared at him for a moment; the horror of it slowly drifting into my brain.

"So, yer see, yer plan betta' be good. We can't get caught this time."

He is half joking, but deadly serious.

I nod, understanding, agreeing, wondering how I am going to get us all out and safe.

Chapter 20

By the time they'd put me back in the hole, I'd got my senses back and was a lot calmer. I felt like I had my own mind back and was the serious, older boy that everyone claimed I was – the thinker once more. It calmed me.

Alex and Elliott had taken it in turns to talk to me, while one of them watched the door. They even managed to tell me a few jokes they remembered. Mostly though, they talked about their past and 'playing the game' - their versions of it. Surviving was all about playing the game. Every kid in the 'gaol' had one! And that's when I stopped calling the kids' home anything but what it was. It was a gaol for kids who'd done nothing wrong. Just because someone was poor, it didn't make them a criminal. Our society had got something wrong. It made me very angry. How could Lacie and Josie be treated this way? Didn't they see what was happening to kids? Didn't they care? I wasn't really sure who the 'they' were, but someone, somewhere must be making the decisions. Still, the anger helped me to be strong again, gave me the determination I needed to get us out of the place.

Elliott had been in about a year and a half he thought. Alex and his sisters longer, nearly two years by my calculations. They both came from poorer backgrounds than myself. Alex's father had died in a factory accident, leaving them without income. They'd tried to pay the bills, but the Evictors had eventually come, selling the kids into this home. He had no idea where his mother or elder brother was.

I shared with them very little of my story, and didn't tell them about the Downers, although I did tell them there was a safe place I could take them to. I hoped four extra kids would be okay, that's not including Alicia – I guess it would be five. I felt a bit guilty, none of the kids in the gaol deserved this place, but I could only take a few with me.

We also made lists in our heads about what we needed to escape and who was responsible. Alex would get three bags of food and water, Elliott would trade for torches and anything he thought would be useful. I would ensure there was a plan that would work and a safe place to go to. I promised them I'd share the next part of the plan within two days. I knew I had to come up with something that would work. We couldn't risk being dragged back.

In the end, they'd given me the torch and Alex had handed me a small piece of stale bread. He said it would keep me occupied for a while and he was right, it was rock hard. I was still afraid, but somehow I felt I could cope. As the trap door came down over my head, I knew I'd be out soon. I sat cross-legged, gnawing at the crust, taking deep breaths. The beam of light also helped. It kept me sane, kept my mind thinking right.

When Crap-Face came back, I quickly switched off and hid the torch down the back of my pyjama top, which was tucked into the bottoms. I prayed to their Maker that he would not notice and I guess, for once, He actually listened. That, or Crap-Face was stupid – which was probably true. As he dragged me out, I pretended to be delirious, for which I received a slap across my face. Crawling upstairs on my hands and knees, I'd never felt so tired and yet, for the first time since I'd been there, I felt some hope. I might actually have some friends I could trust. I couldn't let them down now. They were relying on me to do the thinking.

I just needed a plan!

Chapter 21

That day was one of the hardest I'd ever known. I kept falling asleep. It didn't matter whether I was standing or sitting, my eyes just wouldn't stay open. I received several slaps across the head and face, and surprisingly more than my fair share of sharp, side pokes from Alex. He used an old, dry branch and was almost as bad as the gaolers. The Kitchen Manager was a large hippopotamus woman, although that might be an insult to the animal. She had volumes of fat dripping off her bones and hanging over the sinking armchair she sat in all day. She probably never got up to go home, too much of a task, just slept there the whole night. She wore a tent-like piece of black material covering her body from her thick neck to her fat feet.

Every few minutes as her head fell forward and her bulging eyes closed, the snoring began. Then, suddenly, she'd jerk up, look around and shout for Alex. He'd go running to her like a lap dog taking orders. At which point he'd attack someone, either verbally or physically. I couldn't believe he was the same person I'd sat with just a few hours earlier. If I hadn't known this was 'his game' I'd have hated him already. Several of the kids in the room already did. They scowled and cursed under their breaths every time he approached. I wondered what it was like to live this every day just to protect his kid sisters from harm. It must have been tough.

Elliot wasn't with me today. They'd kept him in the laundry for some reason. I wasn't sure what it was. It made me a little nervous. What if they'd found out? What would happen? Would Elliott betray us? No, surely not, not now! I'd find out later I s'ppose, but still I couldn't help thinking about it.

In the kitchen I washed vegetables, chopped and sliced, but didn't cook. That was left to Alex and whomever he decided could help him. I wasn't sure where all the food was going, 'cos I didn't see it land on my plate for lunch. All I got was a thin soup and stale bread. After the meal, we washed and scrubbed the kitchen before starting preparation for tea. The same routine until four o'clock.

Then, to my surprise, there was a flurry in the kitchen. Even Miss Fatty managed to haul her great beast of a body up from her chair. I couldn't immediately see what was happening, but soon I heard his voice.

"Right everyone. Gather round."

The Mantis had entered the kitchen.

"As you know, at four every day the laundry van comes."

He waited whilst we all drilled in unison.

"Yes sir."

He seemed satisfied enough to continue.

"Is this a chance for you all to escape?"

"No, sir."

I was trying to hide at the back, but he spotted me.

"Come here Lazy-boy. I particularly want you to see this."

I shuffled over towards him and the back door, not sure what would happen, but I kept my shoulders slumped, my head down. I didn't have to pretend submission too much,

141

I could barely make an effort to move; my feet were like lead weights.

"I am pleased with your progress Lazy-boy."

He was being sarcastic. He hated me, I could tell.

"We have had worse...some have even tried to escape in their first week, but they learnt."

"Yes sir."

That was Alex's voice. He must have been directing his comment to him, but I didn't look up.

"I think you will fit in nicely Lazy-boy. You learn quickly."

"Yes sir."

"You should be thanking me."

"Thank you sir."

He wasn't quite satisfied with my level of humility, but then he was never happy with any of the kids. He had such a 'God' complex, (or as he would say, 'Maker'), he probably wanted us all shuffling along the floor, bowing our heads before him.

"Anyway, let's move on. This back door has two keys – mine and the Kitchen Manager's. Do you understand Lazy-boy?"

One hundred and forty-four thousand times I'd heard that....at least!

"Yes sir."

"They are also linked to our palm IDs for security."

I already knew this, but didn't say anything. Perversely, his chopped off hand came floating back into my mind.

"That means you cannot open the door."

"Yes sir."

I felt he was addressing all his comments to me as I was now the only one responding. They'd probably seen this 'game' before, but I no longer felt scared, I knew this was temporary and I'd win in the end.

He was now pulling open the huge double doors. For a moment the cold air whooshed in and I gasped. The noise of an engine caused me to look up and I saw a large van backing up towards the archway of the entrance. I could hear it beeping as it came closer. At one point I thought it was going to crash into the walls, but it didn't. It stopped, blocking off the fading light of the day until it was only a thin line around the edge of the doorframe.

There was a low whirring noise and then a sudden snap as the van's back door opened automatically. A man and a boy jumped out. The man was heavy, with broad shoulders and a thick torso. His rolled up sleeves showing muscular, hairy arms.

"What you doin'? Get back in there and bring the load out."

His voice was rough, the arm carelessly lashing out at the boy as if he were made of rubber instead of flesh and bones. The boy went red and climbed back into the van. He was tall and skinny, with buck teeth, dark hair and a light coffee complexion. He began dragging out heavy wicker baskets.

"You, you and you..."

The Mantis pointed at me, Alex and another older boy named Byron.

"Help him or we'll be here all day."

We all jumped up and crawled into the van and began dragging off the dirty laundry baskets. My mind was racing, I was now wide awake. My plan had involved the laundry run; somehow I'd thought we might all escape in the baskets, but with all these people around, I wasn't sure how.

I helped Alex with the last basket. It was wide and had handles at the side to help carry it. To the left of the kitchen, I noticed some kids from the laundry room were struggling with clean laundry baskets. This was the first time I'd seen this happen. It was obviously a swap.

The guy from the van was talking with The Mantis.

"Just a few baskets tonight Warden. Usual agreement?"

"Yes John."

Money passed between them. It seemed peculiar that the 'John-man' was paying The Mantis, but I didn't care. The Mantis was a crook as well as evil. It didn't shock me.

The laundry boy was about to lift one of the clean laundry baskets onto the van, when John swiped him across his head. It was a vicious attack.

"Are you stupid boy? Checks first. How many times...."

He sighed and looked at The Mantis tutting.

"I bought him cheap 'cos of his colour, but I think I made a mistake. He needs at least half a dozen slaps a day to keep him in line. My knuckles are sore!"

Turning to The Mantis, John missed the split second look in his Laundry-boy's brown eyes. For one second he could not hold it back, could not play the game, but it was clear he hated his owner with every ounce of strength he had. I don't think I've ever seen so much loathing, not even in the gaol. He noticed me looking and turned his head quickly.

The Mantis was still talking.

"I thought all 'coloureds' had been evicted."

"They ought to be, but there are some still floating around. London has most, but I wouldn't advise it. I'm going to sell this one on as soon as I take my next trip south."

"Right, are these the clean baskets? Would you like to have the pleasure or should I?"

"Tonight I have a lesson to teach."

"Then it's your show."

John grabbed his 'slave' by the arm, pulling an angry face.

"Be ready to load stupid."

My attention was so caught up with the laundry boy – we were staring at each other - that I almost didn't hear The Mantis. I knew the boy was wondering if I was going to say something.

"Lazy-boy, come here."

I quickly stepped forward.

"Yes sir."

"Take this."

He handed me a long metal stick with a thin blunt end. I had this strange impression he wanted me to beat the laundry boy. My heart skipped a beat. I knew I couldn't do it. I stared around at the kids; some watched out of the corners of their eyes, most had their heads down and hands clasped like pious monks, as if they were praying, but they weren't. They were hiding, not wanting to be noticed or called upon in case they were punished for something.

"Stick it through the middle of all the baskets."

I stood there perplexed. What was he talking about?

"Do not rip the material."

I still stood there. This didn't make sense. His temper flared.

"Give it to me. I don't have time for this."

He snatched the rod back and began jamming it into the centre of the wicker baskets, about half way down. The more he did, the more impatient he became. As he finished each one, the laundry boy jumped to lift the basket onto the van, straining as he did. I wanted to help him, but I'd not been told to move and The Mantis was irritated.

For a moment, I hadn't a clue what the he was doing. Was he going mad? But a comment from John made me realise.

"No one escaping today then."

"Seems not. What a pity? I should have liked to slice them in half."

The Mantis then looked at me and sneered.

"What do you notice Lazy-boy?"

I knew what he wanted me to say, knew he wanted to be proven right. There was no chance of escape in the laundry van, but I couldn't....wouldn't accept it. There must be a way.

"Get out...all of you. I don't want to see your pathetic faces."

Chapter 22

We were all pushed into the garden after the van sealed its doors and pulled out to leave. It surprised me that the boy was driving, although possibly it was on auto-pilot. He didn't look more than fifteen. It surprised me more that I was breathing fresh air for the first time in over eight days. It was freezing but the air smelt of the sea, and so I didn't care. The thought of waves not far away made me think of sailing out to freedom, away from this place forever. There had to be a way to get out of here.

"Boots."

Alex, under the watchful eye of the Kitchen Manager, was still in charge. The Kitchen Manager lurched from one foot to the other as if she were going to fall at any minute. She breathed heavily as if the effort of movement was a challenge to her heart. I wasn't even sure how she'd managed to get out of her seat, I thought she was glued in.

Alex prodded me towards the left and handed me a pair of muddy wellingtons at least one size too big. I watched him put on a similar pair. He didn't bother taking off his plimsolls, rather just put them on top. Others were still trying to find a pair that would fit them. The boots were all mismatched sizes, different colours and very muddy.

As Alex and I bent down to pull up the boots, our eyes met and somehow he managed to smile without using his lips. I had to stop myself from giggling; as if we were little kids playing a secret game. It would have been really stupid, but Alex turned away and began shouting at the kids to get on with the digging. As I didn't know what I was supposed to do, I followed them all out.

This was our half hour in the sun, only the sun was rapidly setting and my fingers were turning to icicles. I knew that was because my body was protecting my vital organs from cold. The only way I could warm up was exercise, so even though I was exhausted, I put my mind and body…and the last bit of energy I had, into digging hard mud. I wasn't sure why we were digging. There didn't seem any point. It was almost winter, the ground was solid, there wasn't anything to plant. And yet we dug!

Suddenly, Alex prodded me again.

"You, come wiv' me."

I wondered what he wanted. Surely he was taking a risk. We'd agreed to talk as little as possible, to make it look like we were enemies. It was part of the plan.

We walked over to a large shed with a concave roof. It was surrounded by a wire fence - maybe it was a tool shed. Alex handed me a small spade which was leant on the side of the building. He took the fork. On entering the shed via a small, side door, I immediately knew it was some sort of house for chickens. Although I'd never seen one, I remembered reading about how they used to breed them in the past. Nowadays, we don't need the birds to grow eggs. LCR – Laboratory Cell Reproduction is cheaper and safer. The screeching of disturbed birds hit my ears, the smell disgusted me.

"We need to get the birds out, gaver the eggs 'n' clean the straw. Yer'll be me' helper from now on. Any egg breakages, yer take the blame. Got'it?"

"Oh-k-ay."

I wasn't sure which Alex this was, so I didn't say anything. He still sounded tough. Was he playing the game?

He shouted above the deafening birds that squawked in terror.

"Open the front and back doors and 'elp me get 'em out."

I did as I was told and then we proceeded to chase the hens. At first I thought it was funny, Alex and I, bent double, kept bumping into each other as they flapped all over the place, trying to avoid capture. But after a while, my back began to ache and I just got fed up. The dust and dirt in the straw flew up, making my nose itch and eventually I was sneezing every few seconds. Alex stopped what he was doing and looked at me.

"Cover yer nose wiv' yer top."

It helped a little, although my eyes began to itch and water, and my nose started running causing sticky liquid goo to pour from every crevice on my face. Having no tissues, all I could do was wipe it on my sleeve. It reminded me of Lissy. Was she safe? Would they have harmed her 'cos I didn't return? I had to get back to rescue her. It made me hate the place even more and somehow Alex became the object of my annoyance.

"What did you bring me in here for? Couldn't you have chosen someone else?"

Alex's response shocked me more than hurt, but still I didn't know what to do.

"'ow dare yer speak to me like that?"

He pushed me with the end of his spade, hitting me on my shoulder. I tried to dodge the second attack and tripped, falling out of the door, my hands scattering a few hens. He came after me, fire in his eyes. Was he mad? He began kicking me in my shins. It didn't really hurt, but I was gradually getting really annoyed.

"Get up Lazy-boy. 'ow dare yer take a rest?"

His voice boomed; the hate and sarcasm clear.

"What's going on here?"

Fatty waddled over.

"Madam, this boy don't like the work our Maker 'as given 'im. I'm just teachin' 'im a lesson."

I was curled in a ball on the ground, protecting my head and so looked up from under my arm. Alex stood there, one foot in front of the other, arms folded across his chest, a look of self-satisfaction on his face.

"Really....and what do you suggest we should do with him?"

"I fink 'e should be made to clear out the chicken shed twice a day."

I couldn't believe what he was doing to me. I wanted to pick up the spade and hit him with it.

"Perhaps a good idea. Doing something one dislikes is a good way of learning how fortunate one is to be in this place."

She gave me a kick for good measure.

"Get up boy."

Without any other choice, I slowly uncurled and stood up. I had pain shooting up my neck again and my legs were bleeding where the metal bit of the spade had caught me.

"The Maker provides us with opportunities to learn, not to decide what we like or dislike. Do you understand?"

"Yes Madam."

"Make sure you learn well or you will suffer for it. It is the only way."

"Yes Madam."

"I shall be keeping my eye on you."

"Yes Madam."

"Alex, I expect you to help him learn."

I didn't like the way she pronounced 'help', like they both had some sort of secret code.

"I'll do me' best Madam."

"Thank you. Now finish your work. It's getting dark and 'outside time' is almost up."

"Yes Madam."

I followed Alex back into the shed. I hated him. Somehow I had to find a way to lose him once we were outside. We needed him only for food.

"Close that door"

We were bending over to get in the shed. There was only the clean straw to lay now and the eggs to collect. As I pulled the door inwards, I watched as the kids, who had been digging, took off their boots, and go in. I wished I was one of them, instead of being where I was.

"Sorry I 'ad to do that."

I stared at him, anger boiling in my eyes. Alex looked back, his eyes shining out in the dark.

"I tried not to 'urt you... did yer notice my kicks weren't 'ard? But I 'ad to make it look real or she wun't 'ave believed it."

"She wouldn't have believed it..."

I was furious. My body was turning into one big bruise.

"...I didn't believe it. You had no reason to do that."

I couldn't take it anymore. I was confused and physically aching. Tears sprung to my eyes. I just wanted to go home, I was tired of all the work, the pain, the humiliation and the game playing. And that's what it had been. Another game! I wiped the tears away.

He looked down nervously, clutching a handful of straw.

"No, really...it was all fake...'onestly."

He pleaded with me to believe him. I was still angry and wanted to hit him back, have a real fight, instead of all the bowing and scraping, all the acceptance of punisment. I glared at him, breathing heavily, barely controlling the need to thump him in the stomach.

"Why?"

My voice was rough with the tears I wouldn't let flow.

"Two reasons. The first yer'll see when we go in. The second is we need a place where we can talk; a place where no one suspects anyfing. The bathroom every night is dangerous. The shed is perfect. No one comes 'ere but me."

I looked away. He was right of course, it was a good idea, but I was too exhausted to do anything but collect the eggs and tramp my way back. He kept chatting to me every now and then. He was worried he'd upset me, but overall pleased with how he'd managed to trick 'them'. That's how he saw it, how he played his game, how he survived. How many times a day did he trick them whilst hurting others? It was twisted and he couldn't see it. They had twisted his way of thinking – it wasn't right.

Twenty chickens, seventeen eggs; I'd already started counting. In the morning there would be more to count. It kept me sane in this crazy world, this crazy life I'd fallen into. Walking towards the back door, I noticed the numbers above it said 1849. It must mean this house was nearly two hundred years old. I wasn't surprised, everything in it was old.

As we walked towards the food cupboard, the Kitchen Manager, now slumped in her chair, yelled at Alex. She had a cup of tea under her chin as she dipped biscuits and guzzled them up.

"How many eggs?"

"Firteen madam!"

"Good. Log them."

"Yes madam."

I looked at him. He was lying, the corners of his mouth twisting into a hidden smile, as we entered a large walk-in pantry. Casually, he slipped two eggs into an old plastic bag, hidden under the bottom shelf and then placed the rest of the eggs in a small basket on the middle shelf. He'd begun collecting already.

I looked around, the place was cold and dark, but my eyes had adjusted and now, my stomach was growling at the smells that filled my nostrils. Cold meats, cheeses, bread, cakes, boxes of dried stuff, vegetables, fruit...I was overwhelmed. This was stuff I hadn't seen for ages.

"Don't want you two in there long."

I could hear Fatty from outside, and now I knew why she was so gross. She had an excess of glutinous food to scoff.

I just stood there staring, breathing in the fumes of food I dare not touch. I was in a trance.

"Wake up!"

Alex was grinning as he stuffed some of the cold meat into the hidden bag. Then he turned round and handed me something.

"Take this for yer 'n' Elliott. 'ide it down yer top 'n' don't eat 'em 'til they're all asleep."

He winked at me as I took his offering of peace – two biscuits wrapped in a tissue. I smiled, immediately tucking my top in my pants so I could stow it away. Now I knew why he'd wanted me to be with him, what he'd wanted me to see.

I had no idea how we were going to escape – the laundry baskets were definitely a 'no', yet Alex was keeping his side of the bargain – already collecting food. He was taking a huge risk for him and his sisters. It was time I kept my side of the bargain as well.

Chapter 23

It was cold and dark, the rain had been crashing down on the roof for a couple of hours and I was exhausted. I'd had stomach ache for at least a couple of hours, it was probably the food we'd eaten at dinner time; it had tasted a bit odd, although no one else seemed to be troubled with it. Still, it hadn't stopped me from hiding under the covers and nibbling at the biscuit. I tried to make it last as long as possible; the sweetness tingled on my tongue, as I kept it in my mouth longer than I usually would, but eventually it was gone. I wondered if Alex would give us more. Working in the hen shed didn't seem so bad if there were rewards.

I whispered Elliott's name, but he didn't respond. Suddenly, I knew I had to go to the loo. I would never sleep unless I did. I'd tried, but the more I thought about it and the more my stomach screamed out in waves of agony, the more I knew I needed to go.

Crap-Face came and went twice before I got up. This was soooo risky. If I was caught, I'd be in the hole again, without anyone to get me out this time. The thought sent butterflies into my stomach, but I had no choice, unless of course I wanted a wet bed.

As quietly as I could, I took out some clean clothes and packed them under my blanket, to make it look like a sleeping body. It might work! Hold him off for a while. Trembling with cold and at the thought of being captured by Crap-Face, I crept along, hugging the wall and hiding in the shadows, planning my every move in case he turned up. I had the torch with me, but daren't use it. What if he came along and saw the reflection?

I'd decided to go to the girl's toilet, even though it was a horrible idea. They were to the right and nearer, but it took forever before I reached the door and swung it open. The hinges creaked, begging for oil. I stopped, holding my breath, waiting, but Crap-Face's tramping wasn't close enough to hear so I darted in.

The girls' bathroom was different to ours. It didn't have any urinals for a start, only cubicles. I didn't care. I dashed into one of them, closed the door and lifted the lid, relieved I'd made it in time.

On leaving the toilets, I heard Crap-Face, his boots on the hard, wooden floors as he opened and closed bedroom doors, checking we were all in bed. He was now so close, he must have been at my room. I gulped, suddenly terrified, how had he got so close so soon? What would he do if he found me gone? Would he notice I was made of clothes? I heard the door close and his footsteps moving to bedroom four. He was pretty stupid not to notice a body of clothes, but still I was now in a rotten situation. For a moment, I didn't know what to do. Should I dash back into the toilets, hide in a cubicle. What if he checked? A sudden bout of panic sent pain to my chest. My stomach joined in as if I'd swallowed curdled cheese. I had to make a decision. Without realising it, my feet decided it would be better to just move towards the back stairs and hide somewhere in the shadows until he'd passed. This was an old Victorian house and had narrow servant's stairs to the rear. My mother loved old houses, my father had always hated them. I didn't care either way, although adapting them to modern life was hard. We'd lived in an old house and couldn't have automatic doors, built in wall screens and lights for our entertainment centre, or automated heated walls and floors, or even shower friendly gadgets come to think of it. We missed out on tons of things, or rather I did. My friends had thought us odd, but my mother didn't care. She always said she didn't want her life controlled by gadgets, she wanted to make her own decisions.

Right now, I'd have been happy to have any gadget-less house, as long as it wasn't this one. Even though I was in a dire situation, I smiled inwardly at my mother's old fashioned ways. She was so in the past, she could have been living at the turn of the century. The only thing she really valued was her personal, lightweight, roll up laptop. She carried it everywhere. It had her life's work on it. Or so she told me. I wasn't sure what her life's work was. She never said. I made a mental note to ask her when I got back. And I would get back, I would not live my life here. It wasn't a life.

Such self-talk , though crazy, boosted my determination and pushed down into the pits of my stomach the daily fear of being caught. I would get home. These monsters wouldn't keep me a prisoner.

I'd reached the top of the back stairs, when I heard his footsteps behind me, doors opening and closing. Crap-Face was near. I couldn't see a place to hide. There was only wall – nothing else.

The light from his lamp swung shadows in front of him, like an enormous creature lumbering down the hallway. I had to think of something….anything. I couldn't stand there like a rabbit with a gun to his head. It was stupid I know, you think if I were in that situation I'd run like crazy, but for a moment I really did just stand still, before kicking myself into action. There was nothing for it, I hadn't intended to, but there was little choice. I had to get ahead of Crap-Face. I slipped into the dark back stairs and tiptoed down the narrow wooden steps. I was scared of tripping; I couldn't see a thing, so held on to the walls at the side of me, my sweaty hands flat against the plaster. I used my already freezing toes as feelers, edging them to the end of the step, before moving forward. It was painstakingly slow, I was sure he would catch up with me. I tried to count to calm me down...step six...step seven...I wasn't sure how many there were even though I'd been down it plenty of times in the day-time. It seemed longer now and the whole stairway coiled like a snake around a post. It was a trap set up to trip me. The walls were useless as bannisters and once I only just managed to save myself from falling.

I reached the last step just in time. The clunk of his heavy boots on the top wooden step sent me into a frenzy, I forgot about being careful. I dashed under the stairway and squashed myself into the darkest corner at the back of the hallway. My whole body pounded as if I were a big bass drum. I leant against the two corners of the wall, pushing myself further in, wanting to melt into nothingness. I felt my clothing sap up the cold sweat as it trickled down my back. I was breathing too hard, pushing air out of an open mouth as if I'd been running in a race, my chest hurt. I had the urge to bend over to catch my breath, but kept myself crouched deep in the shadows like a tiny creature of the night hiding from its huge captor.

He was down, only a couple of metres in front of me. If he turned this way, the lamp light would spot me. I was praying he turned right. For a moment, I could see the arched door in front of me. I pushed my back harder against the corner, as if I could dissolve into the walls.

He stood, as if wondering what to do next, and then suddenly turned to the right towards the kitchens. My whole body breathed a sigh of relief although I wasn't sure where he would go next. I couldn't move yet. I heard him rumbling around, checking the doors and locked cupboards, before returning along the same path. He walked straight passed me, without even looking to the left, through a side door and onwards towards the front of the house.

Crouched, unable to move, unsure whether to make a dash for it, I sat for at least five minutes, until his footsteps had quietened with distance and my pulse no longer raced at a zillion miles per hour. I'd been lucky this time. Now I needed to get back to bed. I unwound my tense body and slowly moved forwards, still hugging the wall. Just as I was about to stand, my sleeve caught on something and I heard at first a click and then a grating sound, like a badly fitted door across a tiled floor. I was terrified, the noise echoed across the hallway. I was sure it could be heard all over the house. I waited a minute to see if the footsteps returned and then quickly felt around the right-hand side wall. To my surprise, there didn't seem to be a wall. Was I going mad? Had I broken a wall by leaning too hard on it? I pulled out the torch, sure Crap-Face was in the other side of the house, and clicked it on. My eyes took a few seconds to adjust to the light, but what I saw made me gasp. It was a square hole in the wall, the size of one of the wooden panels. It looked as if a panel had fallen in. Someone was bound to notice and then the punishments would be handed out. I wondered if I could fix it, pull it back so no one would notice.

I shone the torch inside, bending my head in, not knowing what to expect. It smelt musty and I imagined spiders and cobwebs at the least. To my surprise, there was nothing but a wall about a quarter of a metre in. It seemed to go up higher than the panel itself, but that was all. I was about to bring my head out, when my torchlight caught something on the narrow side wall. I crawled into the tiny space on my hands and knees to have a closer look.

Sticking out of the wall were thick pieces of heavy metal about thirty centimetres long. I shone the torch all the way up the wall. Both the wall and the metal pieces went up at least four metres. It seemed the spikes had been placed there purposely, to form some sort of ladder. I hesitated for a moment, unsure what to do. This was obviously some sort of secret passage, it must be. I'd read about such things. Old houses sometimes had secret passage ways. I wondered if anyone else knew about it, wondered where it might lead. If I explored, would I get stuck?

It was tempting to go in, my life had been so bad of late, I needed something different, something with excitement. Surely, I could explore and still be back in bed before anyone knew. It would be my secret place to get away from everyone – to hide if necessary. In fact, one day it might be necessary to hide from danger. It might even save my life. I looked up again, having almost convinced myself. It was so narrow. I didn't like narrow spaces, but on hearing Crap-Face's steps getting louder, I made a quick decision. I crawled through the hole and sat with my back against the wall, my knees up to my chest. I could feel the grit and dirt on my numb feet. I shone the torch around the opening and realised the panel was like a sliding door. Pushing it to the right, the grinding of dirt and age made me cringe; it was so stiff. I was sure the noise could be heard outside. I was going to leave a gap, so I could get out again, but it automatically slipped into place and clicked shut.

Immediately, the walls seemed to close in on me. I tried not to worry, not to bring on panic. There must be some sort of mechanical device to open it. Feeling around the rough edges of the panel, I finally found a piece of wood sticking out on the left and pushed it. Nothing happened! My breathing was increasing in pace. I tried again, but this time pushed it up. Still nothing happened. Panic, in the form of bile, began bubbling up in my throat, but I swallowed hard, pushing it away. I held the wood between my thumb and finger and tried to wiggle it around from left to right and back again. I didn't want to break it, but didn't want to be buried alive either. Long ago tales of skeletons being found inside walls flicked into my mind. I whimpered, pushing the images of me forever trapped, no one knowing where to find me, away.

The relief I felt when I heard the click and watched the panel grind open again was huge. I snorted and grinned, it was a miracle it worked. My spine tingled, I wasn't going to be a bag of bones after all. I could now see out again. Crap Face was just on the other side of the connecting door to the front part of the house. Quickly, I closed the panel again, using the small lever, hoping it wouldn't break with age.

Chapter 24

I knew I would be filthy by the time I dragged myself out again. I could feel the dirt clinging to my hair, my face, my hands - sticking on my clothes. How would I hide dirty pyjamas? I pushed the thought to the back of my mind and shone the torch upwards. There were about ten metal prongs.

Quickly, I put the torch in my mouth and grasped the spike just above my head. Carefully, placing my foot on a lower one, I began to climb. At first slowly, I wasn't sure of my grip or where I was placing my feet, but I gained confidence quickly, not wanting to spend too long in the narrow passageway. It was like crawling through a tunnel only upwards. I pushed ahead hoping it was leading somewhere and that no one lived in that somewhere. I imagined it led to another part of the house. The metal pieces were old and rough, possibly rusty, and were freezing cold. They stung my feet, but it didn't matter. They were numb with cold anyway, so it didn't make a difference. I kept my eyes focused upwards, my teeth clenching the torch. Dribbles of saliva kept running down the back of my throat, but I swallowed hard and ignored it. I could feel air coming down the tunnel, which was a relief, at least I would be able to breathe. It turned the earlier sweat cold on my forehead, replacing it with grime and stickiness.

Finally, I reached the last rung, my arms aching. Peeking over the tunnel edge cautiously, like a rabbit watching for a fox as it comes out of its burrow, I strained my eyes to see what was above, before eventually hauling myself up. All was quiet.

I sat on the edge of the parapet, my legs dangling over the side, one foot balanced on a metal spike. With the thin beam of torch light, I could make out a further tunnel-way. I would have to bend to walk along it. At the end there was an opening of some kind. I sighed and heaved myself on my knees, ready to stand. I'd come this far, I might as well see what was at the end.

It was a short walkway and as I went along it, the wooden floor creaked and moaned as if I were walking across an old man's bony back. I tried to tread lightly, but it didn't help. I couldn't be any quieter and so I took larger strides. At least that way I would get wherever I was going faster. Cobwebs attacked me and I flayed around, trying to push them away with my hands before they hit my face. I wondered if there were rats up here and whether they would like me for dinner. Shuddering as a particular large web hit me in the mouth, I had to stop and spit it out. Wiping my arm across my face, I found even more dust and sticky webs. It was all disgusting and horrible. I almost turned back, but without noticing it, the tunnel had gradually widened, until eventually I stood in a small room about three by two metres. It smelt old and musty, left to the creatures that inhabit such spaces when humans go away. With the exception of a support stanchion, it looked unused – a forgotten space. My mind raced. Possibly, it had been a small, storage room, and yet it would be difficult to bring stuff up. It could have been a part of the attic, but it was too small to be the whole of it. Perhaps there'd been an alteration after the house had been built, now it was useless, forgotten for years – the only footprints in the dust were mine.

My eyes immediately set upon something against the wall opposite me. I walked over and stared at it – an old chest, made of dark wood and corroded metal; it was covered in years of dust of course, and as I lifted off the lid, plumes of it hit the air, making me sneeze five times in a row and drop the lid. The rust had destroyed the hinges and, without anyone holding it up, it fell to the floor with a huge clang, echoing in the silent room. I stepped back startled, not sure where I was in the house. Could someone have heard? I stood quietly for a moment, waiting to hear any movements below, but there were none.

Shining the torch in the chest, I saw old bottles, some empty, some full. I picked one up and wiped the dirt off the label. *Scotch Whiskey* was the name on the bottle. Underneath it, it said *Brewed in 1859* For a moment I just stood there, my brain clouding over. This couldn't be right. I looked again at the bottle. Then I began picking up and looking at the others. There were six altogether, all saying the same thing. Some were empty, one was broken. I stood there like an idiot wondering what it all meant. I shone the torch around the room again. What was this room?

In the far corner, I saw a small door. It looked like a cupboard of sorts and so I walked over to it, wondering what I would find now. The door handle was loose, but it still worked if I jiggled it a little. Shining the torch into the dark space, I found it wasn't a cupboard, but rather old, wooden stairs going downwards. I hesitated. I didn't know what time it was, it could be close to 'getting up time', and if they found me gone....should I go?

It was pitch-black, could be full of rats, definitely spiders and cobwebs...and the door didn't work properly. And the batteries in the torch might go. And I could get stuck in there and die a terrible death alone and in the dark. I looked back at the chest, then at the door.

Making a terrible noise with clinking bottles and scraping wood against wood, added to which I couldn't stop sneezing, I heaved the broken chest over to the door and jammed it open. Well it wouldn't close shut anyway. With that, the excuses evaporated and I made my way down the stairs. There were only ten steps, before it turned into a dark passageway, only just high enough not to hit my head, and an arms-width wide. It smelt the way I imagined an old coal mine might have smelt. I'd read about them in our history lesson when I used to go to school. It was only twenty years ago that all mines were eventually closed down in England, due to the method of fracking, which was said to be a cheaper alternative. Only, it was the fracking that caused the tremors and earthquakes in England. Only then did they admit their mistake and stop, but it was too late. I can't understand it myself! Why didn't all those scientists back then know that blasting high pressure water, sand and chemicals at rocks deep below the earth's surface would cause fracturing? We only use natural energy at home.

Some people still remembered what coal was like. When I was about six, my Nan told me how coal fires were hotter and cosier in winter. She even used to toast bread over them. Dad and I tried it with an outside fire, but burnt the bread. We did manage to bake potatoes though.

My mind had wandered, I had to stop thinking about the past and focus on where I was going; it was dark and probably dangerous. The walls were made of rock, roughly dug out to make a tunnel. Sliding my fingers along to help feel my way, the cold and damp made me shiver. It all smelt of fungus, dirt and salt. The torch only shone a narrow beam, so I didn't really know what was ahead of me more than a few steps. I didn't want to know. My imagination was playing havoc enough. Anything could live down here, if they could get in. I tripped a couple of times, my toes taking a battering. They stung, probably cut and bleeding by now. There was nothing I could do, but I wished I'd put my plimsolls on.

I started sensing that the tunnel was going down and had to lean backwards slightly to balance and stop myself from sliding forward. I was aware it was getting steeper and steeper and began to think I might just end up being in a vertical free-fall. I stopped for a moment. How long had I been walking? I couldn't tell, it seemed like hours.

What if I was just going round in circles?

What if it ran out of air?

I laughed at myself, trying to shake the nervousness, trying to be brave – I'd only wanted to go to the toilet. At least I didn't have a stomach ache anymore. But my heart wasn't to be fooled. It pounded hard, surging oxygen around my body. I pushed away the thought of being trapped. I could easily turn round.

Perhaps that's what I should do, turn back. This tunnel could go on forever. I needed to get back.

The voice in my head was convincing.

But what if it was a way out?

The other voice argued.

Just a little further.

I walked on for about ten minutes and had decided to turn round, when I felt a waft of cold air on my face. It tingled across my cheeks and sent a shiver up my spine.

There must be another room ahead. I'll go that far.

Within a couple of minutes, I came to a large room. Empty boxes were littered all over the floors. I could hear a noise ahead of me. It sounded strange, like an engine whirring in the dark of the night. I moved towards it cautiously. Someone might be there. As I did, cold, dank air struck my whole body and I shivered uncontrollably. I switched off my torch in case someone was there and moved closer to the wall to protect myself, leaning against it and feeling my way with the palms of my hands against the rough rock. The noise, though distant, got louder, until eventually I came to the end of the room and stared out shocked. It wasn't a dug out room, it was a cave. I was standing at the edge of the opening, gaping out at the world I'd been a captive from for so long. The horizon was invisible in the dark of the night but a black line indicated the sea was at a distance. The sound I'd heard was only the waves hitting a section of a long beach lying below the cave. My heart skipped a beat, as I realised it was reachable. I couldn't believe it! I'd expected a room and had found the world. I was free. I didn't have to go back. My mind buzzed with excitement, adrenalin rocketing around me, charging me with energy and a heat that warmed my cold toes. The joy and thrill of the world made me dizzy with delight and I laughed out loud, bending over double as the ache in my stomach returned; only this time, I didn't need the toilet.

Chapter 25

I carefully climbed down to the beach, jumping the last half metre. The moist sand between my toes was soft and cold – it made me smile into the darkness. I wanted to shout something stupid like 'whoopee' or jump up and down laughing out loud. Instead, I whispered 'yes' to myself with all the emotion I could muster whilst still being quiet.

Jogging along the beach, my hair flying back, the torch beam shaking light in front of me, I started to plan how I'd get home. There must be a train I could take from somewhere.

My mind turned to the practical things. I needed to find clothes and food though. That was okay, I am a Collector. I can do that as I go along. I slowed to a walking speed. I needed to get Alicia out as well.

I placed my foot on the first of some rough-hewn steps against an old sea wall, ready to make my way up, when I looked back at the cliff. It was a black silhouette against the star-lit sky. I couldn't see the cave from this angle, only the jagged shape of a cliff about one hundred metres high. I couldn't see the home-gaol either, it must have been further back. I thought about the kids in there.

What about Elliott and Alex?

I saw Alex smiling as he hid the eggs and handed me the biscuits. I pictured Elliott proudly giving me the torch he'd traded for; both desperate to escape. And then I saw Lacie and Josie.

What about the little girls? They'd only just learnt to smile.

I imagined them being sent to the hole and shivered at the thought, and then shivered more with the cold.

Could I just walk away and leave them?

Yes, go. This is your chance. They'd leave you behind if they had this chance. Take it. You may never get this chance again.

But even though the voice in my head tried to convince me, I knew I wouldn't.... couldn't just leave them behind. Maybe before I'd got to know them I might have, but not now.

Head down, I slowly walked back to the cave thinking. We needed things to escape anyway. Needed to plan it properly. With more of us, and two kids, we'd have to be careful. I looked out at the dismal sea. And what if the tide comes in? How would we escape the cave?

As I climbed the rocks to the cave, I shook with cold and a sudden drop in energy. I'd been surviving on adrenalin, fear and excitement. Now, I was exhausted and disheartened. It was hard forcing myself to return to the horrid gaol, but it had to be, for now. I looked around the cave and saw I'd missed some dust covered objects strewn around. It was too late to look now. Could look at them the next time!

And there will be a next time! Now I know how to get out, I will!

I wondered what all of it was for; the secret room, tunnel and cave. What could it have been used for? Staring at some old empty containers, and remembering the old whiskey bottles, a possibility suddenly hit me. This must have been an old smuggler's cave. Boats could have come up to it in high tide and unload their goods for storage, ready to be sold on. I was sure I was right. The house was so old, out of the way and on a cliff; the perfect place. It had probably been built for that purpose. I considered whether anyone used it now, but with all the dust and the lack of footprints, I doubted it. I doubted anyone ever came here now. Why would they? Maybe it had all been forgotten.

As I skulked back through the tunnel, into the room I thought about what had happened. By pure chance and accident, I'd found an escape. Not only that, I'd found a storage room to go with it. We could hide our stuff there until we were ready to leave. My mind raced at all the things we needed to do, at how long it might take, but for that one moment as I entered the house again, I was completely happy; our escape was really a possibility. It was the best thing that had happened to me for ages.

I knew it was getting late and I had to get back to my room. Quickly, I pushed the panel back into place and heard the familiar click. The house was not as dark as it had been and I switched off the torch. I could see from the faded light that the sun would soon rise. I had to rush. I looked down at myself. I was so black with dirt, even my feet would cause a trail. I couldn't take the risk someone would notice, find the panel. Not now, when everything was so ready for the taking.

I took off my pyjamas and turned them inside out, thinking I might put them back on, but it was impossible. It seemed the dirt had crawled up the inside of my legs – there was even dried sand, but I could at least use them to wipe my feet. Fortunately, I still had underclothes on, although they didn't do much good, I was freezing. I spat on a clean-ish spot on my top and rubbed my feet until I was sure they wouldn't leave a trace. For good measure, I wiped the floor of dust and sand as well. Next I ran to the only place I could – the kitchen. In the corner, there was a small sink for peeling vegetables. I stood in it and turned the tap on, trying to keep it at a minimum to reduce the sound. Picking up the only thing available, I began cleaning my feet with a metallic pan scrubber, and continued upwards towards my neck. My toes were sore with cuts and small wounds and I winced, trying to be careful. The scrubber cut into my skin, and caused a red rash all over, but I didn't care, rather red and sore than dirty in this place. There would be so many questions if I turned up covered in even the tiniest bit of filth. And someone would notice in the showers and tell on me.

I had to be fast. I was praying Crap-Face had fallen asleep, but it was getting lighter by the second. I jumped out of the sink and used a kitchen cloth to dry myself. The last thing I did was throw my head under the tap to wash away the dirt in my hair and on my face. I scrubbed until the water no longer swirled black down the drain. Hoping I'd managed to get all the filth off me, I made a last ditch effort to leave the kitchen clean, before throwing the pan scrubber and cloth into the rubbish shoot and running up the back stairs. The caution I'd used earlier was totally absent. On the landing, I charged to my bedroom, throwing the dirty clothing in the basket outside as I did.

My mother's angel – she believed in angels – must have been watching over me, as just as I closed the door, the bell to wake up sounded. Elliot was just waking up as I threw on some clothes and made my bed. He looked at me strangely.

"You don't look good."

"I'm okay."

"Why's your hair wet?"

"Oh God…do you have a towel?"

We were whispering so the other two didn't hear, though they looked over at us oddly. Elliott went through the morning rush of dressing and bed making.

"Where 'ave you been?"

I was rubbing my hair and neck, trying to stop it dripping down my back.

"Great news, but talk later?"

"Okay, but your face is red, and your arms. What's wrong with you?"

He seemed genuinely concerned.

"No, I'm fine. Just reaaally cold."

At that point I realised I was shivering, really shivering. I couldn't stop. My teeth chattered and my bones shook. As we walked out the door for the morning line-up, my stomach joined in the dance and I suddenly felt the heat rise in my face. Standing in the line, I wasn't sure I could remain upright, my legs felt so weak. I didn't know what was wrong with me. Elliott kept looking at me, as if to say 'are you sure you're alright?'

I'll be okay. Just tired from no sleep.

I tried to reassure myself and stepped forward. My legs weighed a ton.

"Respect, cleanliness and hard work is the will of the Maker and………"

But I couldn't say anymore. I tried. I knew I'd be in trouble, but the words wouldn't come out of my mouth. My brain was confused and my speech slurred. I felt a spurt of heat shooting through my body and my head started spinning. The Mantis was in front of me, screaming something into my face, but I couldn't understand what he was saying and his face was blurred. I couldn't react.

Instead, I felt my legs buckling beneath me, like thin twigs snapping in the wind. And just as day returns to night in a full solar eclipse, the world disappeared from me into a shadowy silence.

Chapter 26

Until I actually woke up, I didn't realise I'd been out of it for two days.   Not only that, but I didn't immediately recognise the place or the boy sitting next to me. I stared around confused.

"You're awake! Are you better?"

"Who are you?"

His face was pale, his eyes questioning.

"Adam, what's wrong? Don't you remember me?"

I looked at his face. He seemed familiar, I was sure I must know him. Why didn't I? I tried to think, but my head hurt.

"You're sick."

Sick?

"You fainted at morning line up. Don't you remember?"

I was sure I should, but none of it made sense. Where was my mother? I tried to lift myself onto my elbows to look around, but flopped back. Everything hurt, felt weak. Even my funny bone ached.

"They think you have flu, but kept you here until they're sure it isn't anything contagious. The Warden wasn't happy."

He snickered into his hand as if someone being unhappy was a good thing.

"You collapsed on a day when 'e 'ad visitors from the local council checking up on the home. 'E's worried 'e'll lose the money, that's all."

Nothing made sense.

"Who are you?"

"I'm Elliott. Don't you remember?"

He frowned, his blue eyes squinting. He was leaning forward, clutching his fingers, fidgeting and worrying.

"Where am I?"

"In the isolation wing."

I screwed my face up, trying to remember where the isolation wing was.

"In the kids' 'ome...remember?"

This was a nightmare. I couldn't remember anything, couldn't remember this boy. Why did he know me? Where was my mother if I was ill? Everything was wrong and I was too weak to fight back. Tears threatened to trickle so I closed my eyes, ignored the boy and drifted back to sleep.

When I awoke again a day later, the boy sat beside me still, mopping my head with a cold cloth, playing nurse. The cloud had gone and I no longer had a defunct memory. That, at least, was a relief.

I tried to sit up.

"Aaag..."

My whole body burned with aches and pains, as if I'd been flattened in a metal crusher and then straightened out. The boy was quietly staring at me.

"What are you staring at?"

My voice was hoarse.

"Do you know who I am?"

"'Course I do....what's wrong with me?"

"You only 'ave flu."

"Only...you sure no one beat me up....The Mantis?"

He knew I called the warden 'The Mantis' behind his back and so a look of relief came over his face as my memory had obviously returned. I suppose I'd been a lot worse.

"How long have I been here?"

"Three days."

"Right...how long have you been here?"

"Three days.....and nights. I've been sleeping in that bed next to you."

I tried for a wry smile, but everything hurt too much and it came out as a painful smirk.

"How come you're allowed here?"

"I got The Mantis to volunteer me, by telling him it would be a good idea if you died with some unknown illness."

"Thanks."

I almost grinned, but my lips were dry, they cracked when I stretched my mouth.

"'E said as I was a terrible teacher who'd allowed you to be off work with illness, I should suffer too and if I caught the illness then all the better. 'E wouldn't allow any of his staff to risk catching something. Although obviously, I didn't want to miss all the work and sit 'ere for hours at a time doing nothing. It would be against the Maker's rules, so I'm reading the 'good book' to you."

The sarcasm ran from his tongue as he held up the Maker's 'bible' in his hands. I tried to grin, but probably just showed a few teeth. I was so tired.

"Have I learnt anything?"

"Probably not, but then, I only read when I 'ear them coming down the corridor..."

"I can't believe he allowed it."

"Oh he 'ates it. 'E's probably 'oping we both die! But 'e 'as to be seen to be doing something. We 'ave people checking-up on the 'ome. They stay for three days every year and you just 'appened to get ill on their first day. 'E even brought a doctor in."

"Wow."

I was stunned, such a place was actually approved by someone.

"Unlucky for you really. You've missed some real food. I ate eggs for the first time yesterday and mashed potatoes. Never tasted anything like it!"

"Right…"

My stomach turned at the thought of food, my throat felt like I'd swallowed gravel.

"Any water?"

"Yeah.."

He handed me a plastic, cooling beaker. Greedily swallowing down its cold contents, I felt the liquid run down my throat, into my chest and finally land in my stomach – all within twenty seconds. The taste was sweet, a little too sweet for water.

"What is it?"

"Doctor prescribed. It 'as energy salts to 'elp you get back on your feet quickly. The Mantis was very specific about that. Can't 'ave you lying about for too long!"

Almost immediately, I began to feel a little better.

"That's amazing….I really do feel as if I could get up. A minute ago…."

I didn't finish the sentence, the feelings of warmth spreading up my limbs and through my body were strange, as if I were standing next to an open fire. I remember we used to have fires in the garden to burn the rubbish. Dad did it just for fun, just so we could watch things burn. It was the only time I actually saw a real fire.

"I'm burning up. What's in it?"

I pushed the blanket off and sat on the side of the bed, placing my scorching feet on the cool, wooden floor.

"Not sure...but your face is really red."

He looked worried as if he thought I might faint again. I thought I might too.

"I feel hot...like I've eaten a bunch of chilli peppers."

"Chilli peppers?"

I thought he was joking with me for a minute, but he wasn't. He'd never heard of them.

"Oh, a type of vegetable that makes you very hot, and burns your stomach when you eat it."

"Why would you eat it then?"

"Actually, I only tried it once. Didn't like it."

I stood up, leaning on the bed for support.

"Are you sure you should get out of bed?"

"Yep...need the loo. Where is it?"

It suddenly occurred to me to wonder how I'd been to the loo if I'd been asleep all this time. I glanced back...nope the bed was dry. It was only on going to the toilet that I noticed a white, plastic ring on my lower, right-side abdomen. I knew what it was, I'd seen them in the Downer's Medical Centre. It was a small device for drawing out toxins, impurities and urine when a person is unable to get out of bed. My mother had been ill once and I'd watched them draw the golden, wee-coloured liquid out of her body when she couldn't get up. I was tempted to pull mine out, but knew it was attached to a long, needle-thin tube which could be dangerous if not withdrawn correctly. So, I did my business and returned to bed, shivering and crawling up into a ball.

"Someone's coming. Pretend to still be asleep."

I closed my eyes just as Elliott started reading. It wouldn't be hard to go back to sleep, but I didn't want anyone doing anything to me without me knowing about it.

"For the Maker is just in all things. It is 'E that decides what is good and what is bad. It is 'E that...oh Doctor, Warden sir!"

I heard Elliott's chair scrape as he stood up. I imagined him bowing as he always did when adults were present. The doctor spoke.

"How has he been?"

"'E woke once, but didn't seem to remember where 'e was. I gave 'im some of your drink, as you told me to, and 'e fell back to sleep."

I felt a strip sticking to my forehead and then another was placed on my wrist. I knew what they were so it didn't worry me. He was taking my pulse and temperature. They normally sent the information automatically to a handheld device, which would beep after a minute. I was worried about trying to look asleep. I tried not to move, not to breathe too hard or too slow. I knew what sleep looked like of course, but did I look like I was asleep....wasn't sure! The machine's shrill announcement that it was ready almost made me jump.

"Well, his temperature is fairly normal, though his heart beat is faster than to be expected. Still, no temperature is a good sign."

"Should we get him up?"

The Mantis sounded too keen.

"No, not yet warden. He could have a relapse. Better to keep him under observation."

"When do you think he will be well?"

The Mantis could barely control his irritation.

"Possibly tomorrow...and this boy...err what's your name boy...?"

"Elliott sir."

"He's doing a fine job following my instructions. Well done Elliott!"

"Thank you sir."

I wanted to snigger. Holding it back was virtually impossible and I was desperate for them to leave.

"Let's go then. No point in hanging around here if nothing more is to be done."

The Mantis was keen to get away and shortly after I heard footsteps and the door close. As they were leaving Elliott began reading again.

"For the Maker is just in all things. It is 'E that decides what is good and what is bad. It is 'E that gives out justice in the end. All thank the Maker...."

There was silence for a moment and I squinted to see what was happening. Elliott was at the door, closing it softly.

"They've gone."

"Good...I smiled. I almost laughed y'know."

"May the Maker look down on you with happiness!"

Both of us laughed then.

"How long have you been reading the same lines?"

"Oh for about three days."

"And they don't notice?"

"Nope! They don't come in often enough. The nurse comes in every three hours to suck out your pee and feed you stuff, and the doctor is from the village – so 'e's only once a day."

I was a little embarrassed at the mention of all the pee sucking.

"Don't worry, they send me away. I don't watch."

"Right....I didn't know we had a clinic or a nurse come to think of it."

"We don't! This ward is never used. It's part of the legal requirements, but is empty most of the time, unless someone dies."

He watched the reaction on my face and laughed.

"No one 'as ever died since I've been 'ere....and besides which, the nurse is not real either. She's one of the Carers. She just pretends to be a nurse when the authorities come in."

"You're joking! And she's allowed to do stuff to me..."

"Oh, I think the doctor's in on it all. 'E's probably paid to keep his mouth shut. 'E put that thing in you and showed her 'ow to use the sucking and feeding machine."

I suddenly feel unsafe. It is time for me to get out of the place. I pause, Elliott looks at me strangely.

"Can you get Alex to come tonight when everyone's asleep?"

"Probably, but why?"

"I have a plan...a way out."

His eyes lit up.

"A sure way out...."

"Yep!"

"Can't you tell me now?"

"No, I want to tell you together, so we can plan the rest."

"Okay, but are you sure it will work."

"We need some outside help to get away, but I got out. I was really outside."

"You got out and came back....came back for us?"

He sounds surprised and stares at me.

"Yeah..."

For a moment, Elliott looks as if he might cry or something. I turn my head away, embarrassed for him. He doesn't know what to say. It is a long time since anyone cared about him.

"I know...crazy or what? But after finding it, I needed a good rest and the Maker's blessing, and you have been perfect for that."

The moment passes with smirks and sarcasm, as he pulls himself together and laughs.

"Well, then, with the Maker's blessing and good planning, this place shall soon be an evil memory!"

Chapter 27

It is dark and creepy in the clinic at night. The moonlight throws tree shadows against the far wall and if I stare long enough, I can almost believe the branches are the arms of monsters coming to get me – their bony fingers reaching out for my throat.

Don't be stupid! You're not a kid anymore.

A shiver runs down my back, even though I am wrapped in a couple of the gaol's rough blankets. I've been waiting for at least half an hour. I was excited to tell them my plan at first, but now am a bit worried. Elliott has left to find Alex. He has to dodge Crap-Face. We had a good laugh at the chosen nick-name for the Night Warden. He really does have an ugly face, as if his features have been knocked out of proportion, along with his brains….if he had brains to start with.

They should be back soon, but if they get caught, I know they'll be thrown in the hole, and I'll have to go and get them out. I'm still weak and my stomach's now demanding to be fed real food. The Carer-Nurse gave me some more of that liquid stuff, but I insisted on drinking it and going to the toilet as normal. I don't trust her to do anything for me, particularly sucking out or putting in. I imagine she might suck out the whole of my insides just out of spite, or inject me with some sort of poison now that I'm getting well…and besides which, I need to be out of here by tomorrow if we're to make the plan work. And now that my mind's working, I'm itching to get started.

I hear a quiet noise outside the door. It has to be them, as Crap-Face crashes round the place, not caring if we are woken. I see Alex and Elliott's eyes shining out of the darkness, like cat eyes, before the rest of their pale faces come into focus. They sit on the bed to the left of me. They're wrapped in blankets and have their knees pulled up to their chests, tucking their bare feet in, cocooning themselves from the cold air of the night, reminding me of the first meeting in the bathroom. It seems so long ago, but can't be much more than a couple of weeks.

"You look betta'."

Alex grins, but Elliott interrupts.

"'E is…but let 'im tell us the plan. I've been waiting ages. 'E wouldn't tell me until you were 'ere."

Alex's grin broadens. He feels part of the gang. I sit up, following their example, wrapping my blanket around me.

"Okay…so I've found a way out."

"Are you sure?"

Alex is nervous. Elliott jumps in.

"'E's been out."

Alex looks shocked, his eyes open wide, I can see the whites getting bigger.

"You 'ave…and yer came back."

"I did!"

"Well it's a good job yer did. I'd've killed yer if you'd left us all 'ere."

We all grin, like a secret society.

"Actually, I'd have probably been dead somewhere if I hadn't."

"Actually…actually…"

It's become a joke between us that they mock my 'posh' dialect, but there's nothing I can do about it, just as they can't do anything about theirs.

"So, you don't want to know."

I turn round, pretending I'm going back to bed, but their 'pleases' and begging bring me back. The three of us have formed a bond. It's amazing how quickly and how I'd never dream of leaving them behind now. I look at them with what I think is a serious face and begin. They stare at me, so serious, not fidgeting or playing games, waiting to hear their salvation from the horror they live.

"Okay, so, I've found an old tunnel that leads to the beach."

They stare at me as if I must be mad.

"Really, I have."

"But..."

"'Ow..?"

"Where...?"

I see they are not going to believe me unless they hear the whole story, but I have to be quick. We don't have much time, so I start with 'I woke up wanting to go to the toilet...' and end with '...and then ran back to the bedroom.' I decide not to tell them exactly where the tunnel is, just in case one of us gets caught. The less they know, the less they can tell. Not that I really think they would. They don't argue with the logic. They trust me.

When I've finished telling them about my adventure they just stare at me for a minute as if I've told them a fairy story.

"It's really there."

"Yes."

"A smuggler's cave."

"Looks like it."

They are grinning from ear to ear. Their eyes alight with a real escape possibility, not only that a smuggler's cave. It seems too good to be true. Alex can't contain himself. He jumps up, throwing his blanket down and walks to the wall and back, with his head down, as if thinking. Elliott and I watch him and shrug our shoulders.

"Are we going to plan the rest or are you just planning to wear out the floor for the rest of the night?"

"'Eh, I already 'ave one bag of food….a lot of eggs, but it's somefing."

We both look at Elliott as if to ask what he's been doing.

"I'm playing nurse at the moment….and anyway, I know where we are and 'ow to get back to Alan's town."

He's still calling me Alan in front of everyone. I wonder if it is time I told Alex my real name, but Alex interrupts.

"'ow?"

"There's an old railway line with cargo trains. They're slower 'cos they don't move on air like normal ones, they still use the ancient trains and metal track system, but they only use them for moving boxes and stuff for warehouses….not sure what's in the boxes."

He pauses a moment, looking at us to see if we believe him. He's still a little unsure whether we're real friends or whether we might leave him behind. He makes a decision, lowering his feet to the floor, leaning forward. Alex leans against the wall as if he cannot bear to sit down.

"Last time I escaped, that's 'ow I got back. I snuck onto one of the cargo trains and 'id behind all these boxes. It took a whole night, but I got there."

"No one found you?"

"They didn't even bother looking. Didn't think anyone was there."

"Can we all 'ide in it? Is it big enough for five?"

"It's as big as a carriage in a normal train."

"There's just one problem."

"And that is...?"

"It took me three days walking to get there."

"How far is it?"

"I don't know really...just that I walked from sunrise to sunset for three days. It was 'orrible! I had to keep hiding from people and cars. Didn't make any difference in the end."

His head goes down with the memory of the struggle he had, only to be brought back again. I move on.

"Right....was it summer or winter?"

"Summer...why?"

"You must have walked about eight to ten hours a day, at a maximum of three kilometres an hour. So it must be between a hundred and a hundred and fifty kilometres away."

We were quiet for a while. That was a long way for a group of kids to go unnoticed, especially with little kids. I was wracking my brain, sure there was an answer.

"Can any of you drive?"

Maybe we could steal a vehicle...not that I was a thief, but we'd really only be borrowing it. Then a thought struck me.

"Alex...?"

He'd started pacing again.

"Yeah?"

"How well do you know Sid?"

"Sid who?"

"Sid, the laundry boy."

He sat down on the edge of the bed next to Elliott.

"Not well. We aint allowed to talk.....but we could."

They picked up on my idea immediately.

"He can drive, he has access to a van. What if he were to pick us up and take us to the tracks?"

"Why not furver?"

"They'll trace the van as soon as it is found missing."

Alex added an idea.

"We need warmer clothes, or we'll all get sick, like yer did. 'E could get some clothes from the laundry."

We were getting excited, a plan was forming....Elliott continued Alex's thought.

"Yeah...and shoes, but we could take our black plimsolls, I s'ppose."

"Do you think he would do it?"

"'e hates his boss...maybe if there was a promise of not only escape, but a safe place..."

"There is a safe place, isn't there?"

Alex asked for the millionth time, staring at me, willing my promises to still be true.

"Yes, I'll take you all where no one will find us...ever."

They smiled. I smiled. Soon it would happen. Soon we could get out. At the back of my mind I was worried. I wasn't sure about what the Downers would say about so many new kids.

"When?"

"We need time to put together more food and to get Sid on our side."

"I'll make 'im be on our side."

I was sure Alex would as well. He thumped one hand into the other and had a wicked grin on his face.

"He has to want to come Alex or we can't trust him. He might tell."

"Oh 'e'll want to."

"I mean it. He has to see it as a way out for him."

"'kay!"

"And don't tell the girls anything. We'll just go get them when we're ready."

"'kay."

Elliot added.

"That will make six of us with Sid."

Seven with Alicia. The number was rising.

I had a nagging feeling at the back of my mind. I just hoped everyone would be accepted. I'd be returning home with a bunch of kids in tow. They just had to let them in.

"... and if possible, better shoes. Does he keep the clothes he takes from us?"

They knew I was talking about The Mantis.

Someone else spoke.

"Sometimes, 'pends on the quality....and by the way, there'll be seven of us, not six."

We all turned in shock at the voice coming from the doorway. We'd been so excited about our plan, we'd forgotten to keep a look-out. Standing at the door was Jasmine. She was the tallest and oldest kid in the gaol, and she was tough. She'd been thrown in the hole for two days for screaming at The Mantis when we were in line one morning, but had somehow survived it.

At nearly fifteen, she was due to be shipped out to an adult camp the next week. Although The Mantis had threatened her for months, he'd now told her the date in front of all the kids one morning. He meant it as a threat to us all.

I didn't know her at all even though I saw her every day, and, although I felt sorry for her, I didn't really care. I had more than enough to do with my own survival. Most of the kids were that way. Kept their heads down and looked after number one.

We stared at her saying nothing. We didn't know what to say. How much had she heard? Her large, blue eyes mocked us. Her full mouth sneered.

"I 'eard everything and wull tell 'em what yer plannin', unless yer take me along."

Blackmail!

I immediately didn't like her. She was threatening us. Alex and Elliott looked to me as if it was my call. I didn't think there was much we could do about it now. It was too late. We should have been more careful.

"We all bring something to the plan. I have the safe place. Alex the food, Elliott knowledge of the area and a way back to town. What will you bring?"

"I'll bring yer sisters Alex without wakin' the others," she paused for a moment, "'n' yer'll buy my silence. Isn't that a good 'nough deal?"

Alex sighed, I could hear Elliott fidgeting again, twisting his fingers, although I didn't look at him.

"And I do know where 'e stores old shoes. It's a cupboard near his office, 'though I dun't know if there are any in it."

We all stared at each other for a moment. Alex, Elliott and I were trying to decide whether there was anything we could do, short of gluing up her mouth.

"There's nuffin' you can do. I'm comin'!"

"Not 'til we say yer can come."

Alex had stood to face her; he had reverted to his 'game playing' tough role, the one that made me nervous.

"Yeah, if you dare tough boy! I'm stronga', olda' and wisa' thun you lot put togetha'."

"Right...."

I didn't want a fight and there was very little we could do

"You can come, but there are some things you need to know from the start."

"Really, who put you in charge?"

She pointed at me and stressed the word 'you' as if I were stupid. It really got my back up.

"I did. You don't know the exact way out and, even if you did, you have nowhere to go. You'll be caught and brought back."

That was a guess, but I knew it was true, just by the look on her face. I continued.

"Until we get to my safe place…"

I emphasised the words 'my' and 'safe' to let them all know I was the only one with that information.

"…I'm in charge."

I paused looking at them. I knew Alex and Elliott would instantly agree. Jasmine, with her short, dark-blond hair and stubby nose wouldn't like it.

"Agreed."

"Agreed."

My friends didn't hesitate. I looked at her, the enemy forcing itself amongst us, waiting. She stood her ground for a while, arms crossed, eyes squinting, considering her options.

"Fine, fine. I 'gree. Anything to get outta 'ere."

"Right then, let's go over the plan and who is to do what one more time. We can't mess this up."

Chapter 28

We'd set one week from the day of the meeting. We all had to keep track of time and days and we all had to stay quiet, obey the rules and not cause any of the gaolers to punish us for anything. We couldn't carry sick people with us, two little kids would be enough. We'd agreed that if anyone was sick, or thrown in the hole on the escape night, we'd leave them behind. Jasmine had been very quiet in the mornings even when The Mantis provoked her with nasty comments and finger jabs in her shoulder. I was almost impressed, but not quite. She'd pushed her way in and threatened us. I couldn't forgive that. Couldn't let it go, even when she came to the second meeting and told us she'd found the cupboard. There were a couple of pairs of shoes, probably fit the girls if they were still there on the night.

I was now back to my normal bed and routine, so every second night we met in the boys' bathroom. Jasmine wanted us to meet in the girls' and even pushed me to take us to the tunnel itself, but I refused. Only on the last night would I risk showing them the panel. They might be tempted to go and have a look. Jasmine might even try leaving. It was too risky, even though storing things in there, like the stolen food Alex was risking his freedom with, would be useful, someone might leave suspicious tracks. On the other hand, I was also praying the Kitchen

Manager didn't get up to check the pantry herself, Alex would be in tons of trouble.

Alex had made contact with Sid. He'd been feeding him precious boiled eggs, secretly placing them in his pocket. Every egg had a message written in ink. It was lucky for us that the kitchen used pen and paper to keep records of what was in the pantry. It felt odd holding a real pen in this day and age, but lots of people didn't have tech and still used manual equipment.

We'd planned Sid's messages for a period of five days and Alex brought me the eggs to write on as his writing skills weren't very good. As it turned out, we only needed four eggs in the end. The messages followed a pattern:

On Monday message one read 'Eat me! From a fellow prisoner.'

We hoped this might show him we were friends – all in the same situation. On Tuesday morning, we didn't get any response from him, although he seemed to be scanning the kids a lot more than usual. It occurred to me Sid might not be able to read. As Alex had said - then we'd be done for!

The Tuesday egg message read 'We are friends!'

On Wednesday morning, he seemed a little nervous, so when he received message three 'Wanna escape to a safe place?' we were a little afraid and had an anxious night. What if he told on us? What if he said no? How would our plan work then?

On Thursday morning as Alex helped him with the laundry, he looked at him without saying a word, communicating through a subtle nod of his head, Sid returned with a 'just-as-subtle' nod, asking how with his eyes. On Thursday, the fourth egg was as follows, 'Need to talk. Toilet tomorrow?'

We weren't sure how he would manage it or how we'd manage to follow him, but we figured Alex, Elliott, (who was now in the kitchen with us), or myself would sneak away, but Sid was cleverer than he looked. It was the afternoon, and so we were all lined up being lectured on not escaping. Elliott and I had slipped to the back, hoping we were temporarily invisible. Sid and Alex were lifting the laundry as usual, but Sid kept bending over, as if he were in pain. Suddenly, he put his hand on his mouth and shrieked.

"Sir, I need the toilet. Really sir, am gonna be sick."

All the kids moved back disgusted and in fear of vomit flying all over them, as Sid began gagging, gulping for air and leaning over one of the clean baskets. His boss immediately clipped him across the ear.

"Get to the toilet yer cretin!"

Sid struggled to stand upright.

"Sorry sir. Where is…."

He didn't seem to be able to speak before gagging again.

The Mantis stepped up, annoyed and irritated.

"If you can't keep your workers in order, you are not welcome here."

The Laundry Boss almost bowed double in apology, but The Mantis ignored him.

"You…"

Everyone looked round to see who he was pointing at.

"Lazy-boy, get him to the toilet, and if he's sick, you'll be cleaning the floor for another week as you've had plenty of practice."

I couldn't believe it. The Mantis hated me, and yet he had done us a favour. I quickly scurried forward, head bent.

"Yes sir!"

All the kids around me pulled faces and stepped further back as I passed through them, dragging a pale-faced, gulping Sid with me quickly towards the back stairs. I could hear the Laundry Boss apologising over and over, and The Mantis being his usual pig-headed self. Sid kept gulping all the way to the bathroom. I shut the door behind us.

"Try not to be sick anywhere but the toilets."

With horror, I imagined cleaning it up every day.

Suddenly, he stood up and smiled, all the gulping stopped. I stared at him.

"I'm not sick, but don't you dare tell."

He threatened me with his fists and pulled a grotesque face, his dark eyes squinting, his mouth puckered. His voice was deep and although he spoke the words correctly, he had a strange, foreign accent, as if he'd grown up abroad somewhere.

"I just needed to go to the toilet, that's all... and he wouldn't let me just go to the loo."

He turned towards the urinals. I was confused for a moment. Surely he'd come to talk to me. It took me a moment to realise what was happening.

"Are you sure you're not meeting Alex to discuss our escape plan?"

He turned round slowly to face me as if he were a lion tracking an antelope.

"Our escape plan..."

"Yes, we've been sending you messages on eggs. Do you wanna talk or not?"

He grinned, showing big white teeth against a white coffee coloured skin.

"How many of 'us' are there?"

"Seven, including you, if you're in."

Eight counting Alicia!!

"I'm in only if there's a safe place to go. I can't hide on the streets. I'm noticed too easily."

"Where I live, there are a few with darker skin than you. No one finds them."

He was desperate; his eyes told me he didn't think he had a choice. He would die if he stayed where he was.

"What's the plan?"

"First, know that everyone must bring something to help. Alex brings the food. Elliott, understanding of the area and how to get back to town and Jasmine's bringing shoes, (I couldn't think what else to say about her other than she's blackmailing us, which wouldn't make him want to come.) I bring a safe place."

"You said seven?"

"There are two little girls who need rescuing. They can't be left."

"I see."

He said it as if he didn't really understand why we would do that, but I didn't care and didn't explain. I leant against the cold, white tiled wall, with my arms crossed and waited. He stood against the opposite wall, mimicking my behaviour.

"What am I to bring?"

"Clothes for all of us. We can't travel in these rags we wear…"

That was the easiest part.

"Okay, and…"

He knew there was more.

"The van."

I waited for him to say 'no', but he didn't. He seemed to be thinking about it, so I ploughed on.

"You'll pick us up at a place on the beach and drive us to another place not too far away."

I didn't want to give too much away. He could just disagree and tell on us.

"We'll dump the van and then get other transport so we can't be followed."

I rattled it off quickly, not wanting him to interrupt me. Saying it out loud to someone outside the group made me see how dangerous it was for him.

"So, you want me to steal clothes...."

"Yes..."

"Steal the van...."

"Well, borrow really...they'll get it back with tracking." He ignored me.

"Pick you all up and take you somewhere..."

"Yes."

It was sounding more implausible.

"What do we do with the van when we get this other transport?"

He still hadn't said yes.

"What do you mean?"

"Well wherever we leave it, will show anyone looking for us, where we went. Is this other transport already arranged? Are we making a quick getaway? Hanging around waiting?"

I hadn't thought of that. He was right. If we left it near the tracks, they would know we were on the train. They could stop the train at any time to search it. We'd be thieves after all.

"Tell me where I'll be driving the van to."

There was nothing else for it. Our well thought out plan had a problem.

"The old tracks, to a cargo train."

He thought for a minute, looking down, rubbing his chin as if he were a great thinker of the age.

"I see."

"See what?"

"I know that area. There is a small wood not too far from it."

I was slow to grasp his point.

"We'd need to hide the van before getting on the train."

Light dawned!

"Yes, we could do that. Throw anyone off the trail until we escaped."

"We also need to know when the cargo trains go by and at what speed? Whether we can jump on them with two little girls."

Another miscalculation in the plan!

"I'll find this out, but I'll need a week."

"We leave in three days."

"I see."

Again he rubbed is chin, thinking.

I couldn't help responding sarcastically even though I knew his peculiar behaviour was some sort of habit.

"You do!"

He ignored me.

"At what time and where?"

"Night, the beach."

"I need to know exact details. I can't hang around waiting for you. I'll get picked up."

I wracked my brains, trying to remember where on the beach I'd been. It came to me suddenly.

"Above the steps at midnight."

I realised I'd told him an awful lot about our plan, and he still hadn't said yes.

"Are you in? Can we trust you?"

"How do I now if I can I trust you? There's one of me and six of you."

"You can trust us. We have to get out of this prison and we can't be brought back. He'd kill us."

I only realised as I said it, that The Mantis would probably beat us to death if we were brought back. Six of us defying him. He wouldn't be able to bear it.

"I see!"

The gesture was beginning to drive me nuts. Worse than Elliott's fidgeting.

"Right, you do, do you?!"

I wondered if he would say, 'I see' back at me.

"So, clothes for six, two small ones. Van at beach, twelve midnight in three days. Knowledge of cargo trains if possible."

"Yes."

"You don't ask much, do you?"

I realised how much risk was in it for him. We basically just had to get out of the gaol we were in without being caught.

"I have the safe place. We just have to get there."

"You'd better be telling the truth."

"I am."

I stared at him, hoping he could read honesty in my face and not fear.

"Well are you in?"

My voice was a little shaky. We didn't have much time left. Someone would come after us, I was sure. The Mantis wouldn't let us out of his sight for too long without thinking something was going on.

He hesitated, looking down, it was almost as if I could see his brain clicking over. He knew it was a big risk. If it should fail, he would probably die too at the hands of either a brutal master or the police themselves. They wouldn't think twice with his skin colour. He was the immigrant they all hated.

He looked straight at me, his eyes delving into my soul as if to find out if I really was trustworthy or not.

"I will die if I get caught...."

My heart sunk. He was too scared.

"...but I will die if I don't. So, yes, I'm in!"

Chapter 29

I had to keep my head down so no one could see the corners of my mouth turned slightly up, the gleam in my eye. I was so excited. I wanted to jump up, do high-fives, chest bounces or punch the air screaming, 'yes..yes', but of course I didn't. It may have been hard, but I played the game for one last day. I slunk down a bit, pushing my shoulders lower as if I was weary and tired, but really I wanted to laugh. Our last day, our very last day! The last time in the hated morning shower, the last time I'd say 'Yes sir' to The Mantis, the last time I'd scrub a shirt.

At the back of my mind was the thought that we might get caught, but I pushed it away. I didn't even want to think about it. My stomach was butterflying enough.

The four of us, (Lacie and Josie didn't count, they didn't even know about running away), had behaved so well over the last week, that none of us received punishments, but The Mantis didn't even notice. He had others to torment. A new boy, Euan had come in. He was skinny, had long, dark hair and looked about ten. He couldn't control his anger in front of anyone and so The Mantis was distracted with him; each morning a new punishment and two out of three meals he was reading. He wouldn't survive long if he didn't learn the game.

It was dinner time. We'd all agreed to eat as much as we could, even if it didn't taste great. We weren't sure how long we'd have to go without much food. I thought it might take us somewhere between three and five days, but I wasn't sure how much hiding we'd have to do or how long the train would take. There were always two or three gaolers walking around the dining tables, clicking their heels on the floor boards, checking we were eating and listening to the readers.

Tonight, The Mantis was one of them, as if he had a sixth sense that something was going on. He was barely ever there at night; the change made me nervous.

I hadn't told anyone, but tomorrow was my birthday. I'd been here longer than I'd wanted to, but spending my twelfth birthday in this place was unthinkable. I looked around from under my fringe. Lights had already been turned off, only a couple of lamps lit up the place. I took in the grey walls, the grey people, the grey life. I felt sorry for those kids we had to leave behind. They had no colour, no future but this. Still, I guess our escape would amuse them for some time.

Elliott sat across from me, three places down. We had to avoid glancing at each other. Eye contact might be fatal, we might snicker or smile. He was the only one who really knew who I was and he never told. In fact, we barely spoke during the day. It was the same with Alex. With the exception of collecting eggs, when he reported to me how much food he'd been able to collect, he went out of his way to be horrible to me, as if he truly hated the little spot on earth that I occupied.

Even Sid had come through. Two nights after our conversation, he'd somehow managed to sneak a tiny piece of scrunched up paper into Alex's hand as they both carried the laundry together. The tides were on our side. At midnight we wouldn't be facing a battle with water to get to the beach.

Yes, we'd all played our games and survived...only a few hours more now.

We were just queuing up to pile our empty dishes on the table when the voice I really didn't want to hear shouted my name.

"Lazy-boy, come here."

I gasped and turned round.

No, not tonight! Of all nights, not now!

I couldn't think what might be wrong. I hadn't done anything.

I walked up to him, head down.

"Yes sir!"

"Show me your left palm."

I lifted my hand upwards. I was trembling, I couldn't help it. I had an irrational fear that being so close to him, he might be able to somehow read my mind.

"Good. Tomorrow, seven-thirty, report to me for scanning."

"Yes sir!"

Was that all?

With my head down, I watched his long, black cassock and sturdy shoes, waiting to be dismissed. My heart beating. My pulse racing. I suddenly felt very hot and my legs were weak.

"You've been too good of late. I've missed you in my office."

He was being sarcastic with me, his voice whispered like a snake in my ear, full of scorn and barely controlled revulsion.

I didn't lift my head. I was convinced if he looked in my eyes, he would know the truth.

"Yes sir."

He grunted, thinking, staring at me, looking through the top of my head, seeing into my mind, delving his evil eyes into our plans.

He knows, I'm sure he knows.

I held my breath, I knew panic would come if I didn't get away soon. Panic did strange things to people, it might make me spurt everything out and then he'd know.

"Take over as teacher from Byron. Euan is now your charge. Any punishments he gets, you get. Do you understand?"

"Yes sir."

Not a problem! I won't even be here!

"Now, get out of my sight."

"Yes sir."

I scurried away, breathing, thanking whoever the real God was that I'd survived. Not once did I look up. Not once did I lift my shoulders. But the relief I felt almost sent me into tears as I joined the back of the queue of silent kids; some of whom still held their breaths, just in case they were next, but so far thankful they weren't the object of his hatred tonight. We walked out of the dining room on the command of a short, skinny gaoler, without another attack.

As we climbed the back stairway, my heart beat returned to normal. I didn't look at anyone or anything. I just wanted to get to my bed and wait the two hours without falling asleep. We were always put to bed at seven, and Crap-Face checked the rooms every hour or so. We'd agreed to wait for Crap-Face to come round twice before leaving and to use clean clothes to make it look as if we were still in bed. No one was to wear their plimsolls, they squeaked on the wooden floors. We'd have to carry them until we got to the secret passageway. We figured we should allow another two hours for us all to reach the beach, even if we ended up waiting for Sid.

So, at approximately nine o'clock, we were all to meet behind the back stair case in the shadows separately, although Elliott and I would probably go together as we were in the same room. In my mind it was all organised, in my mind it went as planned, like a clock forever ticking into the future, but my mind couldn't account for things I didn't know about.

"Lazy-boy."

"Yes Madam."

The skinny, short gaoler was trailing behind us to make sure we all got into our beds.   I stopped in the hallway as the others filed into their bedrooms.

"You are Euan's new teacher?"

She raised a thick eyebrow.

"Yes madam."

"Then he has a punishment to perform tonight."

"Err...I mean yes Madam."

Oh no...I hated him...not tonight!

"Good, he's in the kitchen. Get to it! The Night Warden will be down shortly to check on you."

"Yes Madam."

Elliott watched me walk away as he entered our room. His eyes prayed things weren't going wrong before they even started. There was nothing we could do about it. I was hoping, whatever the punishment was, it didn't take too long.

With the exception of one lamp in the far corner, the kitchen was dark. Euan was scrubbing one of the deep sinks. I purposely made a noise so he would turn round.

"Oh, it's you!"

"Yeah...what are you doing?"

"Got to scrub the sinks, the tops and the table."

"What did you do?"

If I was going to share the punishment, I wanted to know why.

"Nuffink!"

"You must have done something."

I stood next to him at the second sink, picked up a metal pan scourer and turned the tap on to only a tiny drip. The water was cold. I didn't want my hands to freeze. The sink was clean anyway, no one would notice. I made a minimal effort. I had more to think about than a punishment I didn't deserve.

"I din't."

For a moment we said nothing. There was nothing to say. He was probably right.

"I dunno how you all do it…bowing and scraping, like he's the Maker himself."

I knew he was referring to The Mantis, and I knew how he felt. I'd felt the same way when I first arrived, still did in fact. If Elliot hadn't helped me, I'd be just like this kid. I glanced at him. He was shorter than me, had narrow shoulders and long, black hair – the barber would love chopping that off. With fair skin and dark eyes, he looked Irish, but he didn't have the right dialect. His voice was hoarse and he was sniffing as if he'd got a cold or something. Tears fell freely down his cheeks. He kept trying to wipe them away on his shoulder, but they kept coming. He didn't seem to be able to stop them.

I knew the feeling, the anger, the frustration. I tried to be kind. He was new here. He hadn't found his game yet.

"It'll be all right."

Why I said that, I don't know. He gave me a nasty sneer as if I was stupid.

"It won't. It'll never be all right. I'll die if I stay here."

He showed me his sore, bleeding hands. The freshly opened scars from The Mantis' punishments covered his palms and fingers. I winced for him. No wonder he was crying, they must have hurt like crazy.

"How many times?"

"Today...twelve on each. Tomorrow it's the whip on my back."

"You need to stop opening your mouth."

"It doesn't matter. I'm gonna escape soon anyway."

"No one escapes. They find you, read your ID and drag you back."

"They won't find me. I'll hide."

"Where will you hide?"

"Somewhere!"

He had nowhere to go.

"How old are you?"

"Nine, why?"

I'd thought he was ten, but he was younger and The Mantis was coming down hard on him. He was only a year older than Lacie. I wondered how bad it would be for him once we'd all escaped. The Mantis would be so angry he would knock any thoughts of rebellion out of him, or kill him trying. He'd switched off the tap and moved onto the metallic draining board. He winced as he wiped, water burning into his hands. I watched him for a moment. He was a loner, hadn't made any friends yet. He wouldn't survive long without friends in this place. If I were staying, I'd probably have helped him, but I wasn't so...

Suddenly, we heard boots crashing against the tiled floors and busied ourselves cleaning sinks that didn't need cleaning.

"You two, hurry up and no talking! I want you in bed in half an hour, otherwise you're in the hole. I'll be back in twenty minutes."

The threat was enough to make us speed up. By the time he returned, we'd done the job. I was freezing and I guess Euan was too, but at least he'd stopped crying. There were dark circles under his eyes. We'd barely spoken after Crap-Face's first visit and ignored each other now, as we were marched to our rooms. He was in bedroom four next to ours. I gave him one last glimpse before he shut the door behind him. I already felt guilty for what this boy would suffer because of us.

Chapter 30

Elliott had to wake me. I couldn't believe I'd actually fallen asleep. He was kicking me awake with his toes from his top bunk.

"Adam, wake up! It's now."

I was confused at first, but then realised he was standing on the edge of my bed, stretching over his bed, pushing clothes under his blanket to make it look like he was still there. I immediately jumped up and did the same.

We said nothing as we closed the door. It creaked slightly and we waited, holding our breaths, but the house was silent, nothing moved. The corridor was dark, but rather than use the torch I had, we felt along the right side wall and kept in close, just in case anyone came round a corner.

Elliott was behind me, a small bag and his plimsolls in one hand. I could hear his breathing and imagined his heart beat as hard as mine, as if we'd been running a marathon.

We came to bedroom four. I thought about no-friend Euan, his bleeding hands, the punishments, how he would never escape The Mantis, ever....and made a sudden decision. One that might prove fatal to our plan, but I couldn't help it, couldn't just walk passed his door. I whispered to Elliott,

"You go on. I'll be there in a minute."

"What..? Where you going?"

He was afraid, his eyes glowing white in the blackness of the hallway.

"Go...I'll be there."

I pushed him forward and watched his dark figure move slowly forward. I had to hurry. Carefully, I opened the creaky door only as wide as I needed it to creep through. Then I waited a moment, listening to the sleeping breathers.

It was pitch black and I couldn't see a thing. I was hoping Euan was on a low bunk. Then I heard it, the same sniffle, the wincing of a person in pain. I didn't need to look for him, I crawled across the floor, following my ears, until I reached the lower left bunk.

Risking being seen, I covered the torch with my hand and switched it on to a dim red glow. Euan had his back to me,

"Euan."

I whispered and knew at once he'd heard me. The wincing stopped and I saw him turn over. He looked at me as if I were mad. Crawling across his floor like some creature of the night ready to pounce on him.

"What?"

"Come."

"Why?"

"Bring your shoes."

"Why?"

I switched off my torch and turned round. I'd done my bit. If he was going to argue, I'd leave him. I was risking everything, and I'd scraped my foot on a splinter of wood, crawling over to him. I wasn't about to sit and have a discussion. Just as I reached the door, I heard him following me. Then I remembered he needed the clothes to replace him. I decided to stand up, but kept low.

Crawling would take ages. Quickly, I created a 'replacement Euan' with clothes from the basket, and left the room. Euan stood looking at me, waiting for an explanation.

"You want to escape?"

I whispered.

"Yes."

"Then shut up and follow."

"But..."

"Shhh..!"

Had I done the right thing? I didn't know, but we were now eight, nine with Alicia.

They were all there, crouching in the darkness, worried. No one knew what had happened. When I turned up, there were some gasps of relief, but on seeing Euan comments of 'why's he here' spluttered out of mouths I couldn't see, but I cut them short, we didn't have time.

"He's coming...now let's get out of here!"

I was glad they all shut up. If we'd started arguing right now, it would be a problem.

"'ow?"

It was Jasmine's voice from the back.

"I need to get to the wall on the left. Move out of my way."

Shaking, I pushed my way passed them all. Everyone wanted to be close, to see what I was doing.

"Give me some room. I can't see."

I switched on the torch and shone it on the panel. Heavy breaths and nervous eyes around me, I spotted the catch.

"What's 'e doin'?"

"Shhh..."

A chorus of responses.

Quickly, I flicked the catch to the left and watched as the panel started grinding noisily open. Gasps around me and whispered amazement made me turn round. I knew what they were feeling. They hadn't truly believed it was going to happen until this very point. Somehow it had all seemed like a dream. Only now it was real. Euan stared in shock.

"How did you find it?"

I grinned.

"Crap-Face led me to it!"

Chapter 31

We were suddenly a lot of people with luggage. I hadn't thought about the time it would take to get us all up the first tunnel until I clicked open the panel and looked in again. Jasmine would struggle the most as she was bigger than everyone, but then the girls were small and would take the longest.

I shone my torch inside just to check it was still the same and then shone it back on the group. Their faces were still pale and in shock. Even though we'd known for a week this was going to happen, the realisation that they could have escaped at any time had they known, turned them into statues. It had all been an exciting adventure. Now it was like risking life and death. The gaol was a horrible place, but at least they knew it and had learnt how to cope. The outside world had become an unknown. I needed to shake them up. We had to move.

"Elliott first with Lacie, then Alex with Josie, Euan and Jasmine. I'll go last to lock it. Elliott, Alex, Jasmine and I will take a bag. Be as quick as possible, Crap-Face will be around soon. When you get to the top, follow the tunnel through and wait in the little room. You can't get lost. There isn't any other way to go."

No one argued. Everyone put on their plimsolls whilst Elliott pulled out a torch from his bag. I wondered what else he had in there. He'd make a good Collector. Surely the Downers could train him like they trained me.

"Don't be scared."

I bent down and spoke to the two girls.

"You're with us now and we'll soon be in a safe place."

Josie whispered back.

"I'm not scared Alan, but Lacie is."

"No, I'm not."

She flapped a hand at her sister.

"Yeah you are!"

"Shh…"

Alex bent down and interrupted.

"No talkin'. This is serious."

"'kay Alex."

They looked subdued at their brother's command, but I was afraid they might start crying once they were in the tunnel.

"You're both very brave girls, I know."

"Lacie isn't."

"I am."

"Both of you are."

Their heads were twitching with fear. I wasn't sure what to say. I was a kid myself. What would my mother say? A memory of when we ran away came to me. Something I hadn't thought about for years.

"We're going on a big adventure."

They smiled, their teeth glistening in the dark.

"And I need you to be very brave."

"'kay."

"When you go in the tunnel, remember Elliott will be in front and Alex behind. You're not alone. We're all with you."

Alex was still crouching with me, looking at his sisters. The others were standing around, straining to hear what the delay was.

"It's a bit dark, but I'll never leave yer. Y'know that right?"

"Yeah."

"It's really important not to make any noise."

"'kay."

I couldn't think of anything else to say, so I stood up, ready.

Elliott stuffed his small bag in his top and put the torch in his mouth as I had done the first time, and started climbing. We had to show Lacie and Josie how to climb. It was hard for them. They were incredibly slow. The rest of us were getting jittery, trying not to move, not to make a sound. We'd been standing around too long. In the quiet of the night, with the panel open, we seemed to be making enough noise to wake the house. Every time someone went in, the grit on the ground sounded as if they were sliding against gravel, bags crinkled, and, although we tried not to talk, whispers of 'You next' and 'They're in', seemed to echo off the walls.

Alex eventually made his way in. We'd decided to pass all the bags up and sort them out at the top. It seemed easier that way. Euan was now ready in the hole to take his first step upwards towards freedom. He'd been quiet but his eyes were bright with excitement as he climbed in the gap. He still couldn't believe this chance had happened to him. Jasmine and I stood in the corner waiting our turn, when our worst fear walked up.

"Who's there?"

Crap-Face had turned a corner without us hearing. We'd been too occupied with looking up the tunnel and waiting our turn to get away. His lamp was casting shadows, just missing us. Suddenly, Jasmine did something stupid.

215

"It's me sir, sorry sir."

She stepped out into the light.

"What...what're yer doin' outta bed?"

"...the toilet sir, but then yer came 'n' I decided to 'ide near the stairs. But yer came this way and so I 'id 'ere sir. I only wanted the toilet sir."

It was probably the longest thing I'd heard any kid say to one of the gaolers.

"How dare you?"

"Sorry sir, but...."

He was moving forward, but she dashed to the left as if she were running towards the main hall, taking him away from me, Euan and the tunnel. Had he come closer, he would have found us all. Euan poked his head out of the gap.

"She's in for the hole."

"Euan, take Jasmine's bag and go up. Tell everyone to go down the tunnel to the small room and take the door on the right."

He looked at me as if I were asking him to fly to the moon.

"You can't go the wrong way. It's dark, but there aren't any other tunnels or doors to take. Wait for us in the cave. Don't go to the beach until we get there. Got it?"

I was whispering quickly, hoping he could follow instructions. He still stood there as if stunned. Time was wasting.

"Go! Start down it. The girls will need more time to get to the beach anyway."

"'kay, 'kay, but whad'about you two?"

"I'll get her out. We'll follow you."

He hesitated.

"Go. I need to close the panel."

I knew were Crap-Face was going. I knew what he would do. We all did. So it wasn't hard to get there or to help Jasmine escape. He'd even conveniently left by the time I arrived. I switched on my torch, removed the 'occupied' sign and opened the trap door carefully so as not to bang it against the floor. Although Crap-Face was back on his rounds, I didn't want him running back in this direction and surprising us.

What did surprise me though was that there were two people in the hole and they were clinging to each other, tears streaming down their cheeks. Jasmine and Molly had both been confined in the tiniest of places. Molly was a girl I didn't take much notice of either. She was younger than I, with a round face, small nose and piercing green eyes. She skunked her way around trying to sink into the floors, but I knew her obviously. They both looked up. Immediately wiping her tears and putting on a brave face, Jasmine snorted, trying to be cool, even though I'd caught her in an act of pure weakness.

"Knew yer'd come."

"Right."

Jasmine helped Molly climb out. I don't know how long she'd been in, but she was shaking and could barely hold her own weight. I stood around, wondering what to say, we needed to hurry, but Jasmine was kind and encouraging. Bent down, one of her arms around Molly's shoulders, she stroked her hair and spoke gently.

"Come on Molly. You can come with us."

"Come www..where?"

She stuttered a little.

"Outta this place."

"Heh!"

"You wunna put 'er back in the 'ole Lazy-boy?"

She was defiant.

"No, but…"

"No buts….?"

She stood up, leaning back, arms crossed, eyebrows raised, as if challenging me."

"Don't we 'ave to go?"

Molly quivered.

"Wwwwhere we goin'?"

The gentle voice returned.

"We're escapin' Mol…"

A huge grin covered Jasmine's face. I don't think I'd ever seen her smile or laugh, so it looked strange as if she was practicing, unused to the facial expression. She grabbed Molly's hand.

"'ow…?"

"We'll show yer. Just be very quiet."

I locked the trap door and replaced the sign, so that Crap-Face wouldn't notice if he came by and we headed back the way we'd come. Just as I was opening the panel, I heard Crap-Face banging down the front stairs, cursing and muttering to himself.

"Where are yer vermin? Yer can't fool me with clothes and yer can't escape. Wait till I find you. Yer really in for it."

He'd found at least one of the beds empty and that was dangerous for us. I wondered who it was and hoped he wouldn't discover more for a while. If he found more, he might raise the alarm and that could be disastrous. I was relying on the fact that Crap-Face was pretty stupid, or at least stupid enough to think the person from the empty bed was hiding in the house somewhere - long enough for us to be on the train anyway.

All of us pushed our way into the tunnel, moving as fast as possible, Jasmine first, then Molly, then me. I was the torch bearer, standing at the bottom of the tunnel, giving them some light to climb. I'd just managed to close the panel when I heard his boots outside.

"Anyone hiding in the corner?"

I stood still in the darkness behind the wall, holding my breath, knowing he was right in front of me. Molly had the sense to stop moving half way up the tunnel. Crap-Face stood there for minute or so, grunting like a hog, before turning towards the kitchen.

"Where are yer, yer little rat? Yer can't get away from me y'know. When I get yer, yer really in for it."

Molly and I both scurried up the dark tunnel, like rats being chased by poisoned smoke slithering down a mine shaft.

Chapter 32

Having plimsolls on made it a whole lot easier than the last time I'd crawled down these tunnels. My feet were happier as we charged forward as fast as we could. The others were ahead of us somewhere, but we'd as yet not caught up with them. With my torch on full, we stood close together in the small room, staring around, taking a breather. In the middle of the room was one of the bags. Obviously, they'd left it for us, possibly to show us they'd passed through. Maybe they were having difficulty.

Molly was still barefoot and in shock, partially from being in the hole and partially because she was now in a dark tunnel. We hadn't had time to explain to her properly and she was looking at us wide eyed.

"Am I dreaming?"

Jasmine snorted – her version of a laugh I think.

"Well, if yer are, stay with it or yer'll wake up back in the 'ole."

"Wwwwhere we goin'?"

"Not sure, 'e knows."

She used her thumb to point to me.

"Don't yer?"

"I do...don't worry."

"What's this place?"

Jasmine was squinting, trying to see round in the dark.

"I think it's an old smuggler's tunnel. It comes out at a cave near a beach."

"It does?"

Molly's voice was high pitched in excitement, but her face was so pale it shone out in the dark – even when I turned my torch away from her. It was the middle of the night and she was tired.

"I've never seen the sea."

"Neither 'ave I."

Jasmine was surprisingly kind. She was cuddling Molly into her, as if she could protect her or keep her warm. Molly was clinging on, her arms round Jasmine's waist. We were all beginning to shiver now we were standing still.

"Time to move on."

"Wait! This is my bag. I 'ave a pair of shoes that might fit Molly."

I didn't want to hang around any longer than we had to, but I knew Molly's feet would be cut and blistered if she didn't have something on them. I pointed the torch at the bag so she could see what she was doing. We both watched her crouch and delve into her bag, which seemed to be made of one of the gaol's brown tops. She'd tied knots at the top and bottom, and filled up the centre with 'stuff'.

At last she dragged out a pair of torn, old trainers and thankfully, another torch, which she switched on and put between her teeth. Strange that everyone could trade for torches. I wondered where they all came from. They must have come in from outside, possibly the gaolers brought them in. What would they trade for? Curiosity almost made me ask, but Jasmine was busy. With the torch in her mouth, the words to Molly came out a bit slurred.

"Show-me-yer-feet Mol."

She picked up Molly's foot and measured the soul of the trainer against the bottom of her foot. They looked slightly big.

"Let's-try-'em."

Molly pulled one on, whilst Jasmine did the other.

"They're a bit big."

Molly was walking around as if testing out shoes in a shoe shop. I was hopping from one foot to the other in my eagerness to move.

"They'll have to do. We need to go."

Molly continued to walk around, testing the shoes, wincing at the rubbing against her heels. Jasmine was fumbling, trying to knot her knapsack and look at me at the same time.

"'ow far to go?"

"At least an hour, maybe more, so we really need to go."

My voice was a little squeaky at the thought we might not make it in time. We'd been delayed a lot already.

"We can't be late for Sid. He won't wait for us."

Jasmine looked down at Molly.

"Wun't a piggy-back for a while."

Molly nodded, a toothy grin appearing.

"'ere take this Lazy-boy."

She handed me her bag, but kept her torch. At least if the batteries went in one, we'd still have another and wouldn't be in the dark completely.

"Nope, not my name."

"What's yer real name then?"

Not telling them my name had been my one source of protection, my last invisible barrier. If they didn't know my name, I was somehow safer.

"When we get to where we are going, I'll tell you. For now, Alan will do."

Fortunately, Molly was tiny and exceptionally skinny. She was probably underweight, so Jasmine didn't seem too bothered about slinging her up on her back for a while, even though we were moving pretty quickly. I went up front with my torch, but kept looking back to check on them. I expected the extra weight to delay them, but it didn't. Jasmine was strong and tough, her words were harsh, but possibly we'd misjudged her. After all, everyone had a game in that place. I reminded myself she had blackmailed us to come, but then wondered if I'd have done the same in her situation. She'd been told she was about to be moved to an adult camp, a place from which there was no escape, only work, more work and eventually death. I shuddered. The cold tunnel and the thought of the camps made my spine tingle.

At some points, the ceiling was so low, Molly had to walk. Jasmine was tall and found it impossible to bend forward and still carry her, but before long, she was limping and whimpering. She had blisters on her heels already. I didn't know what else we could do until we got out of the cave.

"How mmmmuch further?"

I wondered whether the stuttering was the result of fear or something else. It wouldn't surprise me if the gaol had caused it. We had been on the steep, downwards path for a while now. Jasmine had nearly slipped and fallen into me several times, so Molly had to walk. Actually, dragged would be a better word as she kept hold of Jasmine's hand tightly and was pulled along.

"How long have we been walking do you think?"

"'bout an 'our."

It was hard to tell in the dark and Molly had slowed us up a little.

"Then we should be there soon...possibly twenty minutes."

After that, other than the occasional whimpers and yelps from Molly, we walked in silence. Only our rapid breathing and the crunch of feet on gravelly dirt made any noise. I walked in front and pushed away as many of the cobwebs as I could. Molly had screamed out at one point when one stuck to her face. She now used Jasmine's back as a barrier. My arms felt like they were layered with dirt-filled, sticky, silk string.

About ten minutes later we felt the first draft of air and knew there wasn't far to go.

The reunion with the others was a relief. Such a relief I felt like hugging everyone, but that would have been stupid. But so far we had all made it out safe. Although I couldn't tell from where I was stood, there must have been a full moon throwing some light into the cave, as there were only four beams of light from torches and I could still see them all scattered around the cave. Euan seemed to be exploring the cave; the rest were sitting against the side of the cave, waiting, watching the dark sea, afraid and yet excited.

Elliott jumped up as soon as he saw us. Lacie and Josie were using Alex's thighs as pillows and had fallen asleep. Molly slunk down near them, as if she were looking to see if Alex had another leg she might use.

I looked around astonished. We looked as if we had been scrambling up chimneys to clear the soot, just like kids did in the Victorian times. It reminded me of a picture I'd once seen in a history book, illustrating the hard life young boys had at that time. I looked at my hands, realising I must look the same, and tried to wipe them down my trousers. It didn't help much.

"Another?"

Euan came up, his hands on his hips.

"We can't carry another one."

I knew what they meant, but felt as if I had to make excuses.

"She was in the hole with Jasmine. What could I do? Leave her in there, alone. What do you think Crap-Face would have done to her?"

Suddenly, Molly was crying; great, heaving, noisy sobs. She was bent over double, her body shaking as if she'd received a sudden shock. She'd been in the hole, escaped, crawled up and down dark tunnels, had blisters, was cold, hungry, tired and no-one wanted her. No one ever wanted her!

Jasmine ran over, cuddling her in her arms, soothing her with 'there, there' and 'don't listen to them'. It was as if I didn't recognise this Jasmine. As if she had shed a horrid skin' and underneath was something different. She looked up and snapped at everyone.

"Shut up all of yer. I'll carry 'er. I'll take care of 'er. She cun share my food."

We all stared and then looked away, feeling a bit guilty.

"Molly is with us now, one of us."

My voice was full of dust, cobwebs and dirt; it felt hoarse. I paused, crossing my arms and leant backwards like Alex did when he was acting tough. I tried to sound as if I were in charge, but wasn't sure if I should be. I wasn't even twelve yet! I forced myself to sound harsher than I felt.

"Any questions?"

I looked round. Everyone was silent except the hiccoughing of Molly's leftover upset and Lacie and Josie who had sat up and couldn't help whispering to each other. Lacie and Josie had woken up with the noise, wondering why Molly was there and why she was upset.

"Okay, so let's plan our next step. Does anyone know what time it is?"

"It's 'leven firty-five."

Euan had spoken from behind us.

"How do you know?"

"The Mantis lent me 'is watch."

He lifted his sleeve to show a metallic surface around his wrist.

"The Mantis leant you his watch?"

Elliott asked naively.

"Well, sort of. It accidentally-on-purpose slipped off 'is wrist when 'e was 'itting me tonight. 'e was enjoying his task so much 'e didn't notice the watch, so I pocketed it."

We all stared for a moment and then as if a chorus of singers were beginning a song, burst out laughing at the same time. Euan stared at us befuddled, wondering if we were laughing at him, but soon a smile was on his lips and then a high-pitched laugh erupted. The girls snickered behind their hands, wondering what all the sudden happiness was about. Alex guffawed, his mouth wide open and Elliott sounded like a wounded horse.

Just as I thought I could stop and had it under control, Jasmine cackled and snorted like a witch, and made me start all over again. One look at one of them trying to curb the laughter made it impossible to stop. Tears ran down our faces creating tracks in the dirt. We held our aching stomachs, giggling, snorting, guffawing and making strange animal noises, until we could laugh no more, until we were in so much pain, we just had to stop, begged to stop.

Eventually, we stood there grinning, looking at each other. The atmosphere had changed. Our eyes were alight with fun. We were together again on the adventure of a lifetime. Then all went quiet. Everyone became serious and looked at me, waiting for direction.

"Right then, now Euan has a new watch,"

...everyone smiled, but kept calm.

"we should leave soon. We have to be at the steps at least five minutes before Sid arrives and it's now....?"

I looked at Euan who glanced at the watch and informed us it was now eleven forty-five.

"Let's make sure we have everything, and get out of the cave. The girls will need help to get down. Is everyone ready?"

As an answer, they all began collecting bags and looking around to make sure they hadn't left anything. I still had Jasmine's bag slung across my back. Molly was limping, following Jasmine around as if she were a mother hen. Lacie and Josie clutched Alex's hands. We all moved to the front of the cave.

Chapter 33

It was harder to get the girls down than expected. We had to pass them between us and hang them over the last half metre to be caught by someone below. Even though Euan was younger, he was determined to be independent and jumped down by himself. As a group, we stared out at the dark sea. It wasn't coming in, but we could hear the waves in the distance, feel the bitter cold wind against our skin. Our clothes were barely adequate for indoors. Outdoors it felt as if we wore nothing. We were all shivering, our teeth chattering as we rubbed our hands together, trying to get warm.

"We 'ave to move, or we'll get sick like yer did."

Alex spoke up.

"We should jog for a while?"

Euan was right.

"The kids wun't keep up."

Jasmine was also right. I thought for a moment. The sand was wet, seeping into our plimsolls.

"Right. Let's move as fast as we can. It's hard to jog in wet sand anyway and the little kids need to move to keep warm."

I thought about Molly's feet.

"It might be a good idea for Molly to take those shoes off Jasmine. The sand is cold, but the blisters will get worse. She nodded. Molly looked relieved and dragged the shoes off, hating them as she threw them to the ground.

"'kay. We ready?"

Alex seemed to speak for everyone and we moved out.

I turned towards the sea wall at a brisk pace. The wall would not only protect us from the cold, but also stop anyone from seeing us. I whispered to Euan.

"What time is it?"

"Five to twelve."

"Right…we're only going to those steps over there, not far now."

We all plodded on.

Five minutes to my twelfth birthday. Five minutes to the van. Five minutes to our escape from this place.

I was hoping nothing had gone wrong with Sid and that he'd be there. Otherwise we'd all freeze to death. We were close to the steps and I was just considering options if he didn't turn up, like staying in the cave, when I heard an engine above me. I couldn't help myself. I ran to the steps, the others ran after me, also anxious to get away. I stopped them and told them to wait. I would look first.

Creeping up the steps like a predator stalking its prey, I kept my head down, trying to see if there was a van. Praying Sid had made it. And for once, my prayers were answered. I could have jumped up and down for joy. Right above the steps, the van sat, engine turned off.

He saw me at once and jumped out of the van.

"Quick, get in. Where are the others?"

"Below. Open the back, I'll bring them up."

"Okay."

I didn't stay to watch. Sid was afraid of being caught. I ran down the steps almost tripping and found them huddling together at the bottom.

"Move...quick, he's here. We have to go."

Everyone ran, as if a herd of elephants, charging up the steps. Jasmine swung Molly into her arms, Alex trailed behind holding on to the other kids. I was afraid the noise would attract attention, but more afraid if we moved slowly. Within seconds, we'd lifted the little kids, bags and ourselves in the van. Sid had closed the doors and we were off.

Chapter 34

The van was probably on auto-pilot as it moved swiftly without banging us around too much. I was relieved Sid wasn't driving; he was underage for manual vehicles and would be easy to spot. Auto-pilots had been known to cause accidents in the past, but over the last five years the improvement of sensors, GPS and the link with satellites had all but eliminated it. I remember my Dad was gadget mad, but he refused to use his auto-pilot. He was terrified he'd cause an accident.

It was dark inside, but not pitch-black, though within seconds of each other Elliott and I had switched on our torches. I looked round. We were all still breathing heavily from the jogging and charge up the steps. It had warmed us up for a brief time, but I could feel the cold seeping into my damp clothing already.

Euan and Alex leant against the side opposite me. The girls were in the middle, leaning against laundry baskets, Elliott and I sat next to each other on the opposite side. For a moment we all stared around, like mice caught in a trap, or as if we were dreaming. We were shivering with cold although it was not as bad as being outside the van.

Suddenly, Jasmine snorted, and with a one-sided crooked smile, she broke the silence.

"We did it!"

Euan responded.

"Well, so far."

Alex jumped in.

"I can't believe we've got this far."

Jasmine threw her head back, laughing again.

"We're gunna make it. I know we will."

She was determined no one would spoil the moment. Everyone smiled nervously for a second. No one wanted to be the jinx. I spoke next.

"Let's look in the baskets. See if there's anything to wear. Sid was supposed to steal some stuff for us."

"Shun't we get some of the dirt off us first? We could get picked up like this."

We all looked around, staring at each other's faces and our own hands.

"We'll just fit in wiv' the other street kids."

"Yeah, but 'aint that bad?"

I tried rubbing my hands on my thighs. I didn't like grimy, particularly when it came from cobwebs, cave dirt and possibly unknown animal waste. Rubbing them helped a little, but not much.

"I think we should look a bit cleaner...maybe just our hands and faces. There's nothing we can do about the clothes."

"Water?"

Elliot jumped into the conversation. Alex did that tough guy folding his arms expression, even though he was sitting down.

"Nope. Water's fer drinkin'. There aint much."

Suddenly, Jasmine turned round and, on her knees, began dragging things out of the basket closest to her. I attacked another and Elliott found a third. We piled the odd assortment of clothing on the floor in the middle. Everyone started grabbing and pushing. The young ones were being trampled over.

"Wait!"

My voice was too loud. I heard a screech from the front of the van.

"Shut up you idiots."

Sid was right. No one moved for a moment as a hushed silence came over the cabin. How stupid it would be if we were stopped because we made too much noise.

"I'll sort it out."

I whispered like a dictator, pulling what I thought might be my own tough face and grabbed the clothes, pulling them towards me. No one argued. Everyone was afraid of being caught. Jasmine sighed.

"I was only luckin' for a bit of cloth to wipe my face."

I ignored her and gave her my torch to hold. There were a lot of socks and I pulled them out.

"Use these to clean with and then put them on. No one will notice."

There were grunts of agreement as I shared out the socks. We got about two pairs each. Everyone started rubbing, but it didn't help much. The socks got dirtier, but the filth was just rubbed in more. Jasmine and Alex were about to get into a fight again.

"This is useless wivout water."

"No, no spare water."

Jasmine sighed.

"Cun I 'ave a drink then? I'm dead firsty. There aint any spit left in my mouf'."

Everyone put down their socks, agreeing. Alex was now the 'kitchen manager's assistant' again...doling out the rations.

"Only three sips each...we don't 'ave enough."

"But I'm thirsty."

"It's three or nuffin'."

"Alex is right."

I decided to back him up.

"We might not find any clean water along the way."

We passed the bottle around our dirty mouths. I don't like germs and wanted to wipe the neck on my clean sock. I was awful at home. No one touched my bottle or glass, but I'd had to be harder over the last few weeks. So, I didn't clean it. I just closed my eyes and cringed as I gulped. As I passed it to Jasmine, I was relieved that I hadn't made myself look like a sissy. Josie and Lacie had the bottles held to their mouths for them so as to stop them drinking more than their fair share. No one cheated and drank more.

Alex put away the half full bottle in his bag. I liked that he controlled the supplies. He was good at it and we needed someone like him.

Unexpectedly, I heard someone spitting. For a moment I thought there was something wrong with the water – it had tasted all right to me – but then I saw what Jasmine was doing. Spitting on a sock and wiping her face. Yuk! She smiled at everyone, a lopsided grin.

"What?"

Her face did look a little cleaner, and then Molly copied. And Lacie and Josie did the same, only they were left with blotches of semi-clean skin, smeared with more dirt. I sighed, but said nothing. None of the boys thought it necessary to waste the only water we had on washing.

I started on the clothes again. Jasmine shone the torch on each item as I held it up, trying to decide who it would fit. We all managed to get something, even if it didn't fit properly. Lacie and Josie had to roll up the sleeves of a pullover and Molly's legs were too short for the pants. I had to tie up the waist of my trousers into a knot to prevent them falling down. And all the socks were from a giant! Fortunately, Sid had brought extra and so we had more than enough to go round. We just kept layering the clothes until there was none left.

"I suggest we all put these on over our normal clothes. We'll be warmer."

Everyone struggled into the garments, even though so many layers were uncomfortable, at least it helped with the cold. At last we sat still, waiting, wondering what to say to each other.   Suddenly, we felt awkward, never having had the chance to really talk in the gaol. I looked at Jasmine. I didn't know much about her, but she looked as if she wanted to say something. I hesitated for a moment.

"When was the last time you were out?"

It was the only question I could think of. I expected her to pull a face or tell me to mind my own business, but she didn't.

"I 'fink I've bin stuck in that place for 'free years, well at least free winters."

"Three years!"

I heard gasps around me. None of us had been there that long. How had she survived? We were quiet a moment thinking about it.

"Didn't you try to escape?"

"Once, at the beginnin', din't get far, they caught me…"

She didn't need to finish the rest. We knew what happened to those who were caught. She changed the subject.

"Molly's bin in for around a year 'n' 'arf."

Molly was nodding.

"I wwwas eight."

You could barely hear the stuttered whisper.

Alex spoke next.

"I rememba' 'er comin'. We've bin 'ere nearly two."

Lacie and Josie were nodding in agreement with their brother.

"And me nearly a year 'n' 'arf."

Elliott piped up. It seemed like we were all making some sort of confession. Euan didn't know what to say.

"Well, y'know 'bout me."

I felt like I should say something, but they all knew when I'd arrived.

"My name is Adam."

I was taking a risk giving away any part of my name, but I wanted them to know. Wanted them to call me by my real name. Elliott smiled as if he'd been waiting for the moment.

"Well, Adam. Where do yer come from? Yer don't speak like us...you speak posh."

"More importantly, where are yer takin' us to? Where's this safe place?"

I couldn't answer their questions right now, even though they were trusting me, someone they barely knew.

"It's safe, clean and there is food.... and other people live there, good people, but it's better that only I know. If we get caught, you cannot give it away."

"Don't yer trust us?"

Alex blurted out. We were all trying to whisper, but his voice was deep.

"It's not about trust."

"But wha' if somefing 'appens to yer? Wha' d'we do then?"

Jasmine spoke up. She was trying to be calm, but her voice showed she was worried. She lost all her word endings and slurred everything she said into one great sentence. She was right of course. They'd be stuck if something happened to me.

"Nothing's going to happen to me."

"It might!"

"Thanks!"

Everyone went quiet.

"I'm sorry, but I can't tell you right now."

There was nothing they could do or say. They couldn't beat it out of me. Elliott jumped to my defence.

"We'll just have to make sure 'e's kept safe then, won't we?"

He probably thought we were going to my old house. He'd be surprised when we didn't.

Euan changed the subject.

"What d'yer fink will happen when they realise we've gone?"

"'e'll go mad."

We all knew who the 'he' was.

"'e'll take it out on everyone."

No one liked the idea of the other kids being hurt.

"When I grow up, I'm gunna go back and get 'im."

Euan was staring at his sore hands, rubbing them. His long hair falling forward across his face.

"I'm gunna beat 'im 'til 'e cries, 'n' I wun't stop even then."

Nobody said anything. Euan's pain and anger slicing the air.

The silence stretched out like a fog in the night.

"I hhhhhope 'e tttakes it out on Crap-Face as well. I 'ate hhhhim."

Molly's tiny voice spoke up out of the shadowy darkness. She, Lacie and Josie were being very quiet and so it was a surprise to hear her whisper. The rest of us grinned.

"Me too!"

"Yeah wiv' that whip!"

"Nah...too gud for 'im, The 'ole fer a week."

Everyone snickered, snorted and guffawed. I looked at Molly again, leaning against her saviour, Jasmine. Her short dark hair, pale skin and wide black eyes made her look ill. She probably was.

"Why were you in the hole?"

"'e 'eard me crying."

"You were in bed."

She nodded shyly.

"And he dragged you out for crying?"

She nodded without a word.

"Why were you crying?"

"Mmme Mum."

Again a silent moment! No one said anything. We all missed our parents,

"Do any of you know where your parents are?"

I couldn't help but ask; all I received was more silence as an answer. It really sucked. Jasmine spoke up first. She was getting good at speaking like a normal person. It was as if she'd changed 360 degrees.

"My Mam was a servant. We lived in a tiny shack at the back of the big 'ouse. But some money went missin' and they blamed us and kicked us out with nuffin'. It wun't us though. We 'ad nowhere to go and one night we were picked up off the streets by some Clearers. They dumped me first."

No one said anything. Alex broke the silence.

"My Dad lost 'is job 'n' we din't keep up wiv' the rent."

He looked down pulling at his sleeve cuffs as he spoke.

"I 'ave an older bruvver who went wiv' 'em. 'e was fifteen and the 'ome wun't take 'im."

He frowned as he remembered.

"They dun't remember Peter."

He was talking about Lacie and Josie.

"They barely remember what Mam and Dad look like. I 'ave to keep tellin' 'em."

Euan was next. His head was still bent, hair hiding his face, but he looked up for a moment, waving his hand as if to say, 'I'm not doing this'.

No one bothered him with questions. He was new and still an outsider anyway. Elliott spoke instead, fidgeting with his fingers the whole time.

"My Mum was a servant, but we couldn't find enough work. We were picked up off the streets too."

They all looked at me, waiting, as if it were my turn. I wasn't sure what to say. Euan and I were the new ones, but it was as if this was an initiation into a gang. I decided to be vague and was just about to speak, but Elliott made what he thought was a joke to lighten the mood. It didn't help and irritated me.

"Oh, 'e 'as an 'ouse with servants."

I glared at him.

"We did live in a house with servants once, but that was a long time ago. My Dad left us and we ran away before the Evicters came. We didn't get caught for a long time because we found a safe place to work and live."

Euan was staring at me in shock. He realised we were not going back to my house.

I was saying too much. I felt nervous but my tongue kept going.

"We've lived in this safe place for years and that's where my mother is now. I was kidnapped and brought here when I was…"

What should I say?

"…out one night."

"Why din't yer tell 'em? They would 'ave to let yer go if yer a contributor."

"I couldn't."

"Why?"

I looked down at the palm of my sweaty hands.

"They'd never believe me."

"Yes, but they'd only need yer ID."

I looked at Alex and then around at the group.

"I'm unscanned!"

They all stared at me, taking in what I'd said. Suddenly, the older ones understood all the secrecy. I was some sort of illegal. I saw a flash of fear in Jasmine's eyes. If they were caught with me, they might get into trouble as well.

I felt bad, like I'd deceived them or something.

"Look if you want to split when we get off the train…."

I left the sentence open. A moment ago I thought we were friends, now I wasn't so sure. They were all survivalists, all had their own games to play, maybe they were playing games now. Could I really trust them? Take them to the Downers. Was I taking the enemy to my home? What if they told?

Euan was the first to speak. He straightened his shoulders and looked round.

"Are yer all daft? I dun't care who Adam is, or where 'e cum from. If it wun't fer 'im, I'd be stuck in that place gettin' beat up every day. I'd ratha' take my chances wiv' 'm than wiv' the warden fer the rest of me' life."

It was the longest speech I'd heard Euan make. He sat back quickly and looked down, embarrassed he'd drawn attention to himself. I muttered a thanks. He flicked his hand again that said 'no biggy' and settled down into hiding his face behind his hair again.

And then to my relief, they all rallied.

"Me too."

"Me too bruv'"

"And me!"

"Yeah, thank the Maker yer walked through that door!"

Elliott exaggerated his tone, like a 'Maker-loving nut-case'.

Everyone laughed.

Chapter 35

Unexpectedly, the van tipped to the right and so did we. It felt like we were falling down the side of a mountain, crashing into one another, screaming and trying to find a place to hold on. Funny bone elbows whacked into metal and other bodies causing screeches and moans. The baskets fell over sideways and we followed, banging our heads. We ended up as one massive pile of limbs and torsos scrunched in the corner.

Trying to push each other away, and comfort Lacie, Josie and Molly who were crying, we managed to right ourselves, just as the van pulled to a halt. I thought we'd had an accident, or maybe we'd been attacked, forced off the road. Terrified, I was about to shout at Sid, when the back door of the van opened. We looked out into the dark night, the cold air blasting in, not knowing what to expect. Were we going to face some sort of disaster? The police? Clearers? Had we been in an accident? My stomach lurched, my brain tried to think of a plan, but my beating heart and surging adrenalin was already taking up effort and energy – instead of plans, my mind was blank.

Straining my eyes, I couldn't see anything for a moment – it all seemed black, but slowly I realised the dark silhouette standing outside was Sid.

"Are you lot staying in there or what?"

He was smiling, his teeth glowing white. I wanted to belt him. Instead I spat the words out.

"What do you think you were doing? You could've killed us."

The smile disappeared instantly, as we all clambered out as quickly as we could. Jasmine lifted the whimpering kids out. All of them were now clinging to her.

Alex, Euan, Elliott and I were standing like animals in front of him, ready to attack. Sid had crashed us into a tree and the van was now balancing on three wheels. We were lucky to get out alive. Sid just stood there, saying nothing.

"Well, answer 'im."

Alex had his arms crossed again. Sid was taller, but there were four of us.

"You lot are idiots. I crashed the van on purpose to make it look like an accident."

"Why d'yer need to do that?"

"Because if they find the van stranded, they'll know where we are headed."

"But it still looks stranded."

I looked back. Gravity was pulling the doors of the van open at odd angles.

"God and the Maker! They don't make you lot too bright, do they?"

He was becoming irritating. Alex stepped forward, I held him back.

"No Alex, let him finish."

I had a feeling Sid had a plan in mind.

"We are here so we can cover the van and hide it. If no one finds it for a long time, we will have a head start."

Now he was beginning to make sense.

"But what about the autopilot? You could have just sent it back."

"This is a piece of old junk. It doesn't have autopilot."

"Doesn't!"

"Nah!"

Elliott joined in.

"You drove it?"

"Yep!"

He said it proudly, pushing his shoulders back.

"'Ow old are yer?"

I hadn't noticed Jasmine step up. She'd been consoling the girls, but now they were quietly sitting down, their eyes watched us, as if we were their parents making all the decisions for them.

"I'm fifteen."

"Yer too young to drive, especially a manual."

"And yet I do!"

I interrupted.

"I suppose there's no GPS then either."

"Nope. No tracking devices, no registration plate finding, no beeping, nothing to find it, should it be stolen or lost. I always thought John was a bit stupid not to have them fitted, but he thought they were all too expensive. Well, now I hope the van rots and he has to buy a new one."

I noticed again his strange, foreign accent. His arms were now also crossed and he was sighing. This was turning into a bad situation. We were supposed to be escaping together and it had become an inquisition.

"Does any of this matter?"

I turned round and looked at everyone.

"Don't we have to get to the tracks."

Sid spoke over my left shoulder.

"The reason we are here is so we can cover the van so no one finds it...at least for a while."

"Wait, where are we?"

I asked looking around at the winter trees and barren branches.

"The woods of course."

"I know we're in a wood, but how close to the train lines?"

"About an hour's walk."

"An 'our?"

Jasmine blurted out, glancing at exhausted kids. I could see her thinking she might have to carry Molly all the way.

"If we were too close, and they found the van, they'd know. This way, it looks like some sort of accident, like I covered the van and ran away. It will hold them up for a while."

He was right. He'd thought this out carefully. We should have been thankful he was using his brains.

"Right then. We have about twenty minutes to do this."

"Which way are the tracks?"

A good question from Alex, not sure why I hadn't thought of it.

"If we keep the road in sight as we walk, it is that way."

The road was now to my right. Sid pointed behind us.

Everyone was quiet for a moment before Sid repeated his earlier request.

"Grab any branches, bushes, anything to cover the van. It can't be found until we've had a chance to escape."

Sid was giving orders, which I didn't like, and by the way the others just stood and stared, they didn't either. Sid had started to panic. His eyes were flitting from one person to the next. He was wondering if he'd made a mistake. I was wondering if we could make it to the tracks. An hour's walk was a long way in the dark with little kids. We'd probably all end up carrying them.

"Wait...did you find out what time the train leaves?"

"There is one that will pass around two-thirty. It stops at the junction. We'll have five minutes to get on."

"What time is it Euan?"

"One."

Euan's tone was sharp. He'd been very quiet. I looked at him. My eyes had adjusted to the dark somewhat, but he was now at a distance. I hadn't notice him step away and it was hard to see his face in the dark. I turned round to face my 'gang'.

"Listen everyone. Sid's right. He's thought this out better than we did."

I hated to admit it, but felt after everything he'd done for us, he needed some support, and besides which I didn't want any fighting between them. Everyone needed to calm down.

Elliott spoke.

"There aren't any bushes around 'ere. It's winter. 'Ow we gunna do this?"

He was right. He'd turned on his flash light to a low level, like a fog light in a car, and was darting the light around and behind us. I was looking around as Sid spoke.

"You'll need these."

He handed out four sharp implements that looked like a cross between long, razor sharp, butcher knives and saws – killing instruments. They'd go straight through bone and skin.

"Be careful! They're sharp."

He didn't need to say it. I gently touched the edge with my finger. Any pressure would slice through the skin as easy as knife through soft butter. The expression was my mothers. Not one I used, so it was strange it came to me now. I brushed it aside and looked around at everyone.

Sid was clever; he really had thought this through and intended to make this escape work. I thought I'd better say something to get us moving.

"Alex and Elliot go that way. Find anything to cover this thing."

I indicated to the right.

"Jasmine and Sid go that way," I pointed to the left, "and Euan and I will go this way."

"What about Molly, Lacie and me?"

Josie's voice was shrill in the night air, as if we were leaving them behind. It was true though, I'd almost forgotten about them.

"One child to each group."

The kids weren't too happy about being separated, they'd started whimpering, but it was the best thing.

"I think that's a bad idea. They're tired."

Jasmine spoke out.

"I think we need to get movin'"

Euan jumped in and Sid supported him.

"I agree with Euan."

"Who asked yer?"

Alex still didn't trust him.

"Right."

I needed to think about it. Jasmine was right. The girls were tired and they still had to walk.

"Right."

I felt daft repeating myself, but I was trying to think. I saw from the corner of my eye
Euan moving from one foot to the other. Sid was worse, he was pacing four steps back and
forth; both needed to get moving.

"Euan and Sid go. Alex and Elliott go too. Jasmine and I will sort this out."

I was trying to think of other instructions that would be useful.

"Try to be quiet....and don't go too far...look after each other's backs."

They were about to move when Jasmine spoke up. She was her tough, calculating self.

"If yer get caught, don't come back this way and don't tell."

Everyone stopped for a moment, realising the consequences of what she was saying.

They stared at me for a response, which I found odd. I still wasn't comfortable with the 'leader' bit of this escape, even though I'd said I was in charge. I was beginning to wonder why I had. I hated to agree with her and wasn't sure if I could really leave one of them behind, even Sid.

"She's right, but be quiet and don't get caught."

They were all about to set off again, when Euan turned round.

"Jas, protect 'im. Don't let 'im get caught."

He was thumbing me. She looked at me, then at Euan. It was strange hearing the assigned nick-name and particularly coming from Euan. I thought she would attack like a panther, or at least pull a face, but instead a strange smile crept to her lips.

"I won't."

Euan and Sid stormed off immediately. I watched their backs as they disappeared into the dark trees. Elliott began walking but Alex hesitated, looking back at me and his sisters in one quick glance, causing his partner to stop.

"Don't worry Alex, they'll be safe."

He looked at me once, before nodding and spinning round to follow Elliott into the dark woods. I heard their footsteps cracking the frozen twigs and bracken scattered across the ground.

Sitting down cross-legged in front of the girls, I looked at them. Jasmine joined me. The ground was cold and hard, frozen from the icy night air. The faces in front of me were dirty, their shoulders slunk down, backs bent with exhaustion they could no longer hide. Josie was picking at non-existent grass, Lacie's head was twitching again, Molly had her chin in her hands, leaning on her knees as if the weight of her head was just too much.

"How old are you Molly?"

"Nine and three-quarters."

Lacie perked up.

"I'm eight and a half Alan...err...I mean Adam."

"Okay."

I smiled at them all. Trying to speak gently like I'd seen my mother do with little kids at the Downers, or even like Jasmine did, I squashed my impatience into my jittery stomach. I didn't want to sort this out, I was itching to get moving.

"So, you're nearly ten."

She nodded wearily. I couldn't believe Molly was as old, perhaps older than Euan. She looked and behaved so differently. The gaol had crushed her spirit and underfed her until she looked and behaved at least a year younger.

"If I find you a nice quiet place to lie down and sleep, and give you a torch, do you think you can look after Lacie and Josie."

"I don't need lookin' after."

Josie, the youngest, gave me a brave, indignant face. Molly's face crumpled, terror in her eyes.

"We won't be far. If you screamed, we'd hear you."

"No!"

Her eyes were filling with tears. She looked at Jasmine.

"Please don't leave me. You promised. Anyone could take us."

"I 'aint leavin' yer Mol. I'll never leave yer and there 'aint no one in the woods at this time of night."

She grabbed Molly's hand as tears dripped off her eyelashes.

"Pleeeease Jas."

Jasmine looked at me.

"Yer go. I'll take care of 'em all."

I was relieved and stood up. I'd tried my best, but didn't think I could handle crying kids.

"I cun 'elp yer Adam."

Josie lent sideways, trying to heave herself up.

"No Josie, lie down. Sleep. Everyone'll be back soon and we 'ave a long way to walk."

Jasmine's voice now kind and encouraging, she reached over to gently push Josie down.

"'kay Jas."

It amused me that everyone was now calling her Jas. Maybe they all had before and I hadn't noticed. I turned to go, looking back as I did.

"You have your knife?"

"Yeah!"

"Right. I'll be within hearing distance if you need me."

"Good. Don't go far and don't get caught!"

She emphasised the words and suddenly reminded me of the words my mother had once used when we were on the run. We were hiding in the woods and I'd needed the toilet. She'd wanted to come with me to stand guard, but I wouldn't let her. She'd said the same words to me in the same tone. I grinned looking back over my shoulder at the four sitting there, watching me go.

"Won't!"

As I strode into the woods, I heard her mutter.

"Betta' not or we're done for!"

She was right. I had the safe place in my head!

Chapter 36

We had almost covered the van in old branches and bushes. Euan had even picked up an old, green tarpaulin that someone had been camping out with – the type soldiers used to camouflage their position. It was a lucky find and hid most of the top and front of the van. We were all even more filthy, if that was possible, but at least we weren't cold anymore. Starving and thirsty maybe, but at least not cold. The exercise had warmed us up. But I was proud! In the dark, you couldn't see the van unless you were really close up.

I was starting to get worried though. Alex and Elliot hadn't come back yet. They'd never stay away so long. We were just putting the final touches to the van, when Elliott came crashing through the trees.

Something was wrong. Elliott's face was distraught. His eyes fearful.

"Alex 'as been taken."

My worst fear. I looked at Lacie and Josie. They, and Molly, were fast asleep, cuddling together under a bush. Better we didn't wake them yet. They'd panic. I looked back at Elliott.

"What do you mean, taken?"

"We were in a clearing when a man grabbed 'im."

"'ow did yer get away?"

Euan voiced my thought.

"Alex fought like crazy and distracted the man long enough for me to 'ide behind a bush."

We all stood there staring at him.

Sid spoke.

"There's nothing we can do. We need to move now if we're to catch the train."

He emphasised the 'now'.

"I know that!"

I snapped at him. Alex wasn't his friend. He wouldn't care. This was not what was supposed to happen...not now. Not after we'd come so far. Sid's face was fuming. He was older than me and I could see the anger in his eyes. We'd agreed not to chase after someone if they got caught and he wanted to move on.

"Which way did 'e go Elliott?"

"Into the woods. That way."

He was pointing in the same direction as the train tracks.

"Can you show me the exact path?"

"Yes."

"Right everyone, pick up what you can of the bags. Jasmine wake up the girls! We're moving now."

The van was covered. We were ready to go and now we knew someone was around, it could be dangerous. He might find us all.

"What about Alex?"

"Just let's go. We'll look at it on the way."

We walked for about ten minutes like a herd of dumb cows, making a racket with cracked twigs and dried leaves beneath our heavy hooves. I'd never seen a herd of dumb cows trotting through a woods in the middle of the night, but then I didn't know if they would be dumb enough either. Elliot stopped and pointed to the right.

"'ere."

"Are you sure?"

"Yes, look. This is where Alex dropped all the stuff 'e'd been collecting."

Sure enough, there were lots of broken branches and bracken on the ground.

"And which way did they go?"

"That way."

I looked in the direction of the woods; it was dark. I could barely see anything. I needed to make a decision.

"No, you can't!"

Jasmine had turned on her 'I'm a hard dude' voice again. I knew better. She had three kids hanging on to her, two of which were shedding tears for their brother.

"She's right. We have to stay as a group."

I looked at them.

"Would you come back for me?"

"Of course...but yer 'ave the safe place."

"And Alex brought the food."

"But..."

"We all contributed. We couldn't be here without him."

No one said anything for a moment.

"Right! You lot go on ahead. I'll spend twenty minutes looking for him. If I don't find him in that time, I'll catch you up."

"How wull yer do that?"

Euan was speaking.

"Keep to the same path, parallel to the road."

"But that's not what we agreed. We said if anyone got caught, we would leave 'em behind."

"We did, but that was when we were in the house. This is different."

"How different?"

Elliott said nothing. I knew he felt the same way as me, but he was also scared that they'd be stranded, alone and picked up again. He looked down at his fingers and began fidgeting. Jasmine spoke up.

"It's a stupid idea!"

I was annoyed. I began to think all they wanted from me was somewhere to go, like I was some sort of precious stone they needed to keep safe.

"What if I'd left you and Molly behind, what would have happened to you?"

She glanced at Molly and looked away, feeling awkward, possibly ashamed, not knowing how to respond.

"Look we don't have time for this. Go!"

"And what if you get caught?"

"I won't!"

I said it as if I believed it. My heart was booming, my mind saying I really was an idiot and they were right, but this was Alex, not some stranger.

"Fine!"

The sarcasm from Euan was annoying.

"Fine, what?"

"I'll come. Watch yer back. Yer not even used to the streets, 'ow do yer think you cun do this alone?"

Euan was becoming irritating. Who did he think he was? He knew nothing about my life or what I was.

"I'll be fine. Now go – all of you."

"Okay, if that's 'ow yer wun't it. Why would I risk myself bein' caught anyway."

I didn't wait for their responses, but turned to go alone into the dark wood. A wood with evil trees that might suddenly wake up and drag me into the pits of hell.

Shut up stupid!

You shut up!

I was being an idiot. I didn't need to imagine anything, the real fears were there to deal with. So, with a knife in one sweaty hand and my torch in the other, my heart hammering and my adrenalin flying, I felt like I was a lion hunter in a jungle, readying myself for an attack. I didn't know what I'd be facing or how many. I had to be prepared.

I kept low, trying to creep along, making no noise, but in the silence of the night, my footsteps sounded like I was crashing through jungle undergrowth. Dried branches and twigs beneath my feet made it impossible to be absolutely quiet. Luckily, Alex had fought whoever had grabbed him and although I was no expert tracker, I could just see the path he'd taken. Bushes had been broken, footsteps pushing down the frozen, wild grass and plants along the way.

Suddenly, I heard a male voice.

"Shut up or I'll bolt yer agin! I wanna sleep."

It was an adult. His voice was deep and grilly. I wondered if there were more of them.

I switched off my torch and tiptoed towards the sound, using gnarled tree trunks as posts to hold on to and hide behind, as I moved. I could hear something crackling and shifted my path in that direction. Peeping out from behind one of the trunks, I saw light and smelt burning. He'd built a fire in the centre of a clearing about two metres wide. Alex lay on his side on the ground; his hands tied behind his back, his ankles bent backwards and secured with the same rope to his wrists, his mouth gagged. He saw me at once and started wriggling and making a grunting noise, his eyes wide with fright. I put my finger to my lips, gesturing for him to be quiet. I didn't want his captor to notice, but somehow he was being stupid. He seemed to be going wilder, moving his legs and body as if he were having some sort of fit. I moved towards him, around the outside circle of the clearing, being careful, hiding behind trees, trying to get Alex to be quiet and to see where the man was. I thought he must be further round. But I'd made a huge mistake. The disgusting fishy smell should have warned me, but my nose registered it too late.

Before I knew it, he'd grabbed me from behind. I dropped the torch and knife as two strong unknown hands pushed my arms up my back, twisting them. My body trembled and I felt a sudden sickness as fear, and realisation of what had happened, kicked in, but I was unable to fight back. He had me in such a tight, painful grasp, I couldn't even struggle. I tried to turn round to kick him, but he only held on tighter.

"What's this? Where you gonna knife me then?"

He picked up my tools, shoving them in his pocket and pushed my arms harder. Pain shot up through my shoulders and I screeched as he dragged me towards Alex, who stared up at me sadly. He'd been trying to warn me and I'd failed to understand.

"I thought there must be more than one of yer cretins, and now I 'ave two to sell."

He laughed congratulating himself on his trap.

"Are there anymore? Should we see?"

He tied rough ropes around my wrists and ankles and forced me to lay behind Alex on my left-hand side.

"Go on! Make as much noise as you like. Call your friends!"

He laughed at his own joke. I felt like a complete fool. Euan had been right, this was a stupid thing to do. Now we were both tied up ready for slaughter.

Neither of us struggled or made a noise. There was no use. I whispered.

"Sorry!"

But Alex didn't respond. As he was gagged, it would have been difficult anyway.

"It's only me. I sent the others on ahead. At least they'll escape."

But no safe place!

I could almost hear Alex say it. I could almost feel his anger vibrating off his body. I shouldn't have come. His sisters would be caught, dragged back and punished for his error, all because I was stupid enough to think I could rescue him. He was angry! I was angry with myself too! I felt like cursing, screaming. It wasn't fair, but what good would any of that do.

"Cum'on little children out there."

The kidnapper was enjoying himself, wickedly teasing us, grinning. In the firelight, I could see him better. He had a dirty boxer's face, with what seemed like years of unwashed grime, but a boxer's face nevertheless – one on the losing side too many times. His eyes had dark circles around them, his nose looked as if it had been broken and his mouth had a hair lip. When he grinned, I saw his front top teeth were missing. He added another branch to the fire and sat back.

"Cum' rescue yer little friends."

He then lay down close to the fire.

"Are there more of yer? Should I pretend to sleep again? A couple more would set me up for a while."

I refused to answer him. I needed to think about how we could escape. Maybe we could manage to untie each other once he'd slept. We had to try. We couldn't be sold again.

I strained my neck to look over Alex's shoulder. The creep had closed his eyes, but I doubted he was sleeping. He was waiting for more kids to show up. Well at least they wouldn't end up like us and maybe they'd find somewhere to be safe. My gut lurched. I'd let them all down.

Chapter 37

We must have been laying there for about five minutes when suddenly I heard a noise coming from the far end of the clearing, behind the boxer. Apparently, so did he, as he grinned and opened his eyes, though he didn't move.

"Shut up or I'll belt yer agin! I wanna sleep."

He was trying the same trick.

Suddenly, from out of nowhere, Euan appeared behind the creep. Shadows from the fire made his face look like something gruesome, like a zombie about to attack. In his hands he held a heavy, thick branch. Just as the boxer was getting up, planning to hide behind a tree probably, Euan swung his weapon up across the back of the creep's head, as if he were swinging a golf club. I heard the crack before I saw him fall forwards, but Euan wasn't satisfied, repeating the action for good measure. I wasn't sure if the branch had broken or the boxer's skull, but right then I didn't care. All I could see was Euan jumping over the splayed out body, with the intent of rescuing us. The creep of a boxer had collapsed unconscious in the dirt.

"Euan, what...?"

"Shhh...talk later, let's get outta 'ere."

In his hand was one of the sharp knives. It crossed my mind he could have used it on the boxer, although I couldn't have done it, and I was two years older. No, make that three, I was twelve now. Although the thought made me shudder, I was in the last place I'd thought I'd be for my birthday, it passed quickly. Action was needed! Euan easily cut through the ropes, releasing our hands and ankles. Alex and I stood up quickly, ready to move.

"You shouldn't have risked it, but I'm glad you did."

I realised Euan, though he behaved tough, was a loyal person...good to have around. I was so very glad I'd brought him with us.

"Yeah wull...now we're even."

"Huh!"

"Figure it out yerself. Let's go 'fore 'e wakes up."

Alex looked over.

"If 'e wakes up...."

We all grinned and was about to turn.

"Wait, he has my knife and torch."

"Leave it!"

But I'd already run passed the fire and over to him. I looked down at his ugly face. Was he pretending? Would he grab me again? I crouched down. I didn't think so. I could hear him breathing heavily and blood was oozing out of a cut on his head, but he was alive. Gingerly, I reached into the pockets of his dirty coat and found my knife and torch. Just as I stood up and was about to leave, he grabbed my ankle.

"No..."

But his voice was frail and his grasp weak. I kicked out at him, managing to accidentally hit his nose, but my toe suffered. The plimsolls were too soft for kicking anything, and I started half hopping around; he still had hold of my ankle and it unbalanced me. He snorted as I tripped and started flailing around with my arms to protect myself. He made a grab for my left wrist. He was growling like a mother bear whose cubs are being attacked. Trying to protect myself, I hit out at him, forgetting I had the knife in my right hand. The blade felt no more resistance than soft jelly, slicing through his forearm, cutting the skin deep. Blood spurted out, splashing across both our faces, as well as my hands and shoes. I yelped and stumbled back. He stopped his attack and looked at me in shock. Then the log crashed down on his head once more and he was at last really out of it. Euan stood behind him, grimacing. I stared up shocked, smelling the rusty, metallic fumes of fresh blood.

"'E'll 'ave a bad 'eadache when 'he wakes up."

"But he won't wake up. He'll bleed to death first."

I stared at all the red stuff oozing out of the cut. It wouldn't stop. Why wouldn't it stop?

"Cum'on. We need to go."

Alex came up.

"'E deserves it. 'E's a scumbag, who sells kids fer money. One less of 'em is a good idea as far as I'm concerned."

"Probably been sellin' kids fer ages."

They were both in agreement, trying to convince me of the same. I pushed myself up, still staring at his arm. All I could think was I'd killed someone. I looked down again, looked at my sticky fingers. My heart stammered, the pulses in my body banging out with horror. I wouldn't leave an animal to die like this.

"We have to do something."

"The train?"

"We 'ave to go."

Alex looked at Euan with a whole different look in his eyes, as if somehow Euan had earnt his badge as a gang member, was now one of us.

"What time is it?"

"One fifty-five."

"We have thirty-five minutes to get there."

"Let's go then!"

"Wait!"

"What? Maybe 'e's got someone wiv' 'im. We need to get away."

Alex was moving towards the end of the clearing, but I stood there, still not feeling good about leaving him to die in the woods alone.

"Euan, throw that log on the fire. Someone might find it."

He did as I said and strode after Alex, his new buddy!. The sparks flew up, eating away at the bark, licking the blood.

Ugh!

By the time they'd realised I wasn't following them and stopped to look back, I'd taken off two of my socks. Trying not to look or get more blood on my hands, I tied them around his arm tight, hoping it would stem some of the flow until he woke up.

"Y'feelin' betta' now?"

I pulled a face at Alex. Euan chimed in.

"Waste of a good pair of socks if yer ask me."

They both grinned; I scowled at them, but said nothing. I wiped the knife and my hands on the hard ground, trying to get rid of the blood. It wouldn't come off my hands. I rubbed them down my pants, almost in tears, but all it left were brown streaks and made me feel worse. I saw some large evergreen leaves on a small bush and began trying to get the blood off my hands with those. It didn't work either. I didn't know what to do. I knew I was making strange, whimpering noises, but I really felt like I'd begun my twelfth year as a murderer with the victim's blood all over me. I was panicking; I had to get it off.

Alex sighed and tutting, came over to me, a half bottle of brown liquid in his hands.

"What's that?"

"It's whiskey I think. 'E was drinkin' it."

He took off the lid. For a moment, I thought he was going to drink it, or worse, give it to me to drink. I couldn't even abide the smell.

"'Old yer 'ands out."

I stared at him, wondering what he was doing.

"'Old yer 'ands out."

He repeated as if I were a child. I did as he said. The blood had got into my nails and changed the colour of my hands. The odour of dried, oxidized blood almost made me puke.

"Now wash yer 'ands."

As he poured the whiskey slowly over my hands, I scrubbed until the blood dissolved. I scrubbed like a paranoid maniac all the way up my arms, but I couldn't help it. I needed to be rid of the rotting smell of flesh on me. Replacing it with an odour of whiskey was not good, but better.

Alex looked at me.

"Now yer face, but close yer mouf and eyes."

Cupping my hands, I held the liquid carefully up to my chin and then closed my eyes before rubbing it all over my face. It burnt my skin and sent its sharp stink up my nose. I didn't care, preferring that to the smell of blood. After several scrubbings, I felt calmer, or at least calm enough to move. I thanked Alex, nodding in appreciation for his care, glad that he was around. Now I was more composed, I felt a bit like an idiot and looked away, but neither of them said anything sarcastic or laughed at me. They pretended my panic attack didn't happen, so I pretended too and we moved on, even though I now smelt a bit like my Dad did sometimes, a whiskey addict. I pushed the thought away immediately. It was not something I liked to think about, so I didn't.

Alex threw the remains of the bottle on the grass near the man's head. I took one last look at our attacker – the bleeding seemed to have slowed down – and then turned to leave.

We ran, not caring anymore about the noise, not caring that the sharp branches and dry foliage poked through the soft plimsolls and socks, tearing at our feet and ankles. We had to get to the train in less than half the time we'd planned and we needed to do it fast if we were to have a chance of actually climbing on board.

Chapter 38

I could hear Alex beside me, his breath ragged. None of us could speak, we were leaning forwards, breathing heavily through open mouths. We'd started off at a run, slowed to a trot and were now unable to go any further before we took a rest. My legs ached and my feet were blistered. I looked at Alex and Euan. They were in no better state. The plimsolls did not protect us. All I needed to spurt me on, was the reminder that getting caught was not an option.

I breathed deeply again, trying to eke out the air going into my burning chest, which felt like it would explode. I was desperately thirsty and needed a drink, but as neither Alex nor I had anything, and the bag Euan had on his back only had boiled eggs, dry bread and stale biscuits - none of us could swallow such food at the moment, even though I was hungry, and tired, and worn out with the stress of running, and the fear of danger – there was no point in thinking about a drink. My brain kept listing my problems over and over.

Shut up! Did you think this would be easy?

The other voice in my head responded.

No, but...

Shut up then! Keep going. No one will help you.

I stopped and leaned on my knees to catch my breath. We'd passed the van, keeping our distance, and had covered at least half the distance to the train, but we still had a long way to go and we had no idea where the others were.

"We need to keep moving."

I heard muttered agreements through the heavy breathing. We all sounded like dogs, which, panting so much, needed to stick out their tongues to cool down. I stood up straight, took one look at them and ploughed ahead at a fast walking pace, leading us into the darkness. My torch flickered.

Not the time for the batteries to die on me. No!

I shook it and it seemed to come back on, but it didn't fool me. We had to get there before it failed me completely.

I looked back at them.

"Caught your breaths?"

They nodded, knowing it meant we were going into another painful spurt of a run. I led them at a jog and then picked up the pace until we were charging through bushes and dodging low hanging branches again, trying to keep hidden, but also trying to keep the road to our left.

At one point we saw lights and ducked behind trees. It was late for people to be out, but it could easily have been the police or clearers. That's how they made their money. Finding those who were desperate enough to live on the street at night, asleep in some corner, and then dragging them away for a quick sale. My thoughts drifted to Alicia. She'd been in a kids' home, a gaol, and on the streets. What would have happened to her if I hadn't come along? What was happening to her now? I had to get back to her soon.

After that, nothing passed by and we were feeling more confident, until suddenly the woods ended and we came to a field of long, wild grass.

"We'll be seen if we walk frough this."

Euan was afraid. His face in the moonlight scrunched up.

"I thought it was woods all the way."

"So did I."

We stood for a moment, thinking.

"We'll have to crawl."

I stated as if it were something we did every day.

"It'll take longa'."

"Then we'll have to crawl quickly. Any other ideas?"

Alex didn't respond. Euan just looked at his hands and I glanced over to see what was wrong, flashing the torchlight in his direction. His palms were sore and bleeding. They hadn't heeled properly yet and the rough travelling was making it worse. He didn't say anything though.

"Alex, I don't suppose you brought anything in that bag that Euan could wrap his hands up with, did you?"

"The food's wrapped up in tea clofs, but they're small. Yer'll never tie them."

"We need to do something."

"It's okay. Let's go."

I watched him kneel down and start moving out into the grass like a ferret, only a ferret would have been much faster. I shrugged my shoulders at Alex. Obviously, he didn't want any help. He was already a couple of metres ahead, but didn't make a sound, even though his hands must have hurt. I knelt down too as did Alex and away we went.

The crawling position was worse than running. The ground was hard and banged into our knees every time we moved forward, our thighs hurt with the effort of continual fast crawling, and all our hands were being cut up now. Not only that, the grass whipped our faces. It had fine hair-like parts to it that seemed to stick and cut into our skin. We had to bow our heads or risk damaging our eyes, but still it attacked our ears, neck, ankles and any other part of the body open to the elements. The socks didn't help much, the material seemed to gather the hairs like little needles, which constantly dug into our skins.

Socks!

I pulled at Euan's ankle to stop him moving. He looked back over his shoulder and whispered.

"What?"

"Socks."

Alex had stopped behind me and I said the same thing to him.

"Put your socks on your hands."

We all sat on our bottoms and stripped a pair of socks off to convert them into fingerless gloves. As I had given away one pair, my ankles wouldn't be protected, but at least my palms would. It would help a little anyway. We all put our heads above the parapet of grass, hoping it wouldn't be seen by anyone.

We were about half way through the field, but had moved across diagonally a little too much and needed to head towards the left a little more in order to stay parallel with the road.

"What time is it Euan?"

He pushed up his sleeve with a socked hand. I shone my torch on it for him to see better.

"Two-twenty."

"We're not going to make it."

"We 'ave to."

He was dragging on the other sock, wincing, but he looked up distraught at the thought of not making it.

"We don't even know how far it is?"

"It can't be far."

I popped my head up again like a meerkat checking for enemies. Everything was quiet, all was dark.

"Let's run…"

"But…"

"No choice, we can't get left behind."

I pulled off the socks and stuffed them in my pocket, along with my torch, and then jumped up and started running, leaving them to decide for themselves. Soon I heard them following me. We charged through the grass, ignoring the aches and pains, the hairy grass attacking us, the dark night half-blinding our eyes and the possibility of getting caught.

Where are the tracks? Where are the others?

We were almost at the end of the field, when suddenly I tripped over something, a stone or piece of wood, or something and crashed to the ground, flattening my face, banging the side of my head on something hard. I tried to get up, but my head was going dizzy and my stomach turning. I was seeing black spots in front of my eyes. I knew I had to get up, couldn't miss the train, but my legs wouldn't obey my orders. I couldn't seem to make sense of anything, couldn't lift myself up to cry for help. I remembered this feeling from before and knew I was going to faint. Desperately, I struggled to fight the sickness off, but…

….the next thing I knew, water was being splashed in my face. I was confused, I couldn't open my eyes, people were dragging me up, pulling me to a standing position. I felt I was being man-handled and I knew I should wake up and run. I was being attacked, that boxer-creep had returned, I should have let him die, but the fear subsided into unconsciousness.

I was drifting in my own world, an easier world, were my parents were happy, not shouting at each other. We were eating ice-cream in the car. Mine was melting and had dripped down the cone onto my sticky hand, but I'd refused to give it up. The sweet, creamy coldness delicious on my tongue as I frantically tried to catch up with the liquefying mess. My mother's tinkling laugh as she turned round and looked at me.

"He's going to make a mess of the car."

"No, he's fine."

"I'm not cleaning it up."

Then the laughter again; one deep and comforting, the other playful and happy.

I heard other voices, people talking, outside the little dream world I was in, I couldn't quite make out what the noise in the distance was. I tried again to come back to the world, but couldn't fight it and faded once again.

Eventually, I woke up. My head pounded and I thought I had one of my Mam's migraines again, and so didn't immediately open my eyes. I was confused. I knew I was laying down on my left side, my arm was numb, but my head was definitely on hard ground. I could smell dirt and blood, and some sort of faint alcohol lingered in the background. It didn't make sense. Was I in danger? There was a constant humming and vibration hurting my head. I wanted it to go away. I knew there was something important I should remember, as if the thought were on the tip of my tongue, but it wouldn't come to me.

Slowly, voices entered my brain. People were talking, laughing, moving around. It was strange. Should I be ready to run? I decided to lay there, say nothing, find out my situation first. Then some words I understood, belonging to a voice I knew I ought to recognise. It sounded so familiar. Was it a friend?

"'ere, 'ave 'nother egg!"

"Nah, can't eat one more. Pass me water 'fore I choke." Snickering!

A girl's voice – someone older. I knew that voice too.

I wanted to look, but didn't want anyone seeing me. I kept perfectly still and squinted. It was dark, but my eyes adjusted quickly. Someone was stroking my hair.

"'e's wakin' up."

A child's voice. I looked up and found Josie gently stroking my head with sticky fingers.

"Josie, of course!"

It all came flooding back to me. We'd been running, I'd fallen. And then I realised, we'd missed the train.

"At least 'e knows who we are. Wasn't sure 'e would wiv' that bang. My Mam once 'ad a bang on the 'ead and lost 'er memory for a day."

Jasmine was sitting next to her. Molly was attached as usual.

"What happened? We didn't get on the train!"

I was distraught, my stomach heaved at the thought; after all the planning and running and hard work, we'd lost the chance.

"Oh, yer found the tracks alright."

There was a short burst of laughter at Euan's comment. I turned over to look at him. Beyond the circle of kids, it was dark. Within our group it was shadowy, but I could just see everyone due to a couple of candles stuck in the middle of the floor. Lacie was laid down fast asleep, her head on Alex's thigh. Thank God or the Maker, or whoever, that everyone was at least safe.

"Huh?"

I knew there was some sort of joke going on at my expense, but didn't know what it was. Elliott put me out of my misery.

"We saw you all charging through the field as if a bull was after you. We were 'iding in the grass and we shouted you, but you didn't 'ear and fell over the train tracks."

"I did.."

I put my hand to my head. There was a huge lump on one side and I flinched when my fingers probed it, sending sharp pains into the right side of my brain.

"Ouch!"

"Where are we Elliott?"

I looked round, needing to know what to do next.

"We're on the two-thirty cargo train."

Everyone was grinning. I couldn't believe it even though I now recognised the humming and jolting of an old fashioned train. How?

"We really made it!"

Chapter 39

I was wishing I had something to take for the pain, my mind flashing back to the cave kids and their trades, when Elliott got up and dug in his bag, and handed me a packet of tablets and a small bottle of water.

"Some sort of pain killers I think...when you were ill, the doctor gave me 'em for you each time 'e visited. I told 'im you'd taken 'em, so 'e would keep giving me some. Thought they might come in 'andy later."

I looked at him.

"Do you know what they are?"

He shrugged.

"Nope! They're called para...something."

I leant up on my right elbow; a dull pain shot through my arm. I'd probably bruised it and so I pushed myself to sit up cross-legged, and reached out for the torch. My head felt worse for sitting. I probably had brain damage after all the bangs and slaps I'd had over the last three weeks anyway. I leaned towards the light and squinted at the packet. I didn't care how much I hurt, I wasn't about to take anything I didn't recognise. Who knows what they were giving me in that clinic? I read aloud.

"Paracetamol....yep, painkillers, unless there's something different inside the packet."

Elliott shrugged again. It was a possibility. He was picking at the skin on his fingers as he spoke, half looking at me, half at the skin flaking away. Without looking, I knew Josie, with her brave face and wide grin, was still twitching beside me. It made me angry, I had no doubt being in the gaol had started the nervousness for both of them. I smiled at Josie, still sitting beside me.

"Thanks for being my nurse Josie. You did a great job!"

She smiled back, her teeth shining out in the dark; teeth that would no longer be scrubbed with twigs and soap every night. That's what they'd made us do. Said we had to be clean inside and out.

"When I grow up, I'm gunna be a nurse."

I smiled. Perhaps, if the Downers accepted us all, she might even be able to do that in the Downers' medical centre. They could train her. After all, I was being trained in three things. The Downers believed in utilising talent from an early age, dependent upon a kid's interests. But every child first had to read, write and do maths to a certain level – a bit like the government really. After that, they chose two or three subjects; one had to be a certain level of technology, (they needed to ensure people were trained in how to keep the base going). Other than that, I chose science and energy. It fascinated me, always had. I was a junior apprentice to both subjects and actually got to go to work, not just sit at a school desk. I was sure they'd all love it. I did!

In addition to apprenticeships, everyone had to contribute to our survival. Some grew food, others built stuff or fixed things. Even those adults who came with a job they'd already learnt, such as doctors, still had to follow the rules about learning and sharing. It was part of our survival, part of everyone being equal. I looked around at the dark silhouettes of my friends. What if they didn't accept us? What would we do?

The thought made me jerk. When had I become one of the 'us'? That was stupid. I'd only known these kids for three weeks. I could go back without them any time.

I looked around at the circle. Euan next to Alex, with Lacie as his extension. Next Sid and Jasmine, with Molly clinging to her and Josie leaning on her arm. Could I really just leave them behind to wander the streets and be taken back to the gaol?

"Are yer okay? Yer not 'bout to faint 'gin, are yer?"

Alex was sitting fairly close by, he leaned forward, watching me.

"I'm fine. It's just the pain."

I undid the packet and sniffed a tablet, then licked it. It was salty, with a bitter aftertaste. I'd had paracetamol before and the taste was the same, so I threw two to the back of my throat before I changed my mind, swallowing from the bottle of water Euan had passed to me. I always hated taking tablets, they made me feel as if I was choking, but I needed my body to function.

"How long have we been on the train?"

Sid responded.

"About half an hour."

Euan corrected, flipping on a torch and flashing it at his watch.

"Nope...exactly forty minutes. It's three ten."

I smiled, I couldn't help it, and then winced. Altering my face, somehow affected the lump on the side of my head.

"What yer grinnin' at?"

"Just thinking of Euan borrowing the Mantis' watch again."

"Mantis?"

Elliot filled them in.

"That's the name 'e gives the warden."

Sid smirked, making a strange guttural sound as if the laugh got stuck in his throat, as if he didn't know how to laugh anymore. No one else said anything.

"Mantis is short for praying mantis – a bug that waits in watch until it attacks its prey, something smaller and unable to fight back."

"Mantis eh?"

"I like that!"

"There are plenty of those around."

Jasmine was the last one to speak, but Euan reacted, scowling angrily.

"When I get bigger, I'm gunna' kill 'em all. I 'ate 'em. None of 'em will be allowed to live."

Everyone was silent, looking down, feeling awkward. Euan didn't speak much unless he felt strongly about something. His hair covered his face for a moment before he looked up again.

"Well...fink of all those kids we left behind. Wun't yer do it, if yer knew it would stop 'em getting' 'urt again?"

Alex answered.

"I would. I'd blow the place up....get the kids out first of course."

Everyone murmured agreement, except Elliott and I. Alex was just warming up to the theme.

"We should blow it up and every place like it."

Jasmine joined in, determination in her face.

"'N' all the adult worker camps."

"Yeah...that too."

"We should do that."

Even Sid added a comment..

"Can we blow up 'slave' factories too?"

"Yeah. We should blow 'em all up, one by one."

I understood them, knew they'd had a hard time and were angry, but even the idea of killing people was wrong. The Downers did no harm. I wondered if they really could fit in to my way of living.

Elliott spoke, his quiet voice reaching them all.

"So, anyone know 'ow to blow anything up?"

They all stared for a moment, before laughing out loud, releasing the angry atmosphere and letting go the tension of the moment. My stomach growled.

"I'm starving. Anything left or have you 'blower-uppers' eaten it all?"

Alex was still smiling.

"Give the posh-boy summit to eat."

We'd decided to take it in turns to get some sleep. We figured we had at least until four before we should worry, depending upon how many stops we had. I decided to keep watch as I couldn't sleep. I took Euan's 'new' watch to keep an eye on the time and every time the train pulled in I peeked out of a gap in the door. Elliott had told me I was looking for a place called Stagton. Once we passed through, our town was two stops after that and we all had to be ready and awake.

The carriage was made of wood and metal. I could hear the clinking of iron from outside as it jerked and was pulled forward. The floor was hard and cold, and every so often I stood up to shake the numbness from my legs and bottom.

Alex had given me an extra boiled egg, a piece of hard bread, three stale biscuits and some water to keep me awake. Jasmine had stolen the candles and matches from The Mantis' supplies and had given me three just in case the others went out.

Everyone called her Jas now that she'd dropped the threatening behaviour. She was such a different person, caring and kind. I wondered what it would take to change her back to her 'gaol' self. Would the Downer rules be too much for her? Could she cope with it? Molly was curled around her, a tiny body trying to attach itself to her substitute mother.

Elliott, Sid and Euan all lay on their left side, curled into tight balls as if someone was going to attack them and they were protecting their heads. I'd never believe Euan was only nine. He was the oldest nine year-old I'd ever met. Although I didn't know much about him, I did know for at least one second, he'd really meant it about blowing up the kids' homes.

My mother always says, 'hate' can drive us in a powerfully wrong direction if we let it. She'd first told me as warning one day when I'd come home from school, stamping my feet, repeating 'I hate him', 'I hate him', over and over, tears of frustration dripping down my cheeks. I was about seven and a boy at school was teasing me, breaking my pencils and making everyone laugh when I'd cried. My mother had sat me on her knee, cuddling and soothing me. The boy at school, Edward, ended up getting detention for his acts of cruelty to younger kids, but at the time, I wanted to get my own revenge.

What Euan had been through in his life was a whole lot worse. I imagined he was like a bottle of fizzy drink that had been kicked around a lot and was only waiting to be opened, so it could hit out at everyone else. I thought he might have the most difficulty adapting to Downer rules.

I nibbled on the corner of one of the biscuits, the same as the one Alex had given Elliott and I the first time I'd cleaned the hen shed with him. I smiled as the memory of the sugar hitting my tongue repeated itself. It seemed like a life time ago, so many things had happened since then. But Alex had been a real horror that day. I could have killed him myself, but he was tough and protective. I was glad he was with us, I could trust him.

I shivered in the cold, wooden carriage. The air from the gap in the double doors was blowing icy. I would have closed it, but we needed both the air, and a spy hole. Otherwise we might miss our station. Worse, there was also a chance that someone might come check the carriage and we needed to be ready to jump off and run. Luckily though, the carriage was empty. Either the cargo had already been emptied or it never had anything in it to start with.

The train jerked again. How everyone was sleeping, I wasn't sure. Alex even snored when he slept. I looked over. He had his arm over his little sisters, as if to protect them even in sleep. Lacie was squashed in the middle of a Josie and Alex sandwich. She was not only weak from the travel, but sick. Alex had told me he wasn't sure what was wrong with her, but he'd been getting worried for a while. No one at the gaol cared enough to listen. We needed to get her home as fast as possible.

The train began to slow again. This was the fifth time. I shone the torch at the watch on my wrist. It was three-thirty already and so I moved to catch a glimpse of the place we were passing though. Rusty wheels squeaked as the breaks went into action, bringing the train to a halt. I peeped out, seeing nothing. The tail end of the long train was outside the station. Elliott had told me he'd chosen the last carriage purposely. If we were closer to the station, people would see us jumping on and off. It meant I had to wait until the train moved again to see the sign telling me where we were. It was freezing kneeling up at the gap, but there was nothing else to do, so I waited.

Suddenly, I heard a voice, two voices shouting as they walked down the length of the train. I heard doors opening and slamming shut.

"Nope, no-one here."

Another slam...closer.

"Or here."

Slam...they were checking the carriages.

Oh no, they'd find us. How were we to get out? They'd see us. I heard the voice again, getting louder, closer.

"No one in here."

Slam.

Elliot was beside me.

"Close the door."

I immediately did as he said. He was waking everyone up as quietly as he could. I looked around. There was no-where to hide. Granted it was dark, could we hide at the back? Everyone, but the girls were instantly awake, terrified, knowing something was wrong by the way Elliott and I were behaving.

"Quiet everyone."

I whisper-shouted as loud as I dared.

"Move to the back of the carriage. Stay in the dark against the carriage wall."

"What's 'appenin'?"

"They're checking the carriages."

Alex was trying to pick up Lacie and Josie. I ran over and lifted Josie and left her in the dark. Our footsteps were loud enough, but she started to cry. Alex shushed her. He was carrying Lacie who hadn't woken up. I ran back and started throwing any bags towards whoever could catch them. Sid did the same. Euan, Jasmine and

Elliott caught. In less than five seconds they were all at the back of the carriage wall. The last thing I did was pick up and blow out the candles before joining them all, pressing my back to the wall of the carriage, trying not to breath heavily.

"Try to hold your breath when he opens the door."

My heart was beating, my chest hurting, the lump on my head joining in with the drum pounding around my body. My stomach burnt with fear. Why were they checking tonight of all nights?

We heard the man getting closer. He was shouting over to his fellow worker.

"Why we doin' this? Waste 'a' time if yer ask me."

Slam!

"Police called in. There's bin some runaways from that non-contributor's 'ome up north."

"What, the one wiv' those kids in?"

Slam!

"Poor blighters if yer ask me. I'd run away too if I were there."

Slam!

"Yeah well, we 'ave our job to do."

Slam!

They knew. They'd found out already. I thought I was going to have a heart attack or black out or something. My chest was tight and painful, I felt sick and little lights were flashing in my eyes. I had to breathe deeper. I needed more oxygen. I knew I was going into panic mode and needed to stop before we all got caught.

"Can yer check the last one Sam. Am off back."

"'kay!"

The door ground open, creating a gap the width of a doorway. I could feel everyone pushing themselves

282

further into the carriage wall, I heard them all holding their breaths. All except Lacie. She was in Alex's arms, fast asleep, but her breathing was shallow. Maybe he wouldn't hear.

Elliot was squashed in next to me, his arm tight against mine. I could feel the pulse on his wrist going mad. The man was staring into the carriage. How long would he look for? Maybe he wouldn't get in. He didn't seem too keen to jump up. To my relief, he began closing the door. I could feel everyone breathe out together. We'd done it. The gap in the door was getting smaller.

And then Lacie cried out in her sleep and the man at the door stopped, opening it up once more and jumping inside. It wasn't her fault. I knew it wasn't. She was sick, but...

...but the fear in me wanted to hit out at her. We'd almost made it. Now, he stood facing us, peering into the darkness.

I heard him shuffling before there was a click and he lit up the carriage with a lighter of some kind. We all stared at him. Our dirty, frightened faces not knowing what to do. We said nothing, just stood there, waiting for him to call the worker, the police, knowing we'd be dragged back.

He was a tall, broad man, with straggly hair and an untidy, dark uniform. He just looked at us, saying nothing, as if he were genuinely shocked to find us, as if we were creatures he'd never seen before. After a moment he moved his light around us to take in the bags, a sick child, a girl crying quietly into the arm of a bigger girl, a dark-skinned boy with white eyes.

There was a call from outside, making us all jump.

"Are we ready to go Sam?"

He moved to the door. This was it. Should we make a run for it? I looked at Lacie, Josie and Molly, who would never make it. I wanted to cry myself. He leaned out the door.

"Yeah, everyfing's okay. Just a rat I 'eard."

He jumped out and began closing the door. At the last minute he whispered into the silence.

"Get off at the next stop. They're waitin' for yer in town."

The door slammed, enclosing us in blackness. We all stood there in shock as the train pulled out of the station, first jolting and then picking up speed. Even when it was charging forward, we still leaned against the wall. They were already looking for us. They knew which route we'd taken. They were waiting for us. Euan woke us all up.

"That man's blind as a bat...he thinks we're rats!"

Our strange laughs at what was possibly the worst situation, melded into one another, like music. He'd let us go. It was impossible to think that he would do that, and yet he had. Jas' voice rung out in the darkness.

"Are we gunna' stand 'ere all cosy, or are we gunna' get off this frigin' trap."

She was right, we had to move.

"Where's the candles 'n' matches?"

I had them. It had been the last thing I'd picked up. I struck a match and lit one, looking round at everyone, at Alex who felt guilty for putting us in danger with his sister, at Josie who had terror in her eyes still and at Sid, who wished he could hide how he looked.

"Thank God for Lacie!"

"Huh?"

"If she hadn't made a noise, we wouldn't know they were waiting for us."

"True!"

"Yep!"

Alex smiled, clinging a now waking Lacie to his chest, before slowly putting her on her feet.

I gave Euan his watch back. Elliott piped up.

"The next stop 'aint far from town. It won't take long to get there. I remember from before. I almost got off, but saw a whole load of warehouses just in time. Not sure why it still stops 'ere."

"Warehouses?"

"Yeah...the old ones, y'know, the ones were all the druggies live. My mam used to tell me never to play over there 'cos of the druggies."

Alex groaned.

"'Ow are we gunna get the kids to town. Lacie is ill."

"We'll be attacked 'fore we get there if it's a drug place."

Euan was being his usual optimistic self.

But the grin on my face couldn't have been wider.

"Perfect!"

"'ow's that?"

"It's closer to where we're going. I didn't know the train stopped there."

For once I felt like one of my Nanna's angels was protecting us.

Sid sighed.

"Oh great, so we're going to a drug den."

"Nope....well, actually, we, or I, have to go to one first!"

Chapter 40

We jumped out of the carriage, throwing kids and bags as fast as we could, before hiding in the long grass, waiting for the train to pass. Once the sound was distant, I stood up and switched on my torch. Elliott, Sid and Jasmine did the same.

"Right we have to go over the tracks to the warehouse site. I'm not sure where we are right now."

There was some mumbling, but everyone started to move. Alex was struggling with Lacie, who was unable to walk.

"Lace, yer'll 'ave to walk fer a bit. Me' arms ache and yer too weak to hold on for a piggy-back."

It surprised me to hear Sid.

"I can carry her, if you want."

Sid was strong, he had muscles in his arms from slinging all the laundry baskets around. Alex looked into Sid's eyes, trying to work out whether he could trust him.

"kay, thanks."

He picked Lacie up carefully and handed her to Sid, who held his arms open. Lacie began to whine and struggle. Alex's strict, 'Dad' voice bellowed out.

"No, Lacie. Sid's a friend and we need to be quiet. No moanin' or yer walk."

Lacie immediately shut up and leaned into Sid, who adjusted her weight for balance and began to walk over the tracks. Jas immediately picked up Molly and slung her into a piggy-back and Elliott allowed Josie to jump on his back.

"Yeh right."

Alex shoved him gently.

"She's heavy. Let me take her. She's strong enough to hang on."

But Elliot held on to her legs and started following Sid.

"We can all take turns. When she's too 'eavy, I'll give 'er back."

Nothing else was said, and the remainder of us picked up bags and crossed the tracks and walked to the outskirts of the warehouse. It was dark, even with the torches. The full moon had disappeared behind clouds. Jas stumbled once, Euan caught her arm before she fell flat on her face.

"Right then. I suggest you all wait here a minute and let me scout around a bit, find my bearings."

We were sitting behind a mound of grass, peeping over the top, trying to see what was in front of us. The ground was damp and the grass smelt of fresh hay on a wet autumn day. In front of us stood a square shaped building with a broken back door, hanging off its hinges, blocking our view to the rest of the estate.

"I've got a better idea."

Sid was speaking.

"There's an empty warehouse down there. Why don't we all hide in it until you find your way?"

"Good idea, but let me check it out first, make sure no-one's in it."

Euan jumped up.

"I'll go."

Before I could say or do anything, he'd pulled out a knife and was creeping towards the doorway. We all watched him disappear, taking deep breaths. We were scared and nervous. It was dark and cold and the warehouse area sounded and looked like every scary story or film you've ever seen or heard of. Creeks and groans echoed off the lonely streets. Bats and owls called out to each other. Scurrying of unknown vermin feet made our spines shiver. We were going into a drug territory and that was definitely a living nightmare.

Fortunately, it wasn't raining or windy, and suddenly, the moon came out again, so it was easier to see as Euan waved to us to come forward. We hefted ourselves up and tramped down the mound and into the building, trying, and failing, to be completely silent.

The bags were dropped and four torches immediately flipped on and were shone around. Jas lit a couple of candles and stood them on the floor.

"Need to save batteries."

She switched her torch off, though no one else did.

Beneath our feet was broken glass, splinters of wood, dirt and the ever present dust.

"Floor needs clearing. Can't sit on glass."

"You do that. I'll go look."

"I'm comin' with yer."

Euan looked at me determined.

"Okay, but I also have to find someone. It might take some time."

Everyone looked at me. This was the moment.

"Look, a friend was kidnapped by a gang here – well they're not really a gang, just kids like us. I was supposed to bring back food – they're starving you see – and then they'll let her go, but I was taken by Clearers."

I thought it better not to tell them I was trying to trade drugs at the time.

They all looked at me as if I were telling them a fairy story. Elliott was fiddling again. The girls were twitching and then Jas and Alex crossed their arms. They were all going into their 'game' mode.

"And when were you going to tell us this?"

"Errr now!"

"Now!"

"What difference does it make? I'm not going to leave Lissy. I promised her I'd go back."

My voice was squeaking.

"Y'know, she's just like you, escaped from a kid's home and then she got captured again by this gang. I can't just leave her behind."

"Yeah, but yer can't just leave us 'ere Adam."

Elliott was trying to reason with me.

"Anything could happen."

Everyone was staring at me. They were right of course. I looked down.

"Okay, I'll just go scout, ten minutes, and then I'll come back. I'll figure out something."

"Am still comin'"

"Good, let's go."

I turned my back and left them to cross arms and stare at each other as much as they liked. I wasn't going to leave Lissy behind.

Chapter 41

I shoved my hands in my pockets and skulked along, keeping my eyes and ears wide open. Euan shadowed me with a torch in one hand and a knife in the other. I was hoping no one was around at this time of night. It was freezing.

We'd stopped on the corner of a building, I was peeping round to make sure no one was there, when Euan whispered.

"So, is this friend, yer girlfriend or what?"

I sighed. Why did everyone always think that? I looked over my left shoulder and whispered back.

"No, just a friend...one I hadn't seen for over two years until three weeks ago."

"Then, why do yer care?"

I wasn't sure what to say and so just looked at his dark profile for a moment.

"You wouldn't understand."

"Why wun't I? Y'think I'm stupid?"

This was not a conversation to be having at this moment.

"Dun't yer think if we're all riskin' bein' caught, while yer rescue sum' unknown person, we 'ave a right to know."

"Probably, but not right now. Let's just look around and get back to them."

He shrugged his shoulders, and was about to say something else, which in itself was strange for Euan, (why did he chose now to get talkative?), when he dragged me into the doorway of the building we were hiding behind.

"A voice!"

Then I also heard it.

"The Maker be damned, am I tired!"

The voice was rough.

"Me too. This was an 'ard night wiv' nuffin' to show for it."

"At least we din't get picked up by that patrol."

The voices were getting closer, they were going to pass us.

"Dillon wun't be 'appy."

My mind was alert suddenly.

"Now't we can do. The trade wun't there."

I turned to Euan and whispered in his ear, cupping my hand so the two outside couldn't hear as they passed.

"I can't believe our luck. It's them."

"Them who?"

He mouthed back at me.

"Dillon is there leader, so they must be going back to the cave. They can lead us."

"Cave?"

"Were Lissy is."

"Lissy?"

"My friend."

"Come on, they'll show us the way."

Their footsteps on the gravel road had now turned the corner.

"Come on, be quiet and switch off the torch."

I crept out of the building, Euan followed me with his knife held higher as if he were going to attack someone. It occurred to me he could really hurt someone with it, or even himself if he fell, but I said nothing. Dillon's gang had scythes, Euan's knife was nothing compared to their 'killing' tools.

The two boys were at least three warehouses ahead, which was good in one sense, as we didn't want them to hear us, but also bad in that it was dark and we might lose them. I couldn't risk that and sped up so that we were only two buildings apart.

At one point, I thought they'd completely disappeared, but then I saw the dark alley Lissy and I walked down and knew they'd gone that way. Suddenly, we were out in open grass and I knew we were close to the cave. It amazed me, we were only about fifteen minutes from my home. How could these kids live so close and we not know about them?

It was a cold, dank night. The long grass dampened my trouser legs, but I was hot and sweaty with excitement and fear. I'd be home soon, I really would   Just this one last thing to do.

Euan pulled me down, hiding me in the grass. I looked at him confused.

"There's only one of 'em. The other ones disappeared."

"What?"

I'd been distracted and hadn't noticed.

"'E might 'ave 'eard us and be comin' back."

"A trap?"

"'Ave seen it b'fore."

"Right!"

I was itching to move forward, I didn't want to lose them, but Euan held me down, as if he didn't trust me. Then, we heard a quiet rustle in the grass. My heart boomed out a drum symphony. Someone was moving towards us.

"Stay 'ere. I'll look 'round. Don't move."

"What?"

Before I could stop him, Euan had disappeared into the night. I could have killed him. He was supposed to stay with me, not go on some sort of scouting mission. We didn't have time for this.

Suddenly, I was being pulled back by my neck. Someone had grabbed me from behind and was hanging on to my shoulders as if they were hugging me. I felt hot breath against my neck.

"So, 'oo are yer...sneekin' after us. Yer think we din't 'ear yer."

I struggled, elbowing him in the stomach and pulling his arm off me, but although he stepped back, he kept his balance and managed to kick the back of my knees, knocking me to the floor. I turned over to face him. In his hands he had one of those scythes. I could see it glistening in the moonlight, which had conveniently come out again. The whites of his eyes glared out at me.

"Well, then..."

But his words were cut short as a butcher's knife reached the front of his throat.

"Drop the knife or die...and believe me, I'll do it."

Euan sounded the part. Although he was shorter than the guy by a head, he was angry enough to make up for it.

"Drop it."

The boy dropped the scythe into the grass. I grabbed it quickly.

"Now kneel!"

Euan was giving the orders. I couldn't believe a nine-year old would do this and didn't know what to say. He was like a little gangster out of an old movie. I remembered his tears at the gaol-home's kitchen sink, and wondered if I was with the same person. We were all kneeling, hiding in the grass.

"'oo are yer?"

"None of yer business. Yer want to stay alive. Yer keep quiet 'n' do as I say."

"Give me one of yer socks Adam."

"Huh?"

"Socks!"

"Oh yeh."

I delved in my pocket and passed it to him. What did he want a dirty sock for?

"Open yer mouf."

"No."

"Open it or I'll 'ave my friend 'ere open it for yer wiv' that piece of metal 'e's wanting to use."

The boy looked at me scared. I probably looked as frightened as him. Euan stuffed the sock in his mouth.

"Keep yer quiet."

"Oliver, where are yer?"

The other 'cave' kid had started moving towards us. I looked at Euan as if to say what now. In the moonlight I could see his taught face and gleaming eyes. I wasn't sure how he would hold on to two of them. And then I realised, he didn't mean to. I was supposed to take the second one.

"Euan?"

I wanted to say more, but couldn't. I was hoping there might be another plan. I didn't think I could do this.

"Oliver."

Oliver was narrow-boned and starving skinny. His eyes flicked over my right shoulder as he desperately tried to think about how he could warn his friend.

"Oliver."

His friend was to the right about five strides away. He couldn't see us in the grass, but if I knelt up, I could see him. Now was my chance to grab him. Euan nodded at me.

"Look Oliver, this 'aint funny. If yer don't anser' me, 'am goin' back wivout yer."

None of us said anything or moved. Euan was glaring at me, pushing me to stick the scythe against the boy's neck. I crouched, ready to leap up.

He passed us by about three strides before deciding to turn back. His voice was worried.

"Right am goin'."

He stood there listening.

"Last chance!"

He was a small lad, possibly only nine or ten, his voice was squeaky with fright.

Euan flicked his head towards the boy and mouthed.

"Take him."

Suddenly, the boy had turned and was crashing through the grass in terror.

"Get 'im."

Euan spoke aloud.

"Why, he's going. We only need one."

"Are there others?"

My brain suddenly clicked. He'd tell the others. They'd know something was wrong and come out looking for us. I jumped up and raced through the grass, scythe in front of me, heart beating fast, pulse throbbing. I felt sick. This was my fault, I had to stop him getting into the cave. I slipped once and almost went down on a muddy mound some mole probably dug. Fortunately, I managed to right myself and leap over it.

The boy in front of me was fast for his age, but I was faster and I had the motive. He could put all of us in danger if I didn't catch up with him and that would be worse. My brain saw a scenario where everyone in the warehouse became prisoners, forced to trade for their freedom. It would be my stupid fault.

His back was now an arm's length away. I reached out for his shoulder, but just couldn't make it. In a desperate effort, I threw my scythe down, leapt and landed on his back, slamming him to the soft, grassy ground, squishing him below me, knocking the wind out of both of us. Luckily, he'd had the foresight to throw his blade away as well, or I really could have hurt him without meaning to. He was screeching like a little kid, terrified, but I found my senses quickly, leaning into his left ear.

"Shut up or I'll sock your mouth!"

Being tough was totally alien to me and so I imitated Euan's tone.

Immediately, he was quiet, which was good, as I didn't know if I could pretend again.

"Better. Now I'm going to let you get up. If you keep quiet and come with me for a while, everything will be all right. I'm not going to hurt you."

I grabbed his bony shoulder and dragged him back a little so I could pick up my scythe. Then I forced him to stand.

"I can catch you if you run, so don't!"

His face was white, his eyes like an animal caught in a trap.

"Answer me."

"'kay!"

His eyes flicked to his knife lying in the grass. I bent down, keeping my eyes on him at all times, and picked that one up too. Both hands were now full, so pushing him gently with the tip of the scythe, I forced him to move in front of me.

Euan had somehow managed to tie his prisoner's hands behind his back with his socks. The boy, Oliver, couldn't say anything, but was fuming and dangerous. From his knees, he glared at my captive as if it were his fault.

"What's your name?"

"Jamie."

"Well, Jamie, if you're good, you'll be okay."

He didn't say anything, looking down at the grass, hands in his pockets, but Euan chimed in.

"But if yer not.."

He stepped forward, lifting the boys chin with his knife, giving him a stark warning. It was obvious the boy was terrified and I wanted to tell Euan to stop, but the older one needed to think we meant what we said. Obviously, no harm would come to them, we just needed their help.

Euan insisted on checking all their pockets and tying Jamie's hands before we pushed them in front of us, back in the direction of the warehouses.

Chapter 42

"What d'yer mean?"

Alex wasn't happy.

At first, when we'd brought in our captives, everyone was surprised, but when Euan explained, (in his own not-so-subtle language), Alex laughed and congratulated him. He'd suddenly become a hero, not in the least because he'd protected me. It was embarrassing, but I had a feeling they'd made some sort of pact to guard me. Their future safety was now in my hands!

I don't know how, with all the noise we'd made, but somehow we'd scurried through the streets and were now standing in the opening of a mineshaft, not a cave. Jamie had been very helpful so far, even though Oliver had scowled at him most of the way. In the light of the torches and candles, I could see Jamie was more like eight. He was filthy black and smelt like a fowl ditch, but once I'd promised him some food if he'd lead us to their hide-out, he was happy to walk ahead.

Both of them were shocked to see so many kids, but when I showed Jamie a boiled egg and some stale bread, his eyes widened desperately. Oliver wasn't so easily persuaded, even though I could see he needed food.

"What d'yer mean?"

Alex asked again shocked. I was demanding they all hid in the opening of the mine and gave me the left-over food, but he wasn't about to agree lightly. He'd gone through a lot of risk to get us food and drink.

"The kids that live here are starving. Look at these two."

Oliver was giving me a peculiar look, like how did I know. Jamie just stood there, waiting for his next orders.

"Look Adam, we dun't know what's gunna 'appen to us. We dun't 'ave much left."

I looked at them all, staring at me. Jas stepped forward.

"I know yer want yer friend back, but we dun't 'ave to give 'em food. We cun just take 'er. We've got prisoners to swap."

He waited a moment for a reaction, before adding.

"What 'bout us? Look at Mol, Lacie and Jo."

They were right of course, but I wasn't sure how many kids were in the mine shaft. I moved away from Oliver and Jamie, who were listening to everything we said, and lowered my voice.

"We're not far now. These kids have nothing."

I could see they weren't going to budge on the issue, Alex, Euan and Jas had gone into their crossed arm stance again. I could've laughed, but didn't. Sid was quiet, leaning against the wall, as if he wasn't permitted an opinion. His job was guarding the kneeling prisoners. The girls were sat on the floor slouching, ready to fall asleep any second. I looked at Elliott, appealing for help. He lifted his hands up, as if he wasn't having anything to do with this.

"Not this time Adam. I agree wiv' 'em."

I stared at the stubborn faces in front of me.

"Okay, what about half what's left?"

"Quar'er."

"How much is a quarter?"

As Alex was in charge of anything food and drink, he dug in the bags.

"Two eggs, piece of bread and four biscuits."

"Give me another egg and more bread and biscuits then."

"Are yer sure we're close?"

"Yes, twenty minutes from here. Honestly!"

Fed up with the bartering, Alex handed me the portions, as well as a half bottle of water, before changing the subject.

"How long will this take?"

"About twenty minutes, I think."

"I'm comin'."

Euan, my little protector, spoke up. I looked at him and the others.

"Fine."

"Me too."

Alex joined in.

Lacie started whimpering at the thought of her brother leaving. We all turned to look at her. She was covering her face with her dirty hands as if she had tears to wipe away. Her head was twitching.

"No, stay for Lacie and Josie."

"I'll come."

Sid called out, before Alex could argue.

"Do I need two of you?"

A chorus of three voices answered.

"Yes."

"Right!"

I sighed and tried to see it from their point of view. They'd have nowhere to go if anything happened to me, but still I wasn't going to tell them where I lived. The Downers might be angry with me.

"Stay quiet, in the shadows, in case someone else comes in."

Sid spoke, pointing to Oliver.

"He should stay here."

Oliver's eyes bulged, but as he had the sock in his mouth, the only sound he could make was a back-of-the-throat gurgle.

"He's uncooperative and will alert the others in there."

"You're right."

I beckoned Jamie.

"Come here."

Sid hauled him up with one hand, which wasn't hard, he was so skinny, and walked him over. His hands still tied behind his back. He looked up under a scraggly fringe. I bent down in front of him, so our eyes were level.

"See this egg."

He nodded, watching it as I moved it from side to side.

"It's yours if you keep quiet and lead us in. Will you do that?"

He nodded over and over, still watching the egg. It would have been comical if it wasn't so sad.

"Good. Here's a piece of biscuit too."

I pushed half a biscuit into his mouth. I could see his eyes light up with the sweetness hitting his tongue and the feeling of real food sliding down his throat. I could tell he would have been a good kid, if life had given him a chance. I stood up again.

"Let's go!"

"Adam!"

Elliott called out.

"This is a mine shaft. How will you find your way out?"

How stupid of me not to think about it.

"Any string or chalk in the bags?"

"Nope."

How could I have forgotten? I could have brought the chalk from the classroom with me. Suddenly, Jamie's squeaky voice spoke up.

"There are markers on the wall. I'll show you."

Oliver went berserk, as if trying to get up and attack Jamie. The noise from his throat was angry and frightening. I looked at him and back at Jamie, who cowered, afraid. Sid walked over and kicked Oliver in his side.

"Shut up or I'll drop you down a well."

As it was very unlike Sid to talk like that, we all snickered.

"I'll chop yer 'ead off first!"

Alex was joking, but all the same, I was uncomfortable when he smirked at Euan, like two thieves in the night. I turned back to Jamie, speaking gently.

"Thank you. For that you can have the rest of the biscuit."

He smiled and opened his mouth like a young bird awaiting a worm.

The painted markers were dark blue, almost impossible to see unless you had a torch and were actually looking for them. They were on the old timber which held up the opening to the mine. Every four had a blue arrow, showing the direction. Once we knew about them, they were easy to find.

Without the hood or blindfold, we moved faster. Jamie's pace was the only thing that slowed us, but within five minutes I could see a larger opening ahead and stopped everyone.

"Sid, Euan, this is it I think…"

I looked at Jamie for confirmation. He nodded.

"Both of you stay here with Jamie. Don't let him back in. He might warn everyone."

"No, I'm comin'."

"Not this time. Stay with Sid. I need you to come and rescue me, if I don't get out."

They both looked at me for a second.

"'kay."

"Good plan."

Sid grabbed Jamie's shoulder. I handed Sid an egg.

"Feed him this."

"Yes boss!"

"Not your boss. Jamie kept his end of the bargain. We keep ours."

Jamie grinned in anticipation.

I moved forward on tiptoes, clinging to the damp, slimy, fungus-covered wall. On getting to the edge of the opening, I peeped round. Other than a distant dripping, there were no sounds. Maybe they were all sleeping. No, nothing was that easy!

My wet plimsolls scratched against a dirt-strewn ground. I was sure someone would hear, but no one jumped up. I kept looking round. I didn't want anyone to attack me from behind. My heart was beating and I wondered how much more terror it could stand. Fear was driving it to have an on-going work-out.

Suddenly, I could smell smoke. When I looked in the direction it came from, I saw a dying fire. Around the embers were the sleeping bodies of kids. From where I was I couldn't see if Lissy was with them. I had to get closer.

I crept further in, barely touching my feet to the floor, slowly placing the tips of my toes on the slippery worn rocky ground, trying not to slip at the same time. I was almost on top of them when I saw her. She was on the far side of the circle, laying with her hands as a cushion for her head on the hard floor. I spotted Dillon, he was closer to me. I desperately wanted to shake him, scream at him for what had happened to me, but my target was Lissy and so I passed him by.

I heard someone snoring. It was Long-Nose. I needed to avoid him. Eventually, I was standing above Lissy. Quickly, I crouched, put my hand across her mouth to stop her making a noise and woke her.

She looked up, fear in her eyes, ready to scream, but when she saw it was me, she stopped and stared as if she were dreaming.

I pointed to the entrance and mouthed, 'Come'. She got up and followed me, sleep still keeping her in shock. Although she kept pulling at my arm and trying to whisper something, I shushed her and refused to speak until we were back with Sid and Euan

Chapter 43

"Why didn't you come back? You promised!"

Lissy and I were just going through the opening on our way back to Sid and Euan. I stopped and turned round. Our faces were close and we whispered into the darkness.

"The trade was a trap Lissy. I was knocked out and taken by Clearers to a kids' home up north."

"Oh no, it can't have been. Dillon wouldn't do that."

"He wouldn't...well he did."

"No, you don't get it Ad. They're really just kids trying to find food. There not like we thought they were."

"I don't care. I'm going home. Are you coming?"

I was irritated. She cared more for these people than me. She didn't even ask how I was, how I'd managed to survive or even escape.

Why did I bother to come back for her?

I turned round and walked to where Sid and Euan were waiting with Jamie. He smiled at me, hopeful of more food.

"Who are these people?"

Alicia looked around.

"Jamie, what are you doing here?"

She went over to him.

"Why are his hands tied?"

She glared at me and began untying the socks.

"Wait!"

Euan stopped her, pushing Jamie to one side.

"What's happening?"

Sid crossed his arms , standing in front of Jamie so she couldn't get around him.

"So, this is Lissy."

"Get out of my way….Jamie come here."

Euan just stared for a moment, a torch in one hand, a knife in the other.

"We goin' now?"

"Yes."

I turned to Alicia.

"He'll be set free once we are at the mouth of the mine shaft."

"But, what are you doing? He's only eight."

"Yes, but he might let the others know we're here."

Euan and Sid had started moving away and I followed them. If she didn't want to come, it was up to her.

"Adam, where are you going?"

"Home…are you coming or not?"

"This is it, you're just going to leave them all behind?"

Her voice was squeaking, as she caught up with me.

"Them?"

"All the kids living here."

"Are you mad?"

I stopped and stared at her in the dark. The others had gone ahead and so I pulled out my torch and switched it on.

"Lissy, they're the ones that brought us here hooded, at knife point, and then sent me out to do a trade for your life. A trade on some other gang's turf, that ended up with me beaten up and sold to a kids' home."

I took a breath and stepped back. My voice was sounding desperate and I felt overwhelmed with the last three weeks. I would either hit out at her or burst into tears.

"I came back for you because I promised, but now I'm going home. You want to stay with your new friends, then go ahead."

I turned and strode ahead. She followed silently for a moment.

"Well, you've collected two others on your way, why not take a few more kids? They need somewhere to live as much as we do. Look at little Jamie."

She wasn't going to shut up. I ignored her, speeding up. She lengthened her stride until she was next to me, looking up. I looked ahead, counting the wooden beams and checking the markings so I didn't get lost.

"I know we were scared at first, but they weren't really bad to me Ad."

She watched my face for a moment, looking for a response. I gave her none.

"After you left, they gave me more food. They shared what little they had with me."

Still no response.

"There's only eight of us now. Some left and others came."

Not even any recognition she was talking to me.

"But Dillon stayed to protect us...there are three around eight, the two black girls you saw are twins – Tilly and Milly, and then there's Jamie. His brother is Oliver. Then there's Mandy, the older girl who looked after me, and Luke, who's Dillon's brother. He's the one with the long nose. Everyone else left to see if they could find food. Thing is, they didn't come back."

She really knew how to chatter on and on and on.

"Adam, please. Surely, there'll be room where you live for eleven kids. You told me it was a new world – a different world to the one we live in."

That stopped me and I looked at her. It was hard to tell from just the torch light, but I could imagine her dirty face pleading at me, the way she used to when we were little. 'Please Ad. Just this game and then we can play yours.' Although we never did. She was doing the same now.

"What do you mean, eleven?"

"Well, eight of us, the two boys your with and you....actually no, that makes ten really. You already live there."

I stared at her for a moment.

"Since when did you become one of them Lissy?"

She stuttered a little, looking down.

"They looked after me...we all look after each other. There's a pact!"

I sighed.

"I didn't know what had happened, didn't expect you to come back."

"I just can't believe you. Only three weeks and you made some sort of 'we all look after each other brainwashing' pact."

"It wasn't like that!"

"There are more kids at the entrance Lissy. I escaped with eight kids, not two."

"Oh."

I turned to walk again. She pulled my arm

"How did you escape?"

Now she wants to know!

"I found a secret tunnel. Now are you coming or not?"

I shone my torch a little higher, behind her shoulder so as not to blind her with the beam. Her face showed first amazement and then determination. I remembered that look from when we were kids, she was convinced she was doing the right thing.

"No Adam. I can't leave them behind, knowing I'm safe."

"Fine."

Why had I bothered coming back? I could be home by now.

"But can you take three little kids in my place?"

"What?"

"They'll die if they stay here."

"And you won't!"

I hadn't meant to say it, but it just slipped out.

"I can look after myself. They need food."

I stood staring at her, perplexed. She'd succeeded in making me feel as if I were wrong, guilty of something though I wasn't sure what. I thought of Lacie and Jo, of Molly and little Jamie. They were all weak.

"Okay, go get the little kids, but hurry."

She grinned.

"I'll be back in two minutes. I'm fast now I know my way along here."

She turned and had taken three strides.

"Lissy……you can still come. You don't need to give up your place."

"Okay….err…thanks Ad."

I stood, flicking the beam around the black walls and ceiling of the mine shaft. It was a horrid place to live, no proper air, just dust to breathe. Imagine living the whole of your life in this way, stealing and trading for a bit of food. I didn't think I could bear it. I looked forward, perhaps I should just walk away. The entrance wasn't too far. It wasn't my problem; the whole world was like this as far as I knew. No one cared! The thought dampened my spirits along with the fungus, clinging on the walls struggling to survive in a hostile environment.

Why doesn't anyone do something about this world?

I turned to leave, but then swivelled round in the direction Alicia had gone.

"What yer doin'? Where is she?"

Euan startled me. He looked around as if Alicia was playing hide and seek.

"Do you still have your knife?"

He lifted it so I could see it gleam.

"Hide it and come with me."

"Why? What's happening?"

"I may be making a mistake, but if I am, I need you with me."

"'kay."

He waited for more, but when I stared marching in the opposite direction he wanted me to go in, he called out.

"What's 'appenin' Adam?"

"We're going to talk with them. Make them an offer."

"What offer?"

But I didn't answer, I wanted to think about what I would say. I still couldn't get out of my head the picture of Dillon and his cronies waving scythes at me.

Dillon and Long Nose Luke stood to my right. Mandy, Alicia and the two eight year old twins, (Tilly and Milly), to my left. Euan was on my right.

"So, this is the deal."

"What deal?"

I looked at Alicia.

"Please listen to him Dillon. He was captured by Clearers and he has a safe place to go to now."

"But I dun't see any food and some'ow 'e found 'is way in."

His accent sounded more like Alex's now. Before it had been barely understandable.

He glared at Alicia as if it was her fault, but in his half asleep, the red line down his face smeared into black dust. He was trying to be tough in front of me, but after all I'd been through, it didn't affect me. I was surprised a little, but also pleased.

"I have an offer. You take it or leave it, I don't care which, but know that whatever you decide, in five minutes I'm walking out of here."

"Go on! We'll 'ear yer owt."

"I can take you to a safe place with food and a place to sleep, but it's run with rules by adults...."

As a sudden afterthought, I added.

"...and you'll have to leave your knives behind."

I didn't want to go anywhere with them if they had those scythes.

"Forget it!"

Euan stepped forward. I was glad to have him at my back, even though no one was playing with their blades at the moment.

"Let's go."

"No, wait. Listen everyone, please!"

Alicia was pleading again.

"On our way, I'm in charge. What I say, goes. Do you understand?"

The Mantis speaks again!

"Why should we trust yer?"

Long-nose Luke piped up.

"You don't need to at all. I don't trust you..... I'm going. I've made you an offer. Now it's up to you lot. Stay here and rot, with no food, no air and danger, or come to safety with us."

"Us?"

Alicia interrupted.

"There are nine of them, including Adam."

I heard some gasps, though in the dark it was difficult to see their faces and gestures.

"Is there doctors...medicine?"

Mandy was talking.

"Yes."

"Milly 'n' Tilly are ill. They need food 'n' medicine. I can't 'elp 'em."

"They can come, but we also have sick kids that need carrying. So, two of you must carry them."

"I'll come."

Mandy was the first.

"I'll carry one of them."

I could see Alicia smiling; her teeth still sparkled in the dark cave.

"You won't be able to Lissy, but I'll help."

There was silence whilst the brothers stared at each other.

"We 'cun always leave if we 'ate it....'n' maybe we'll get sum food."

Dillon looked at his brother. Long-Nose was quiet.

"But we said we'd never 'ave adults rulin' us 'gin."

Instead of answering his brother's question, Dillon looked at me.

"'Ow long 'ave yer lived there?"

"Since I was eight."

That was enough chat.

"Right. You do what you like. I'm going."

I turned, Euan walked beside me. I half expected to be attacked from behind, but didn't look back. Alicia caught up quickly. She grasped my hand and squeezed it tightly. I quickly pulled away embarrassed.

"Thank you."

"Their choice Lissy."

"Yes, yes, I know, but thanks anyway."

I could hear Milly and Tilly behind me. Their steps were shorter and they were whispering to Mandy. She shushed them and made them hurry to catch up.

The first thing I did on seeing our group huddled against a far wall was untie Jamie and take him over to Oliver, who was now leant up against a jutting out piece of rock. Mandy followed me, her two charges in tow. The others looked at me. Alex was about to say something, but Euan silenced him.

"It's okay. We're takin' a few extras wiv' us."

"We are?"

"Yeah! The kids are sick, like Lacie."

"Our boss 'as decided."

"I'm not your boss!"

I responded hastily, irritated with the comment, as if suddenly I was one of the gaoler-carers telling them all what to do. No one said anything. I'd probably reacted too harshly –

Euan could have been teasing I suppose – but at that point I didn't care. Lissy had annoyed me and now Euan's comment annoyed me.

I sighed and let it pass, tried to be calmer. We were nearly home and I should feel happy, but all I felt was more anxious, a painful tingling in my bones. Just when I thought we'd be home, something else stepped in to stop it. I had the urge to turn and run, leaving them all behind, but I didn't. Instead, I just looked at Euan and smiled an apology of sorts and moved on.

After the darkness from the cave, the moonlight shining in the entrance seemed like a light bulb. I crouched in front of Oliver.

"We're going to let you go."

The anger in his eyes was still present. I didn't blame him.

"I'm sorry we had to do this to you, but it was only to find Lissy. We weren't going to hurt you really."

Lissy was crouching on the other side and couldn't help contributing.

"Oliver, don't be mad. Adam's a good person. He's offered to take us all to his home."

She leant over and untied the sock.

"What? I'm not goin' wiv' 'im."

He was struggling and spitting like a dog on a tight leash trying to escape.

"That's your choice, but we're taking Jamie."

"Yer can't, 'e's my bruvver."

This boy was stupid, although I doubt I'd have trusted me if I'd been tied up like him for nearly an hour.

"He needs food and warmth or he will die. Is that what you want."

"I'll protect 'm Oliver."

"Yer goin' wiv' 'em Mandy?"

"I'm takin' Milly 'n' Tilly. They need a doctor."

Her voice was hoarse as if she were trying to stop tears, causing me to look at her. If she washed off the dirt, she might only be about thirteen. I'd thought her older before.

314

"Oliver, 'e gave me an'egg...an 'ole egg to m'self."

Oliver stared at his little brother.

"Yeah, fer betrayin' us."

The words were like a slap in the face. His eyes crinkled up as if he was going to cry and he hid behind Mandy, but the condemning brother continued.

"Look what 'e did to me Jamie."

As we had yet to untie Oliver's hands, he was struggling again.

"Yer not goin' 'n' that's my final word."

I stood up.

"Let's go."

"What 'bout Oliver and Jamie?"

Mandy asked.

"Not about to have him chasing me. Jamie or one of the others can untie him."

"No, Jamie needs to come. I'm bringin' 'im."

I looked at her determined face as she stared at me.

"You sort it out then. You have two minutes and we leave."

I walked away, leaving Alicia and her pact brothers and sisters alone. Briefly explaining what had happened to my friends, I listened to their reactions.

"More to feed?"

"Told you, we're nearly there."

"Can we trust 'em?"

"Not sure!"

"Why are we takin' 'em then?"

"They need help."

"What if yer place wun't take us all, 'oo will yer chose?"

There were some sounds of general agreement.

"It's a big place...lots of people."

I was really worried they wouldn't take any of them.

"Right, let's move out. We need to be there before it gets light."

"It's four forty-five."

The timekeeper Euan reported.

"When's sunrise?"

"'bout 'arf an 'our, maybe forty-five minutes."

"Let's go then."

Lacie, Josie and Molly were asleep on the cold, hard floor. They were using the almost empty bags as pillow. Sid automatically picked up Lacie. Alex had to coach a sleepy Josie onto his back and Jas did the same for Mol. The rest of us picked up the left over bags.

I looked over my shoulder at Alicia.

"Are any of you coming?"

A noise and then a voice came out of the dark.

"We're all comin'."

Dillon and his brother were striding up.

"Oliver, get up, stop arguin'."

"But Dillon?"

"Do as I say or yer'll be left 'lone."

I waited, standing my ground.

"Drop all your weapons."

"What?"

Oliver was furious.

"You don't come with any blades or scythes."

He looked at Dillon.

"We'll 'ide 'em in the corner. If we 'ate the place, we'll come back."

Oliver looked at me.

"Do yer lot 'ave blades?"

"Yes, but only as far as the entrance."

Then it was my groups turn to react.

"What?"

"Yer never told us this."

I sighed, my brows furrowing. I just wanted to get home. Fed up, I raised my voice.

"What did you all expect? Would you let unknown people into your safe place with weapons?"

They were quiet for a moment. Elliott doing his usual fidgeting, Euan crossing his arms, Alex glaring. I'd had enough. My own group were reacting as if I was the enemy suddenly.

"Look, all of you. Do as you like. I'm going home. I want to at least have a good meal on my birthday!"

I dropped the bag I'd picked up, (thinking if they didn't come they might need the food in it), and strode away.

Chapter 44

Euan was the first to reach me, my little shadow protector. He said nothing, just kept pace with me as I walked. Elliott caught up shortly after.

Within a few minutes I heard Jas.

"Adam, yer 'aint gunna lose us that easy!"

I smiled and slowed down a little. Several of them were carrying the sick kids.

"Well, yer can't blame 'im for tryin'."

They all laughed, even I grinned and turned round. They were all there, struggling with kids, bags or just their own heavy and tired bodies as we trod through the long grass. The sun had begun to rise and for the first time I could see clearly what I was dragging in to the Downers.

To start with, everyone was filthy black, our faces, hair, clothes, nothing shone through, just dirt. We looked like coal miners leaving a nightshift. Molly, Lacie, Josie and the twins were fast asleep, either in someone's arms or on backs, their heads drooping across chests and shoulders. We all walked with weariness in our bones, or at least they did. I'm not sure how I looked, but I felt how they looked. Tired and worn out. Desperate to just lie down and sleep. Yet deep inside me, there was a tingling, excited feeling. I was ten minutes from home.

On the whole, the kids from the mine shaft stayed behind my group, though Jamie was happy to walk ahead, away from his brother. I had a feeling Oliver wasn't very kind to him. I needed to rectify that once we were home. I was surprised to see Long-Nose Luke carrying one of the twins, Mandy had the other.

'Home' – the very word thrilled me. I imagined my Mam would still be asleep. She was an early riser though, so she might be out of bed by the time I arrived - having her breakfast cup of sweet, milky coffee to wake her up.

Suddenly, Elliott began singing, shaking me from my thoughts.

"Happy Birthday to you."

I stopped, looking over at him.

"Seriously Elliot!"

He sang really badly, his voice creaky, the effort great. It was a really old song, one my mother sang to me when I was a little kid. He ignored me and continued.

"Happy Birthday to you."

Some others joined in. I turned around unbelievingly. After all we'd been through; they still had the energy to croak out this old tune.

"Happy Birthday dear Addaam."

Alicia was giggling. I could feel my face getting hotter and hotter with embarrassment. I was too old for the birthday song, but they finished it off anyway.

"Happy Birthday to you."

And then even worse, Lissy shouted.

"Hip-hip hooray. Hip-hip hooray. Hip-hip hooray."

With the exception of Oliver, Dillon and Long-Nose, who just looked confused, they all laughed out loudly, giggling and guffawing like crazy creatures from another planet. I looked at them and grinned. I was bringing a little mob of madness with me, but I was happy to be with them. I bowed as if I were performing an act of some kind.

"Well, thank you kind ladies and gentlemen!"

"'ow big are yer then?"

I knew Euan meant how old, but chose to avoid the answer.

"Oh, as big as you, plus a head!"

As he snorted, I turned, my heart lighter and my determination greater. They had to let them in.

"'ow far Adam. Mol is getting' 'eavy."

"About five minutes."

"Which way?"

"See that over there?"

It was already getting light, but we were nearly there.

"Yeah, what is it?"

"It's an old solar farm set up by the local government years ago."

It still glistened in the morning light.

"Solar farm?"

Euan interrupted me.

"That's 'ow the cities get their electricity, 'ain't it?"

Alex exclaimed.

"But it's 'uge....goes on forever!"

Jasmine asked.

"'ow does it work?"

"From the sun. Rays shine down and it sort of collects them and turns them into electricity."

"Really?"

"Yes, but the government closed this down before I was born."

I turned round and smiled at Jas, who sounded shocked.

"Yeah, but it 'ain't fer us, it's fer the rich 'uns."

Euan added irritably.

"I seen it b'fore in the city."

No one said anything. Perhaps that was were Euan came from. The city generally referred to London, though I'd never been there.

"Anyway, we're going to the woods to the left of it."

Chapter 45

"A drainage pipe?"

"Yes, a drainage pipe."

"You live in a drainage pipe under this solar thing?"

"Sort of...this is just the entrance."

We were walking into a large, disused pipe that ran at a slope into the ground. The gradient was no more than a gentle downwards hill, but the pipe was big enough to get a tractor down it.

I went in a few steps and turned round. The light outside was now white against the hole of the entrance. It smelt of murky water, tadpoles and fish, although I'd never found any water bound animals living in it. As I looked back, they were all in silhouette against the sky. We all stopped and I faced them, speaking with what I hoped was authority in my voice.

"This is your last chance to change your minds."

I said that mainly for the benefit of Dillon, Oliver and Long-Nose, who were grumpily bringing up the rear. No one said anything.

"At the end of this pipe is the first entrance."

"You live in a pipe?"

Sid asked again.

"Nope!"

I continued.

"There you will have to leave any weapons you have on you."

Euan and Alex were the most uncomfortable, apart from the three un-wise monkeys at the back.

"You will only be allowed to go further, once I've checked you haven't got anything on you. If you can't do that, you might as well turn round now."

I waited and watched. Some grunted, Euan avoided eye contact, Jas hiked Molly higher on her back, but otherwise, no one moved. They just stared at me, waiting to be led into a pipe. I was nervous for them, but excited as well. They didn't know what was coming. They'd be so happy once they knew. I wanted to say 'trust me', but it wouldn't make any difference. Most of them hadn't trusted anyone for a long time. They were exhausted and just putting one foot in front of another was hard. The last bit of energy was on the hope that I knew what I was doing. They had nowhere else to go.

I started walking forward again, switching on my torch at full beam. Those that had torches copied me. Shadows bounced off the pipe from behind me. My own shadow elongated like a stretched being, extending down the pipe I knew so well. I was always happy to walk down it, knowing I was going home to safety, but now I was delirious. I thought of my Mam, knew how amazed she'd be when I walked in. But they couldn't share my delight, they were afraid right now; they'd be okay, once we got there – I hoped.

The echoes of shuffling feet kept us company as we reached the end of the pipe. If it wasn't for the torches, we'd have been enveloped in darkness, unable to see in front of us.

"Where now?"

Elliott asked looking round.

"First we drop every weapon."

I threw the knife I had in my pocket against the back of the wall, were it disappeared into darkness. Elliott did the same.

"Come here Elliott."

He stood in front of me, fingers fiddling with each other again, biting his bottom lip.

"Don't worry, I'm only checking you. Once you're cleared, you stand behind me. Got it?"

He nodded.

"Lift your arms."

I patted him down as if I were a policeman, along his arms, down his sides and along his legs and feet.

I knew Elliott wouldn't have anything, but I wanted the others to see what would happen.

"Good. You're free to go on."

I turned to look at the rest of them.

"I don't have anything Adam."

Alicia stood in front of me, her arms spread out. She grinned at me as if I were her confidential friend, or worse, girl-friend. I wasn't, I hadn't even seen her for years, but I was determined to treat the girls the same way as the boys. No exceptions! I tried not to pat too hard in the wrong places, but was still embarrassed and flushed hot. I had to remind myself how terrible it would be to take danger into the Downers. They'd never trust me again.

Just thinking about the Downers made me feel strange, as if that life had been so long ago, a life I wasn't sure was me anymore. I felt odd and struggled against it. Of course it was me. It was my home.

Jasmine flung a knife to the back of the cave and came forward with Molly, who hadn't even been disturbed by all the clashing of metal against rock.

"Go on then!"

Somehow she managed to balance Molly and still lift up her arms. They both passed, as did Sid, Lacie and Jamie, whose eyes could barely stay open.

"Alex, Euan?"

I looked at them.

"Not until they 'ave. I dun't trust 'em."

Euan added.

"Me, too!"

Oliver's voice was deeper and echoed loudly.

"'Ow do we know if we can trust yer. This might be a trap."

"Fine. Leave."

Dillon pushed him forward and then Long-Nose Luke, his brother."

Oliver had nothing. I'd forgotten we'd taken his scythe off him. The rest of them were supposed to have left their weapons in the cave, but Luke had a scythe and two shorter blades down the sides of his torn boots. Dillon also had a scythe, which clanged as he angrily dashed it against the bottom of the wall in the darkness. He walked forward as if he were in charge.

"Get it over wiv' and I'm tellin' yer, if there 'aint food at t'end of this, am gunna murder yer wiv' my own 'ands."

"Yeah, right!"

I was in my own territory now and didn't feel afraid at all. I wondered why I'd been scared of him before. As I patted him down, I could feel his bones sticking out of his thin skin. I could have knocked him over....and knew there was no way he could have frightened me, had it not been for the red stripes and slight issue of the sharp scythes!!

Alex stood forward next and then, with everyone behind me, Euan faced me.

"Are yer sure 'bout this?"

"I am."

"This ain't a trap, or 'owt?"

"After everything we've been through, do you think I'd do that to you?"

The cave was full of silent breathing, all listening to what we were saying.

"Yer a good 'un Adam. I'd trust yer wiv' my life, but what about those inside, can I trust my life to 'em?"

For a nine year old, he was a clever boy. He had doubts as did I, but not for the same reasons. Once they were accepted, I was sure they'd be okay. It was just the acceptance part.

I held my breath, staring him straight into his dark eyes as he held onto the scythe we'd stolen, not really wanting to let it go.

"I promise you, I won't let anything happen to you."

He looked at me for a second longer, before throwing the scythe and three other knives, (I didn't know he had), in the corner one after the other as fast as he could, as if to do it before he changed his mind.

I patted him down and led them all through into the next section.

Chapter 46

Unless you knew were to go exactly, the next section could easily be missed. There was a wall jutting out, that looked like it was the end of the pipe, as if the pipe had been filled in with bricks. I knew what they were thinking as we were coming up to it, that it was a dead end. I remembered my amazement on the first night I'd been brought down here. My Uncle Mark guided us. He'd done the same 'weapons' thing, in the same place, so that's how I knew what to do, but at the dead end I'd thought he'd gone the wrong way. Then, somehow, he's disappeared behind it, as if he'd walked through a wall.

I did the same and listened to the gasps, as I peeped out, smiling.

"It isn't a dead end. It's an optical illusion."

"Opti-what?"

Elliot asked.

"I mean, you can't see it unless you are up close, and even then it's difficult to spot."

As they came through, they marvelled at the way the wall had been built at an angle, allowing a body to slip behind it, though looking from the front as if it was cemented to the side of the pipe.

"That's brilliant!"

Lissy spoke for everyone. They grinned and smiled as they came through, struggling with bags and kids. We had to pass sleeping children between us through the narrow gap, as if they were sandbags in a flood being passed along. They were really a dead weight, but no one complained. It was at this point, I noticed Jamie again, barely able to stay awake on his feet.

"Oliver, can you carry Jamie for a while please?"

I decided to take charge as he didn't seem to care.

"Nope! 'e needs to toughen up. 'e's a weaklin'."

"You're wrong. He's an eight year old boy, who's been awake all night and is weak. Carry him."

"Yer can't tell me what to do."

"I can. I'm in charge, remember. Do it!"

I used a voice that I remembered my Dad using. It was the 'or else' tone that I hated when I was younger. Not sure how it popped out.

Everyone stared at Oliver. Eventually, Dillon spoke.

"'e's right Oliver. 'e's your bruvver and 'e's delayin' us. Carry 'im."

I didn't like that Dillon had to repeat my order, but nodded at him to show appreciation for the support. Oliver huffed, but slung Jamie on his back.

"'old on weakling. If yer fall, am not catchin' yer."

The next section was totally underground, the earth piled in around it. Standing still, the only sound was our breathing and the echoing of our whispers. Moving sounded like an elephant herd moving across a hard, barren wasteland.

"'ow far Adam?"

"We're going to rest at the end of this tunnel."

It wasn't an answer, but they were all too tired to question it. I thought it better not to tell them my plan until we sat down. It only took around three minutes anyway. Everyone immediately slunk to the ground, dropping bags and burdens. The younger kids didn't even wake up. Whether it was hard ground or someone's back, they'd given up on trying to stay awake.

"How's Lacie?"

I asked Alex, and then remembered the twins were ill too.

"And Tilly and Milly?"

Alex looked away, his torch falling to the floor. His face saying it all. He'd been very quiet most of the way and now I knew why. He didn't think Lacie was going to make it. I needed to get help fast.

"The girls are weak."

Mandy answered.

"..but not as bad as Lacie."

She looked over at Luke and then at Alex sadly.

"Right!"

"What now?"

Euan asked.

"I have to leave you for a while."

"What?"

I saw them all straighten their bent backs, staring at me as I knelt before them.

"This is not a trick - just a security procedure. Everything will be okay. I just need to get you passes to come in."

I hoped!

"Yer can't leave us 'ere. Yer promised."

Euan sounded as if I'd betrayed him.

"I won't. I'll be twenty minutes. I won't leave you.....look why don't you share the rest of the food and water."

I took out the bit of bread and the biscuits I still had in my pocket and gave it to Alex.

"By the time you finish, I'll be back."

"Are you sure you're coming back?"

Elliott asked.

"Can't you take me with you?"

Alicia spoke as if she was a special friend that could have an exception.

"No, all of you need permission. I did when I first came. This is just routine."

I didn't like to mention my mother and I already had permission before coming in. My Uncle Mark had arranged the approval in advance. New people did come into the Downers, I just wasn't sure of the procedure.

I stood up to go. Euan pulled me over away from the others. They all stared wondering what was going on. So did I? Euan whispered.

"In this safe place of yer's."

"Yes?"

"Is all the rich 'uns kept young?"

I looked at him for a moment. I knew what he was talking about. My teacher had told me as part of my apprenticeship in science. In London, older people took Telemar drugs to keep themselves from aging. The discovery had been made years ago using something called 'Tiron' which reduced pollutants in the body and mended the skin. Since then, tons of companies had discovered and produced more.

"No, we don't use drugs to keep ourselves young."

I wasn't sure what frightened him about it, although I did know only the rich could afford the drug. Poorer people just grew old naturally. For the second time, it crossed my mind that Euan must have come from London, but I was too pre-occupied to give it much thought.

"'Kay, that's good."

"Anything else?"

"Nah!"

He seemed a bit embarrassed, so I walked back to the others.

"I'll be back very soon."

And then I left them to share out/argue about the last bits of food between sixteen kids. Sixteen kids! What was I thinking about?

Chapter 47

The way in was ingrained in my mind. So much so, I usually went in without even thinking about it, but this time it all meant so much more. I slipped to the right, knowing Euan was watching me; he always watched and I needed to make sure he didn't follow. It would be impossible to find the way unless you knew and I couldn't risk him getting lost. Although my torch was small, the beam was strong. I shone it back one last time and mouthed 'Stay here', pushing down with my hand as if I were patting a seat. He was close and could see quite clearly what I was saying. He shrugged and sat down with the others.

From where we were, it just looked like the pipe bent to the right, but on turning the corner, there were five possible ways to go as the larger drain split into further smaller tunnels. From each, there were many other directions, but all led away from the Downers.

I knew I had to take the second from the right, then the first on the right and then the first on the right once more. If a person, by chance, had taken the right direction, they ended up in what looked like a small, damp cave. I'd been in enough caves to know this looked and smelt like the real thing. I shone my torch around. The fungus was almost luminescent down here.

"Nothing's changed."

I whispered to myself, smiling. I wanted to rush in and shout out I was back. Run home and see my mother's face, but before I could, I needed to find our leader. I knew where he lived and would go straight there. It was early, but he should be up.

Anyone looking wouldn't find it unless they knew exactly where to place their fingers. I slipped mine into a crack, just big enough for a hand, pulled back on an internal leaver - cold and metallic, and watched as the door slid open, grating slightly.

I passed through quickly. It automatically closed after three seconds. My head started planning how I'd have to stay on the other side opening the door for the kids several times to get them through.

I was now on a narrow shelf that ran vertically around the inside of a gigantic cavern. I knew it did 'cos I'd had a tour and seen it lit up, but now, in the dark, I could only see the path in front of me. Looking over the half a metre shelf was an endless pit, except I also knew it wasn't. Below me was our city, a city of light that was hidden by technology. It was not only a clever invention, but truly amazing. But it was not just for fun, it was a good way to secure the place. If someone, by chance, found their way in, they would only see darkness below them. As if they'd walked into an underground cavern. What they were actually seeing was a holographic projection that not only convinced the eyes there was nothing there, but silenced any sound. It was like a grid over the top of our magnificent city. Only when the lights were turned on, and the holographic image was switched off, could the city be seen.

I remembered how I'd felt when I'd first realised my eyes were deceiving me. I thought it was a trick at first, but when I eventually accepted it wasn't, I just stood and stared for ages. It was then that I'd decided I wanted to work with whoever built it. I wanted to know how it was done and be able to create stuff like it. That's why I loved my apprenticeship; I got to do stuff like this.

I couldn't wait to show the others, I knew they'd be really stunned. I wanted to be there to watch their faces when they saw the city light up below. But first I had to get them in! Suddenly, I missed my easy life, my mother and my friends. These new friends I'd made seemed like a burden for a moment, but I shook it off and moved forward.

Right now, the whole area was on 'secure' mode, but I knew the way in. That's not to say the shelf wasn't dangerous. Slipping off it would kill you as you plummeted through the image into whatever was below – a building or home, or possibly even a person. And so I stepped carefully, shining the beam ahead of me along the path.

It wasn't far, just up the slope and down the other side. Then there were two paths; one led upwards, widening out, leading to a pipe and the way out, (or round in circles if you lost your way). The other led downwards to a narrower path that suddenly crumbled away and made you turn back.

I took the downwards path. It was another 'trick' image that kept the curious trekker at bay. As I stepped over the crumbled path, I had to overcome my own doubts and fears. I knew there was really a path beyond it, but it felt so real.

But what if it was real now? What if something had happened since I'd been away?

I pushed my toe through the holographic image, feeling the buzz of the barrier as I did and the strange, contradictory knowledge that although my foot looked like it was floating in mid-air, it was actually on solid ground. I also knew once I'd crossed over, I couldn't be seen from this side.

I stepped through. I was home!

I knew security would have been alerted that someone had come through the barrier, but, as the barrier also scanned my genes at the same time, which would register 'citizen', they would let me pass. Although, I would probably also be registered as 'missing' by now. My Uncle Mark had gone missing, no one could find his tracker, no one knew where he was. That was when I was nine and a half. My mother had been devastated, but we still hoped he would come back. He was an electrician and had taught me a bit about electricity in his spare time. I wondered if security would alert my mother that I was back.

I only had a few steps and then I took the lift down about one hundred metres. The lift was made of glass for both security and delight. From outside, anyone could see who was coming. From inside, I could see the expanse of the underground city, which had grown to five times its original size over the ten years it had been here.

I looked out smiling. This was my home. Although deep inside the ground, the area was lit up with reflector panels which stood high above the buildings. The reflector panels were linked to the solar panels above us. All our electricity came from the panels free of charge - no one knew we were linked up to it. The reflector panels had five settings, from bright to dim. They gradually changed throughout the day, moving us from morning to afternoon, and evening to night.

There's an old football pitch in town – not far from the central part of town. My Mam said that years ago thousands used to go and watch football there, but the club ran out of money and stopped playing. The pitch is still there, over-grown and full of rubble. Some of the seats have been stolen and the wood has been taken to make into other things, but the lights still remain. They're so high no one has been able to reach them to take them down and so they just stand alone - witnesses to a history not many remember. Our reflector panels look a bit like these old lights, only ours our more technological.

The whole of the layout and how we use energy is organised down to the tiniest detail. There are too many of us to waste anything. Space is distributed based on family members, so my Mam and I have a two-bedroomed house allocated to us. The houses are really made from the rock itself, either dug out or built up with large stones. They are on the right-side, grouped together. That's where I'm heading. The Leader, Alan, along with the committee, decides who is permitted to stay and who cannot. I want to get to him first before anyone else informs him of all the kids lurking outside.

The lift stops and I climb out. It's quiet, no one's around. I turn the corner to the right, feeling the buzz as I walk through yet another security barrier. It will register me again. I'm looking down, thinking about what I will say to convince Alan, our leader, head scientist and my boss, to let them in, when I see several pairs of feet in front of me. I look up. Standing in front of me with Alan are three security guards. They wear the usual clothes; tunics and pants, with their job insignia strip sewn onto their top right-hand side pocket.

Alan has pulled a coat over his pyjamas, although he is wearing shoes. He stands in front of me and even after all the planning in my head, I don't know what to say. He's obviously only just got up. His grey hair, usually tidy, is sticking up and his chin is unshaven. His arms are crossed as if he's angry or something.

I just stare at his green eyes and all I want to do is cry. I don't know why, I'm safe at last, I should be happy, but my stomach is burning, my chest is heaving. Salty saliva is building up in my mouth as if I'm going to be sick. My mind is blank and I don't know what to say.

"Adam."

I hear my name, though his lips don't move.

"Adam."

Again, her voice. And then the guards and Alan are being pushed aside and there she stands. My mother is in tears. Her long hair un-brushed and messy from just getting up. Her blue coat flares open, showing her white nightie beneath as she flings herself at me and pulls me close. I almost fall over, but she grasps me, crying and laughing at the same time.

"It's you. Really you!"

So many questions.....

She pulls back, but still holds on to me.

"You're in trouble, young man, and you're filthy. Where have you been?"

But she doesn't give me a chance to say anything as she holds on tight again, as if I'm not real and I'll drift away like a spirit in the night. I too hold on tight and breathe in the smell of my Mam, slightly sweaty from running through the streets to me. Tears are falling down her cheeks and I realise mine are wet too. I try to control them, but my chest is heaving, the relief of being safe suddenly pouring out of me. I am just a child again and willingly let her cling to me for a while. Eventually, I feel a bit saner and a lot embarrassed. I wipe the remainder of my tears on my mother, knowing her clean clothes will be black, but not caring. I am home.

Alan interrupts.

"Amy."

He is trying to be kind, doing a lot of harrumphing, but my mother doesn't hear.

"Amy."

I have to push her away and face Alan. I feel like a baby crying in front of my boss, and wipe my face to make sure my face is dry. It probably has streaks down it, but I don't care. I know what he's going to say, he has a security tablet in his hand; he can see the kids outside, but my mother asks before he has a chance to speak.

"Adam, what happened? What have you been doing all this time?"

My mother can't help interrupting again.

"What happened? Why didn't you come back? We tried to find you. Did you lose your tracker?"

I look at her, then at Alan's serious face. He sent me out on a mission, I had a task to do, but I didn't collect the stuff I was supposed to. Well I did, but I didn't have it anymore. Dillon probably did, maybe I could get it back to prove I'd done my job.

My heart is pounding. They need permission to come in and I'm afraid the committee won't let them. I don't know why, but what I say next just pops out of my mouth as if I haven't been planning what to say the whole way, as if I have no control of what I'm thinking.

"I've been collecting."

She looks confused. Alan laughs out loudly tapping the screen in front of him with his forefinger.

"I think we'd better have a chat about what you've collected."

Chapter 48

"Alan, we can't just chat. Lacie's dying and little kids are starving."

My Mam responded.

"Kids dying? What are you talking about?"

"Kids that came with me from the home and the mine shaft."

"What home? What mine-shaft?"

"It's a long story Mam. Can we just help them first?"

"Of course we can help them...can't we Alan?"

Alan had said nothing. He was looking at us both.

"Are you talking about one of the Non-Contributor's Homes, that's where you've been all this time?"

"Yes."

I emphasised the word, flapping my arms in frustration. I'd told them twenty minutes. I needed to get back.

"I think Lacie's dying Alan. Can't we just help them first?"

He hesitated.

"There are protocols for allowing people in."

"Alan..."

My mother stood by me, staring him down, her voice sounded as if she were telling off a child. Had the situation not been so serious, I'd have laughed.

"These are kids that are dying and starving. Is this what we're about? Letting children die whilst we decide what to do! I thought the Downers were different."

My mother's voice had taken on an edge, but I was proud of her for sticking up for my friends. She had her face stuck out, like she was a bull threatening to attack.

"Aren't we about helping those who are desperate... who come to us for help...who need a place to stay?"

Alan looked away for a moment, thinking about what my mother had said and his dilemma of keeping the place secure. Then he looked down at his security screen.

"How old are they?"

"There are six kids under nine. The rest are between ten and fourteen I think."

"So, not yet adults."

"No, but a couple could be older, I'm not sure really."

"You said some were from a mine shaft."

"It's only ten minutes from here."

"Yes, we know of it. I didn't know kids were living there."

"They weren't. They're dying there."

I knew it sounded dramatic, but I wanted to hit home about the dying part.

He was still hesitating.

"Did you tell them the rules Adam? Are they willing to live by them?"

"No."

I looked down, feeling a little like Elliott as I twiddled my thumbs.

"We were escaping and running, trying to get here. I didn't have the time."

I turned to my mother.

"Alicia's one of them."

For a moment she looked at me as if the name didn't register.

"Little Lissy?"

"Yes. Her parents have gone and she was put in a home."

"Oh dear God! Poor child!"

She seemed to be calculating something.

"We can take her in Alan. I'm sure others would be willing to take an extra child as well."

There was silence as we both looked at our leader, pleading for the right decision. He made it suddenly. Turning to the security guards, he said.

"Matt, go wake Doctor Sahid and ask him to come to the outside cave. Explain the situation and tell him to bring medicine for viruses, colds, headaches and fevers as a minimum, and anything else he might think of. Also bring plenty of blankets, hot soup if possible and those rehydration drinks we have. Have you got that?"

"Yes sir."

He turned to go.

"Oh and Matt..."

"Yes sir!"

"I expect you and your crew at the cave with the food, drink and blankets within fifteen minutes. I'll call Ahmed and inform him of our needs and that you will collect them shortly."

The guard nodded and turned away.

Using his tablet, Alan called our Stores Manager, Ahmed, briefly explaining the situation and what was required, then he turned to me.

"Well, Adam..."

I was grinning from ear to ear.

"...do you think your friends will mind meeting me in pyjamas?"

I laughed.

"Do you have a torch?"

"Yes."

"Then would you please lead the way?"

"I'll come too."

My mother was buttoning her coat. Alan did the same.

"Thank you!"

"Don't thank me yet. They still have to agree to our rules."

I pulled a face.

"Everyone has to swear to them, before they come in Adam. You know that!"

"But…"

"No buts, let's get there quickly. If it's as you say, and I don't doubt it is, they need our help now."

There was nothing I could say, so I spun on my aching, plimsolled feet and headed for the lift. We passed through the barriers and round the cavern quickly. All the time I was thinking about who might and who might not agree to our rules. I figured the younger kids and those attached to them, like Alex to Lacie and Josie, Jasmine to Molly and Mandy to the twins, wouldn't have a problem. With Alan there, I knew Oliver wouldn't have a say about Jamie, which I was pleased about. Elliot and Alicia would agree too, I was sure of it. Who would that leave? Euan! I wasn't sure he could adapt. I hoped he could, I liked him for all his toughness, but he didn't trust easily. He'd had a difficult past, I was sure of it. Sid was also an unknown, but not so much as Dillon, Luke and Oliver. Had I left anyone out? There were so many and I was outrageously tired, I could have left someone out. I started counting names again. All I could hear behind me were shuffling footsteps. We didn't talk in the dark, preferring to concentrate on not slipping off the ledge.

We all stepped through the door with the secret handle quickly, whilst it was wide open and before it automatically closed. Within seconds we'd turned the corner and there they were, slumped on the floor, bodies hanging, shoulders rounded, little kids leaning, eyelids closed. Jas had lit the last two candles and put them in the middle of the group, although they were almost burnt down. I had a second to see them before they noticed me. Surely, Alan wouldn't refuse anyone just for a few oaths.

Alicia was the only one who jumped up when she saw my mother.

"Amy...Amy!"

The others just stared, not sure who I'd brought back. Seeing the skinny, short-haired, dirty girl racing towards her, didn't stop my Mam holding out her arms and welcoming her.

"Lissy...oh Lissy. You poor girl."

Lissy was crying as she crushed herself into my mother. They had once got on really well, I remembered. Lissy's sobbing echoed off the walls for a while. My mother stroked her hair, trying to comfort her.

"It'll be okay Lissy. You'll be fine. Don't worry now you're here."

With the exception of Lacie, the other little kids were waking up, wondering with sleepy eyes where they were and who the adults were. Not sure if they were going to be hurt, they huddled behind their own protector.

Alan knelt down in front of them. He was a tall man and could be very frightening, especially at the moment in the dark cave. Euan spoke.

"Adam, what's goin' on?"

I sat down as well, crossing my legs. Lissy had stopped crying, but was clinging on to my mother as if she might disappear at any minute. My mother didn't seem to mind.

"This is Alan and this is my mother. They have come to meet you all."

I could see them all staring at my mother hugging Lissy and almost felt guilty. Their mothers had disappeared years ago. Alex could barely speak up, his voice hoarse with fear for his sister.

"Lacie Adam!"

Alan answered.

"A doctor is on his way as is food and blankets."

No one said anything. They weren't sure how to react to adults being kind, so they just stared with blank faces. I looked at Alan. I didn't know what to say either.

"Why don't you introduce your friends Adam."

He was trying to be encouraging. At least he wasn't going straight into rules bit.

"Okay…."

I wondered how to do this.

"This is Elliott."

I vaguely pointed in his direction.

"I met him first. He showed me how to survive in the home."

Elliott smiled wanly and nodded.

"That's Alex. I met him next with his sisters Lacie and Josie. He fed me biscuits when I was starving."

The memory of it brought tears to my eyes. I couldn't help it. It had meant so much to me at the time. I rubbed my eyes and yawned. I was tired. We were all tired so hopefully they wouldn't notice.

"I thought Jas was an ogre at first, but she turned out to be kind and generous."

Jasmine was embarrassed, I could tell. She looked away.

"And that's Molly leaning on her."

"Sid…"

I stopped for a second and looked at Alan.

"If it hadn't been for Sid's driving and thinking ahead, we'd never have got here."

At each person, Alan nodded, but said nothing.

I looked round, coming to Mandy, Tilly and Milly introducing them as the kids from the mine shaft. I did the same with Oliver, Jamie, Dillon and Luke, although I neglected to tell Alan how they'd treated me and Lissy and how I'd ended up at the home in the first place. I wanted them to have a chance.

My mother said.

"This is Lissy. She was Adam's old school friend. I don't know how they found each other."

"Adam found me on the street."

Lissy answered, looking up at my Mam as if she were her saviour.

I looked at Euan. He'd stood up and was leaning against a wall, separating himself from everyone again. His arms were crossed as if he needed protection. I was about to say something, but he interrupted, frowning.

"I'm Euan. Yer've said sum really nice things 'bout everyone Adam, even those that dun't deserve it."

He glared at Dillon's group.

"But I wunna say summit."

He took a breath and looked around. I was afraid he was going to spoil it. I wanted Alan to have a good impression of everyone.

"Adam took me wiv 'im 'n' 'e dint even know me. If it 'adn't bin fer Adam, none of us would be 'ere now. We'd still be at the 'ome, bein' beaten and starved to death."

Everyone was nodding their heads, agreeing with him. I felt the soft pressure of my mother's hand on my shoulder for a moment. Quiet praise for her son! Under the dirt, my face was heating up. I wasn't good at compliments, but Euan hadn't finished.

"You.."

He pointed at Dillon, Oliver and Luke.

"Dun't know 'ow lucky yer are to be 'ere."

He stopped for a moment.

"I'd 'ave left yer behind."

I felt Alan look at me and raise his eyebrow, which I knew meant 'we need to talk'. I'd seen it many times before. I shrugged, but just said.

"That's the introductions done."

"Good. Now, I need to know who are the urgent cases for the doctor."

A chorus of 'Lacies' answered him.

He smiled.

"Glad we agree. Who else?"

Mandy spoke up.

"Milly and Tilly are in bad shape."

"Okay, we'll have the doctor start with these girls and then the younger kids. Is that okay?"

Everyone nodded.

Chapter 49

The ground was getting cold and uncomfortable, but I couldn't be bothered to move. Alan stood up to use his tablet. He was speaking to Matt about how long they would be, when a movement came from behind us. We all looked over.

Sahid, the doctor, stepped out from the dark. He was short and stubby, and had grey hair. Sahid's ancestors had originally come from India and so he had dark skin and eyes – the type of person purged from England a few years back. Uncle Mark had told me he'd been one of the first to come down and has lived here with his family ever since. His children have lived mainly underground for their own protection. On his back was the rucksack of supplies he always carried.

When he saw us, he looked shocked, but on scanning the room quickly, he saw the sprawled kids and frowned. Briefly he welcomed me back, then he looked at Alan.

"Which first?"

"Lacie."

Alan pointed to her, and he immediately bent down in front of Alex, whose thigh must have been numb as Lacie had been resting her head on it for ages.

"I need light."

After a bit of scuffle, pulling out and re-arranging torches and moving of candles, he seemed satisfied and began his examination. Jas moved closer to see what was happening, but the doctor's back was in her way as he spoke to Alex.

"Who are you?"

"Her brother."

"And how low long has she been like this?"

"Weeks, but it's got worse over the last few days."

He nodded and then used a high-tech, digital metre for testing temperature, blood pressure, heart rate, pulse and other stuff. It was a great gadget. It only took a few minutes of holding it to her wrist and reading data, before he was administering a needle with some sort of clear liquid-medicine. We all watching silently, awaiting the verdict. He looked first at Alex and then at Alan.

"I've given her something to help reduce her fever, but she needs to be at the clinic as quickly as possible. I suspect she has bronchial flu, but her immune system's probably low due to extreme malnutrition. She'll need constant care and observation for a few weeks."

He examined everyone, including me and those kids who thought they didn't need him. We all had malnutrition to varying degrees. Josie had flu too, but was fighting it better. Milly and Tilly he wasn't sure about, but said they needed to be in the clinic at once. Out of all of us, he said six needed to be hospitalised, but we all needed further tests to check we didn't have any other, more contagious diseases. He left saying he'd ready the clinic for the arrival of so many. We'd all be put on a separate ward, in isolation, until it could be confirmed we weren't contagious.

That's when the blankets and food arrived and no one had eyes for anything, but what Ahmed handed out. There were tons of bread and flasks of hot, tomato soup, sweet cake and biscuits, apples and rehydration water. As he handed out cups to all of us, and began sharing out the soup, all you could hear was slurping and mashing of mouths. The last bit of energy focused on the food in front of them. Content to be silenced, I joined in. The soup sliding down my throat was bliss. I felt it burn through my chest and all the way into my stomach, heating my insides. It was as if I'd never tasted tomato soup before and this was the most delicious thing on earth.

Stuffing more bread, I watched as Alex coaxed Lacie to drink a little of the liquid, blowing on it to cool it down first. She wasn't quite with it, but still licked the soup off her lips, not wanting to miss a drop.

Chapter 50

None of us were able to eat as much as we wanted to, our stomachs had shrunk with weeks – in most cases, years – of so little. I noticed Alex collecting what was left and stuffing it into bags – habit or did he think they wouldn't be allowed in. Alan noticed it too, but didn't say anything. Instead, he knelt down again and spoke in a calm voice.

"I am Alan. I am the leader of the Downers. Adam is my apprentice in science and technology and I am glad to have him back."

He put his arm around my shoulders and pulled me into his side for a brief, manly hug. I felt embarrassed, but didn't resist.

"You are all welcome to our home. We will make you well, feed you and find you somewhere to live."

He spoke in a clear, strong tone.

"Everyone either learns, works or helps our little community survive."

He paused, letting them take in what he'd said.

"We are all equal here. It doesn't matter what the colour of your skin is, where you come from or what your beliefs are."

As he said this he looked particularly at Sid, Tilly and Milly.

"But once you step through the door, you are bound by our rules. At your age, they are simple. Once you reach sixteen, they become a little more complicated. They allow us to live in peace without being found, which is vital to our survival."

He paused again. Even though he had a gentle voice, I was nervous. I didn't want any of them to walk away, even the mine shaft gang. It was hard out there for kids to survive. No one deserved that.

"I know you have all suffered under the rules of others. Rules that were unfair and wrong, but our rules are not like that. They are there for everyone to live happily and fairly."

I realised Alan was trying to prepare them, convince them before he told them what the rules were. He wanted them to stay. That made me happier. Dillon spoke up.

"What if we come in 'n' then decide we dun't like the rules."

"We'd hope that never happened...what's your name?"

"Dillon."

"Well, Dillon...."

He folded his hands on his knees and continued.

"Why don't I tell you our under 16 rules and then you can all decide for yourselves."

He nodded as if he were being reasonable. Everyone else looked wary as if they knew there was a catch to all this.

"Rule number one: Never tell anyone about the Downers even if you are in trouble."

He looked at me and then at the others.

"Did Adam tell anyone about us?"

Elliott replied.

"No, he never did, even though we asked 'im tons of times."

Alan smiled at me.

"Was that hard to keep Adam?"

"Sometimes yes, but I knew if I ever told anyone, you might all be in danger."

"And that is the reason for rule number one. We always protect our own. Do you think you could keep it?"

He was asking Dillon directly. Dillon looked uncomfortable and got up to lean on the wall and cross his arms as if that made him tougher somehow.

"Yeah! We 'ave that at the mine, dun't we?"

Some of them nodded agreement.

"Good. Rule number two: Stay invisible!"

He looked at Euan.

"I bet you know how to stay invisible when you're on the streets."

Euan didn't answer, just kept staring at Alan, hiding what he was thinking.

"We train all our citizens to be invisible, to blend in, so they are not followed, so no one finds us."

He paused again, giving them a chance to think. I wondered if he was going through all the rules like this. It would take ages if he did, although he seemed to have everyone's attention.

"Rule number three is an add-on to rule number two. Don't get distracted! It means know your purpose and stick to it. Getting distracted can cause you harm. Someone can pick you up for example."

Just like I did!

I was glad he didn't look at me again.

"Rules numbers four, five and six are about how we behave with each other. We live in harmony, we are all equal, we work for the benefit of all and we do not harm another intentionally. When we talk about harm, it can be physical or mental."

There were some frowning faces at the front of the group. Was he now going too fast or didn't they understand the words, but he'd already picked up on it.

"Mental can mean bullying or shouting, upsetting someone on the inside."

Surprisingly, Josie spoke up in her brave little voice.

"The warden was a bully."

Alan nodded, observing the twitching of her head. I'd got so used to it, I barely noticed, but Alan spoke kindly and gently.

"We don't have wardens here. What's your name child?"

"Josie."

"I'm sure you're a very brave girl Josie."

"I am."

She beamed at the praise. Several of us smiled at her. Alan continued.

"Physical hurt is when someone uses an object to hit or damage a person in some way."

"That's why Adam took our knives off us?"

I gulped at Jas's question, but Alan just glanced at me with approval in his eyes, taking Jas's question in his stride.

"Yes, that's right! No knives, guns or any tool which is being used to harm is permitted."

He stopped and looked at me.

"How am I doing so far Adam?"

I shrugged. I didn't know why he was asking me. Alex spoke, surprising me.

"So far, you're doin' okay, 'cos I'd agree for the sake of the girls."

Sid also surprised me, speaking with determination.

"I think everyone should be equal and work the same as others."

Alan nodded and continued.

"Rule eight is about money. We do not use it in our city. We believe it is an evil that is manipulated..."

He corrected himself, not sure if they would understand the word.

"...used in a wrong manner, to allow some to have more power than they should. It creates greed and wars."

He said it with a passion he usually held for his science work. Elliott was paying attention.

"How do you buy things then...food and clothes?"

"We all work to earn food and clothes. Some other things can be traded."

No one said anything else even though Alan waited and looked around to see if there were more questions.

Rules number eight, nine and ten reinforce helping each other, leaving no trace so that no one can find us ever..."

He stressed the 'ever'

"...and the freedom of a person to leave and return as they wish."

Dillon stood up straight.

"So we cun leave if we wun't?"

"Yes, but as children, we'd strongly suggest you stayed with us until you are old enough to learn a trade and make your own way in life."

He was quiet for a few seconds. I looked around, trying to measure their reactions, but some of them were in shadow and it was hard to tell. Alan continued.

"We worked hard to create a caring society, to build a new world with different rules of governing. As you understand more about us, about our city and how we live, you'll be able to decide whether it's for you or not, whether you can commit to our way of life."

Everyone was quiet. I didn't know why he'd had to do this now. I wasn't sure they quite understood everything. We were much too tired.

"What now?"

Mandy asked, her voice not much more than a whisper.

"Usually, a parent swears the oath for their children, but you have no parents and so you will need to take the responsibility. It will be the first time the Downers have done this, but if you decide to come with us, I will take it you accept the rules and will, at some point quite soon, swear an oath to them. Later on, when you are older, you will be asked to swear to the senior rules."

This was getting so serious. You could feel the atmosphere vibrate with fear. I stood up. "Who wants to come in with me?"

Euan answered.

"But we 'ave to swear oaths to rules Adam?"

"But the rules are good ones Euan. Think of all the rules that were forced upon you in the home. They were bad rules."

He stared at me, his arms crossed, a frown on his face. Elliott stood up, anxiously fiddling with his fingers as usual.

"I'll trust yer Adam. Yer'v kept us safe this far, but promise yer'll still be on our side."

"I'll always be on your side Elliott."

He sounded like a little kid, but he smiled and stepped forward, standing next to me.

Alex got up, carrying Lacie, Josie following.

"We'll come. I dun't 'ave anywhere else to take 'em."

Jas stood with Molly and Sid behind them.

"Us too."

Mandy did the same with the twins. I assumed as Lissy was still clinging to my mother, (who was strangely quiet), there was now only the boys left.

Alan spoke.

"What's your name child?"

"Jamie."

His voice was quiet, but Oliver, who was sitting next to him, spoke up.

"'E's my bruvver and he dun't go anywhere wivout me."

"He's young. It must be hard for you to take care of him."

Oliver was surprised. He'd expected to be told what to do.

"Yeah it is."

Alan waited, giving him a chance to make his own decision.

"I fink I'll 'ave to cum for 'is sake, but I might leave if I dun't like it."

"Me too."

"And me!"

Dillon and Luke were ready to come. Euan was pale in the dim light, standing there alone, leaning against the wall, not sure what to do. He looked afraid and lost. And then one of those things popped out of my head, which I wished I'd thought twice about before just sprouting it out.

"You can live with us Euan, if you want. I've always wanted a brother."

My mother would probably kill me. She'd now have three kids instead of one. It startled him, I know. With all the torches switched on and pointed in his direction, I saw it in his eyes before he went back to his glare. I didn't know how to make it easy for him. He was troubled and everyone was now staring at him.

"Is 'e tellin' the truth Adam. Cun I leave if I 'ate it?"

"Yes."

He was silent for a second longer before seeming to leap off a cliff.

"'Kay! I'll cum, but am not promisin' I'll stay."

"Okay!"

My mother suddenly spoke up from behind me.

"Why don't we all get moving? It's cold and the children need to go to the clinic."

She was right, but I also wanted to get them in before anyone changed their mind again. This had been a nightmare!

"Yes, let's move."

Alan agreed.

"If everyone's okay with it, our guards can help carry those who cannot walk."

I added.

"We have a narrow path to go along. It would be safer."

Although they looked as if they wanted to argue, with full stomachs and exhaustion kicking in, no one disagreed. The guards picked up the twins, Jamie and Josie. They were gentle and whispered kind words. Alan crouched in front of Alex.

"We'll get her well, don't worry. Dr. Sahid is an excellent doctor."

Alex glanced at me, before nodding and giving up his hold on his sister. He watched as Alan carefully balanced the sleeping child in his arms and stood up. She never even noticed.

The guards went first, one of them had a large torch. Those carrying children followed. At the door, my mother pulled back the leaver. With what had happened, I'd somehow forgotten they hadn't seen this before. As the door creaked open, they all gasped.

"What's that?"

"'Ow did it open?"

"Is it magic?"

I almost laughed.

"No Elliot, it's a leaver. When pulled it opens the door for three seconds, but then automatically closes. I'll show you, watch."

I stood back and let them all watch and then walk through. Euan wanted to work the lever for himself on both sides and so went through several times, wanting to make sure he knew how to get out.

If they thought that was crazy, just wait till they see the rest.

We came to the ledge.

"First time walking across is a bit nerve racking, but it isn't far."

Alan was looking over his right shoulder, trying to reassure them.

"Stay close to the inside and don't look over the side."

All of them immediately looked over the side.

"Ah....I cun't see a thing...it's black."

Euan said, trying not to sound scared.

Elliott screeched.

"I dun't like being so 'igh."

He crawled along the wall like a snail, whimpering. Alex was behind him trying to push him forward.

"Cum on. You're slowin' us down."

My mother took his hand.

"It's okay Elliott. Stay with me on this part."

For all his bravery in surviving the kids' home, Elliott was terrified and glad to hold her hand. My mother dragged him along and after that we moved quicker. I decided not to tell them that our city was hidden below. They were having a hard enough time crossing the path.

"'Ow did yer build this place?"

Jasmine asked as we came to the end of the ledge.

"We didn't."

Alan's voice boomed out from near the front.

"It's a natural underground cavern."

"What's that mean?"

"It built itself over many years."

"Oh!"

We managed to make it across without further discussion or hold up. Alan was giving orders to the security guards.

"Go through. Wait on the other side."

"On other side of what?"

Mandy was anxiously watching the twins leave without her. Alan turned round. It was dark, but there were enough torches to just about see his face.

"Don't worry. We have a barrier. It won't hurt you, but you will need to walk through it."

"'Ow!"

"When we get there, Adam can show you one by one."

I was at the front with Alicia and Alex. I thought we might do this two at a time so they weren't so nervous. If they all tried pushing forward, there might be a real accident. Lissy spoke first.

"What are you doing Adam? There's nothing there."

"What you see is not really there. It's a false image if you like."

"Like a projector."

"Thank God Lissy was bright enough to get it quickly; those behind her were listening, but couldn't quite see anything yet.

"But the path crumbles."

Alex was hesitant.

"It doesn't really. That's just what it's supposed to look like, so people don't come in."

"'Kay!"

He wasn't really okay. I could tell by the way he was staring at it, as if he could make it go away.

"That's the only way in?"

"Yep!"

I waited.

"Watch."

Then I stepped through and they all screamed out in terror. I'd disappeared and left them in the middle of nowhere.

"Adam!"

"Argh!"

"'E's dead!"

"'e's gone, left us 'ere alone."

Trust Euan to think that.

"'E wouldn't do that."

I stepped back through the barrier and startled them.

"No, I wouldn't!"

"Yer can 'ear us!"

"Yep. It's not real….only a picture, remember. Now, who's first?"

Lissy stepped up.

"I'll go. Your mother's on the other side waiting for me, isn't she?"

"Yeah!"

"Okay then, I'll go."

"You'll feel a slight buzz. Don't worry about it. It won't hurt you."

"Okay."

And she stepped through.

"It's okay everyone."

We could hear Lissy's voice from the other side.

"It's amazing!"

She'd spotted the city.

"Come through."

With that, everyone trod through, leaving me at the back, the last one to enter.

I don't think I'll ever forget the look on their faces when they first saw the city. Now lit up like early morning, they could see the rock houses, the pathways, buildings, and even trees, all underground. They stopped, unable to believe their own eyes, their mouths gaping open.

"Is it real?"

"It can't be."

"It's a trick. It's one of those pictures."

"A trap."

"No, this is where I..."

I corrected myself.

"...we live. I told you, in a safe place. No one can find us here."

Seeing their faces delighted me, I grinned at them, remembering my first day here as strange, but amazing too.

"But how...?"

"Years of working at it."

Alan was waiting.

"Anyone afraid of lifts?"

As none of them had ever been in a lift, they didn't know. We got in, in three different groups. Alex, Euan, Elliott and Jasmine waited with me for the lift to come back up. We were the last to get in.

"It's a moving glass box."

"I suppose."

"'Ow do yer control it?"

I joked, moving my fingers in front of Euan's face.

"With my mind."

He looked so serious for a minute, I thought he hadn't got the joke, but then he grinned.

"Yeah...and more leavers and stuff."

He was looking out of the window at the mechanics of the lift.

"If you're interested, you can take classes in it."

I was trying to interest him in something other than how to get out.

"Really!"

Alex looked at me.

"I dun't like learnin'. Do we 'ave to go to school 'ere."

"A little, but school is great here."

They all looked away, grunting.

"This world yer live in is strange Adam."

Elliott added after a few seconds.

"No stranger than the world outside, but a whole lot safer."

As we walked through the narrow streets to the clinic, people going to work stared at us. The kids looked down, sneering, feeling bad as if they were being judged. They were completely overwhelmed. None of the passers-by even recognised me in my filth, even though I knew a few of them, but Alan cheerfully wished them all good morning as if this was normal. He was carrying Lacie at the time as well. Leading the troupe, it was a bit like that old Pied Piper story were the man takes the kids away, only he was saving them this time, like he'd saved so many other people in the past.

Epilogue

It was around two o'clock in the afternoon. I was sitting on my bed in my room smiling, a towel wrapped round me. I still hadn't slept and couldn't believe I was still awake, but the smile on my face grew. It turned into a huge grin that sent a warm glow to my cheeks and happy butterflies to my stomach and chest area.

I felt silly just sitting there grinning, but after the steam shower, all my limbs felt weaker, if that was possible. I loved wet showers more than dry, but we were only permitted one a month. We had to recycle water and take care not to use too much, so mostly it was dry showers. I'd watched as the dirt ingrained in me slipped down the drain along with all the struggles of the last three weeks. The gaol-kid's home now seemed a million miles away.

I had to move to get dressed, but it felt as if the puppet strings attached to my limbs had been cut and I couldn't move. I had one more meeting before I'd be allowed to sink into my own bed, my own soft pillow. I stood up and looked around the room. It was strange, I felt a bit like an alien who'd just landed, but everything was the same, nothing had changed.

As I dug out my tunic and trousers, I thought back over the amazement they'd had on walking through the tunnel and then how it had taken eons to get them to go through the barriers.

When we were all in the clinic having tests, they kept asking me questions about the life here, each of them interrupting the other. We were sat on the beds, making them incredibly dirty.

"How do ya breave?"

"We have natural tunnels which run outside, blowing in the air."

"Even when it ain't windy."

"Yes."

Euan frowned, trying to understand how that worked.

"Where do ya get food from?"

"We grow it."

I had several responses of...

"Underground?"

"Yes, it's something I work on. I'll show you if you want."

"And we just get given food, real food, just like that?"

Dillon had joined the conversation.

"Yes, but we all do some sort of work."

"And 'ow cum it's light?"

Alex asked.

"We use the old solar panels."

"'Kay!"

He didn't really get it, but most of the stuff was so high tech that they'd have to see it to understand.

By twelve I'd been given the all-clear sign by the doctor and was allowed to go home. The others had to stay for a while until they'd finalised tests and figured out where to lodge them. Lacie, Josie, the twins and Jamie would probably stay longer as they were ill. Dr. Sahid had told us they needed rest, medicine and decent food, but they would, with care, all get well. I was relieved to hear about Lacie as was Alex.

My mother had waited outside the ward and hugged me all the way back to the house. I was almost as tall as her and felt a bit awkward, but didn't push her away.

"I've missed you so much Adam."

"Missed you too Mam."

I had, but I felt daft saying it, so it came out odd.

"I thought you were gone like your Uncle Mark."

I knew she'd be thinking that.

"I know your tired, and you can tell me everything later, but I really am so very proud of you. You're a good kid. The best, really."

Now I was going red from my neck upwards. I was glad of the dirt for once.

My mother knocked on my bedroom door, reminding me of the time. The meeting I was going to was procedure, a report to the committee. I was a bit nervous about it. The committee was a serious thing and I had to detail everything that had happened since I'd left. I hoped they'd go easy on the mine shaft kids, understand why they'd behaved as they did.

But it would be my chance to discuss rescuing the others as well. Surely, now they'd seen them, they'd want to get all the kids away from those horrid places. Euan was right, we couldn't just leave them there, couldn't let the creep-adults get away with it anymore. It wasn't fair. We had to do something. I would even go with them, show them the way in through the tunnel. Euan would probably go with me. We could slip in at night, wake the kids and get them away.

My mother stood at the door waiting for me to come out. She was going with me.

"Penny for your thoughts!"

I grinned. It was such an old expression she'd almost made it hers. I never heard anyone else say it. I stood up, wanting to get the meeting over with and get back to my bed. Tomorrow I'd be able to face whatever, today, I just needed to close my eyes in safety.

For some reason, the committee was in the hall, instead of in the usual offices. My Mam said something about redecoration, but I wasn't really paying much attention. The streets we walked down were a blur. Now that I was clean, I was beginning to feel a little more normal, but not quite my old self. I couldn't quite leave behind everything that had happened, nor could I talk about it all to my Mam, so we walked side by side in silence. I wondered if I would ever be my old self again. I didn't even know if I wanted to be.

We opened the frosted-glass panel doors and walked in. For a moment I thought we'd gone to the wrong place, no one was there. But then suddenly people came out from behind doors, chairs and tables and a huge noise screeched at me.

"Surprise!"

"Happy Birthday!"

"You didn't think we'd forgotten your birthday, did you?"

The committee was there, my friends, the people I worked with and other neighbours. I looked around missing my new friends – the ones that had become a part of me and who I now was. Suddenly I felt lost without them. The eight older ones were there, huddling in two groups in the corner, not sure how to behave. They looked nervous, eyes flitting around the gathering, wondering who these 'happy' people were and what sort of life they would have. The doctor must have given the 'all clear', no contagious diseases. I was glad they'd come. I stared, understanding how strange it all felt, how hard it was for them to be here. I wanted to hide away from all the noise and people as well.

I couldn't figure out what else was wrong though, they seemed different, and then I realised what it was and smiled. They were clean! Lissy rushed over to cling onto my mother, smiling as she passed me by.

Then, everyone was grinning at me, waiting for me to say something. I tried to think of something clever but I didn't know what to say. I was so shocked.

"Errr...thanks."

They all laughed at me and I felt my face heating up from the back of my neck to the tip of my ears. I glanced at the corner again, even my new friends grinned a little, though I could tell they felt out of place. For a moment, I wanted to dash over and protect them, or at least be one of them, but I didn't. They needed to figure some things out for themselves.

And then, my mother started singing that horrible birthday song. I didn't need it twice in one day, but it seemed everyone was delighted and joined in. In the end, I just laughed with them. What else could I do? I was at home, with friends, in my safe place.

But what about the others, the ones we left behind?

The thought in my head voiced a question that bothered me. I pictured The Mantis' anger – the punishments after our escape – I just couldn't have taken them all.

Eventually, Alan walked up, distracting me and shushing everyone.

"I know all these kids want to do is find a bed and go to sleep, so I'll keep this simple. There will be time to welcome, talk and figure things out over the next few days."

He's making a speech!

"So, I'd just like to say, I've never bestowed a new status on anyone more deserving."

Status? What's he talking about? This is not what I expected. This was supposed to be a report.

He placed his hand on my shoulder. I felt its weight and Alan's reassuring squeeze as he looked around first, and then looked at me again.

"Congratulations Adam. You are now officially a Collector."

Look out for Adam's next adventure:

The Collector

Coming soon.....

Or take a look at the website:

www.tracytodd.co.uk

8147378R00218

Printed in Great Britain
by Amazon.co.uk, Ltd.,
Marston Gate.